ROSA

THE

Ann

C000186366

MILLS & BOON LIMITED
ETON HOUSE   18-24 PARADISE ROAD
RICHMOND   SURREY   TW9 1SR

First published in Great Britain 1988
by Mills & Boon Limited

© Anne Herries 1988

Australian copyright 1988
Philippine copyright 1988
This edition 1989

ISBN 0 263 76336 6

Set in Times Roman 10 on 10¼ pt.
04-8902-83817 C

Made and printed in Great Britain

CHAPTER ONE

A GREY mist hung over the land, partly obscuring the white cliffs that heralded the ship's safe arrival. England! Rosanna was home at last after three years of travelling in Europe with her father. Memories of the man she had loved so dearly clouded her eyes for a moment. His death in Spain some weeks previously had been a severe blow. They had been close these past few years, but his health had been failing for a long time and she had grown used to the idea that she would one day be alone. Perhaps that was why...

'We'll be docking at any moment, Miss Whitby.'

Rosanna turned to look at the man who had spoken, her green eyes lighting with warmth. Captain Robert Henderson had been more than kind to her on the journey. On hearing of her plight from the British consul, he had accepted her as a passenger without full payment of her fare.

Her financial embarrassment was, as she had explained, only temporary, the usual funds from England having failed to arrive in time to meet all the extra expenses Mr Whitby's death had incurred. Thomas Whitby had been a wealthy man and she would be a considerable heiress when her affairs were settled.

'Then I should go below and see to my luggage,' she said, realising that she would only be in the way amid the flurry of docking. 'I must thank you once again for your care of me, sir.'

'It was a pleasure.' Captain Henderson looked at the girl's beautiful face and sighed. That dark hair and those eyes! It was a pity she was spoken for, he thought.

Once in her cabin, Rosanna's smile faded. Now that she was actually in England, she was beginning to feel

nervous about having come home to marry Harry
Bellingham. Whereas in Spain it had seemed so simple,
now she was suddenly seized with doubts. The Bellinghams were old friends of her father. She had known
Harry when her mother was alive, before she had been
sent away to school for ten miserable years. On her sev-
enteenth birthday she had finally escaped the dull routine
of Madame Belvoir's academy for young ladies, per-
suading her father that she was old enough to accompany him on his travels. Harry had journeyed
independently to Rome, taking a grand tour, as the sons
of gentlemen often did. It was the romance of blue skies
and ancient temples that had led Rosanna to listen to
Harry's impassioned avowals of love.

'You are the most beautiful girl I have ever seen,' he
had declared. 'If you refuse me, I shall die!'

'Oh, Harry, you idiot!' She had laughed at the sight
of him kneeling awkwardly amid a riot of oleanders in
the gardens of the Roman villa, but her heart had
quickened with the romance of it and her lips had been
eager for his kiss. 'I think the sun has gone to your
head—but if you still feel the same in a year's time, I
shall come back to England and marry you.'

To her surprise, Harry had produced a beautiful
diamond ring, slipping it on to the third finger of her
left hand. 'We're engaged,' he announced with an almost
pompous pride. 'Let's tell your father—though I spoke
to him first, naturally.'

Rosanna had felt a spurt of annoyance, but then her
pique turned to amusement. That was very much more
like the Harry Bellingham she had known in England.
Tall, lean, with fair hair and blue eyes, he was every inch
an English aristocrat. Sometimes she thought there was
a touch of weakness about his mouth, but she enjoyed
his company and there had been a moment in the moon-
light when he had made her heart beat faster. Besides,
as his wife, she would have a settled home at last, something she had not known since her mother died.

Was she really prepared to marry for the sake of a home? Rosanna had asked herself this question several times and was still not sure of the answer. She was twenty, quite ancient in terms of marriageability, and like most women she wanted a home and children. Harry was well qualified to be the father of those children. Of good family and pleasant mannered, she suspected him of having a selfish streak, but believed he was genuinely fond of her. Indeed, she thought she might be a little in love with him, if only she could be sure what it felt like to be really in love. She had felt something for the Russian count who had tried to abduct her, and she had been charmed by the Italian prince who had sworn eternal love and then abandoned her hurriedly when his wife arrived on the scene. She had fallen in and out of love a dozen times, enjoying it all hugely, but none of her romantic followers had really touched her heart.

A bell was ringing on deck, warning the passengers to be ready. Rosanna turned as two of the sailors came to collect her bags. One of them gave her a broad wink; the other nodded his head respectfully.

'Will Mr Bellingham be here to meet you, Miss Whitby?'

'I'm not sure if Harry will come himself, but he will be certain to have sent a carriage for me. I sent word of my arrival, and . . .' She broke off as footsteps came clattering down the steps and her fiancé appeared in the doorway. 'Harry—you came!'

'Rosanna!' he cried, moving impulsively towards her. 'Of course I came myself.' He took her in his arms, ignoring the crewmen's grins. 'It's been such an age!'

'Nine months,' she said, her mouth quirking. She looked up at him as the sailors tactfully departed with her bags. 'How are you, Harry? And your parents? Helen and Mary?'

'My parents are eager to greet you. My sisters are enjoying themselves at Devonshire's estate and I am miserable. Or I was until a moment ago. It was dashed unkind of you to insist on a long engagement.'

Rosanna frowned. 'My father's health was uncertain. The English winters were too harsh, and I could not leave him, Harry.'

He looked at her uncomfortably. 'Forgive me, that was tactless. You know I'm very sorry about... Well, you know.'

'Yes, I know.' She smiled at him. 'You needn't feel awkward, Harry. I shall miss him terribly, but I've learned to cope with my loss. We both knew it was coming. I was lucky to have so much time with him.'

'You are very brave,' Harry said. 'Making all the arrangements and travelling by yourself. You should have sent for me.'

'There was no time to be lost. Besides, I had many good friends to help. Father always had people around him, you know that.'

Harry nodded. Privately, he felt that Thomas Whitby had collected every scrounger and ne'er-do-well in Europe. He had been far too trusting and, in Harry's opinion, a little foolish—but of course, it would not do to tell his daughter that. Besides, Mr Whitby had been wealthy enough to spend whatever he pleased on his friends.

'Shall we go?' Harry asked. 'The carriage is waiting.'

'Yes, I'm quite ready.'

There was a sharp breeze and some fine drizzle as they left the ship. Rosanna pulled her cloak tighter as she felt the cold strike. It was only October, she thought ruefully: in Italy the sun would still be warm enough for her to seek the shade of a tree as she sat reading Lord Byron's poems—poems that he had been moved to write after making his own grand tour a few years previously. For a moment the girl regretted the life she had left forever, then she straightened her shoulders, a look of determination on her face. She would not pine for the past but look to the future. Travelling with a sick man had taught her to be self-reliant, and she was quite capable of facing this new life in England.

Feeling Harry pull at her arm, she moved forward without looking and collided with something hard and ungiving. A cry escaped her and she hastily apologised as she discovered that the unmovable object was a large and angry-looking man in a cloak with several capes over his coat and tight-fitting breeches. He was also wearing a pair of shining hessians, one of them now sadly scuffed where she had trodden heavily on his foot.

'I'm sorry,' she said. 'It was all my fault.'

'Why don't you look where you're going?' the stranger replied rudely. 'Why don't you take care, instead of charging about like a mad heifer?'

Harry stiffened, his face going red. 'How dare you insult Miss Whitby! You will apologise at once, sir.'

'Or what?' he drawled insolently. 'Will you challenge me to a duel?'

Rosanna's eyes flashed. 'No apologies are necessary. As you obviously have no manners, you were not aware of the insult. Come, Harry, waste no more of your breath.'

She swept past the stranger with dignity, leaving him staring after her in surprise. Harry followed in her wake, feeling rather like a puppy dog running at her heels. He had always been aware that Rosanna had a strong will, but her travels seemed to have made her more determined. He looked at her stiff back doubtfully. He hoped she would not become too dominant over the years. For a moment he wondered if perhaps he had made a mistake, and then she turned and smiled at him, and he remembered the magical evening when he had asked her to be his wife.

'Forgive me, Harry,' she said. 'I should not have interfered, but where Father and I have been these past years, they still fight duels all the time. I was alarmed…'

'You were frightened for my sake?' His eyes caressed her. 'That was sweet of you, my dearest, but I couldn't have fought him. From his manner, he wasn't a gentleman.'

'Oh, Harry,' her laughter rang out joyously, 'I'm so glad you asked me to marry you!'

She squeezed his arm as they turned towards the carriage, her heart lifting. Harry was kind and gentle and he would be a thoughtful husband. She had been worrying for nothing.

'Rosanna, my dear!' Lady Bellingham gathered the girl to her ample bosom. 'How lovely to see you again. We were devastated to hear about your poor dear father. How difficult it must have been for you, all alone in that dreadful place!'

'Spain is a very beautiful country,' Rosanna said, crushing a tiny spurt of annoyance. 'I had friends to help me. Besides, I am quite capable of managing alone. My father relied on me to make all our travelling arrangements after his health began to fail, you know, so I was accustomed to dealing with all sorts of people.'

Lady Bellingham frowned. There was something a little too bold in the girl's manner for her taste. Her tone dropped several degrees as she turned towards her husband.

'Come and say how d'ye do to Sir Harold. He has been telling everyone what a delightful gel you are, and our neighbours are impatient to meet you. We have arranged a little party for tomorrow—just twenty couples, you know.'

Rosanna smiled. She had noticed the new coolness in her hostess, but decided to ignore it. After three years of being her own mistress, she would find it difficult to adopt the manner of a girl just out of the schoolroom, which was how Harry's mother seemed to see her. She moved forward to the fireplace, making her host a slight curtsy. He caught her in a hearty embrace, kissing her cheek and calling her a pretty puss.

'She's a fine gel, Harry,' he told his son. 'You were lucky she wasn't snapped up by some foreign fellow.'

Rosanna smothered a smile. It was as well that Harry's father didn't know how close she had come to running away with a Russian count!

'We must go up to town quite soon,' Lady Bellingham said, casting a critical eye over the girl's travelling attire. 'That gown is a little dowdy, don't you think?'

Rosanna glanced down at herself. 'I suppose it is. I have many newer ones, of course, but this is the warmest. I think that is a very good suggestion, Lady Bellingham. I must in any case see my father's lawyer. The last payment due to Father did not arrive on time. I have some small debts to settle, and I shall need money to buy my bride clothes.'

'We must discuss the wedding later,' Lady Bellingham said. 'It should not take place just yet, of course, but perhaps in the spring?'

'There's plenty of time to think about that, Mother.' Harry frowned at her. 'I'm sure Rosanna is tired from the journey. Will you take her upstairs, or shall I?'

'I was just about to do so.' Lady Bellingham looked annoyed. 'Rosanna, please come with me.'

Rosanna dutifully followed her from the room. Bellingham Hall was large and rather draughty, and the long passages seemed endless. A little shiver went through her as she was at last shown into a dark, cold room. The furniture was old and ugly and the decoration decidedly tasteless. There were many things that would have to be altered if she were to be comfortable here.

'Do you think I could have a fire lit?' she asked.

'A fire?' Lady Bellingham's brows lifted in surprise. 'But it's only October. We do not normally start fires for another month...' She saw the girl's pinched look, and gave an odd laugh. 'Since it is for you, I'm sure it could be arranged. We must remember that you are not yet used to our climate.'

'Thank you. I should like to rest for a while and change my gown, ma'am.'

'Very well.' Lady Bellingham's manner was icy. 'Dinner is in an hour. Sir Harold insists on punctuality. Even from you.'

Rosanna realised that she had upset her hostess, and bit her lip, annoyed with herself. That was the last thing she wanted to do. She would have to be more careful in future, but something about Harry's mother had got under her skin. After a much freer way of life over the past three years, she must be careful. Until she and Harry were married and living in a house of their own, she must adapt to Lady Bellingham's ways. Left to herself, she lay down on the bed, but it was impossible to rest. She felt uncomfortable in the strange room, and recent memories chased through her thoughts. Sighing, she changed into a pretty gown for the evening, determined to make an effort to please her host and hostess.

Dinner was a complete success. By the end of the evening Sir Harold was calling her his dearest daughter, and Lady Bellingham's face had lost that frozen look. When Rosanna left the drawing-room to retire, she was assured that a fire would be waiting for her upstairs.

'My parents adore you already,' Harry said as he escorted her to her room. 'I knew they would.'

'I'm glad,' Rosanna said, smiling. 'I want to be on good terms with your family, though we shall of course have our own establishment. Have you been looking for a suitable house for us?'

There was surprise in his face. 'But I imagined we should live here, Rosanna...there's so much room. I know it's what my parents expect.'

'I should prefer a home of our own. After all, we can afford it.'

Harry frowned uneasily. 'If it's what you want, I'll have a word with Father.'

She felt a tingle of frustration. Why should he need to discuss their affairs with his father? It was on the tip of her tongue to ask, but she held the words back. She would have to learn to curb her impatience. Marriage entailed more than kisses and a gold ring; she must respect Harry's wishes and not seek to have her own way all the time. Ruefully, she realised that it was not going to be as easy as she had imagined.

As Harry took her in his arms to kiss her, she pushed her doubts to the back of her mind. It was pleasant to be kissed by such a gentle man, and surely that was why she had chosen him. She had seen enough of passionate rogues who sought her only for her father's fortune. What she wanted was a solid, dependable man who would provide a good home.

It was what she wanted, yet she could not entirely smother her feeling of disappointment as Harry released her and she entered her bedchamber alone. He had never shown any sign of impatience or of wanting her so much that it was an effort for him to tear himself from her side. Undressing, she scolded herself. If she had wanted romance, she should have run off with her Russian count. He would probably have abandoned her by now, but she could have found herself another protector. She thought she might have done rather well as a courtesan, and suddenly she was laughing. What a fool she was! By now she should have learnt that romantic love was a dream, all very well for schoolgirls, but not at all practical. Harry was reality, and she was lucky to have found him!

The Bellinghams' dinner party served its purpose of introducing Rosanna to the neighbourhood, but was otherwise rather dull. There was no dancing or music, and the gentlemen stayed a long time over their port and brandy, leaving the tea-trolley to the ladies. After questioning Rosanna briefly about her travels, without bothering to listen to her answers, they plunged into gossip about people she had never heard of or complained about the lack of any decent hunting that season.

Rosanna found herself missing her father and the sparkling conversation of the colourful people he had always managed to collect about him. Poets, writers, artists, great opera singers and politicians had flocked to his table, drawn by the generous hospitality to be found there—and by the desire to sell their work. Mr Whitby had bought many art treasures, having them crated and sent to his agent in London. Wherever he went, he had been surrounded by people of wit and intelligence.

It would be better when they went up to town, Rosanna told herself. At least there would be music and dancing, so perhaps then she would not feel so bored. Catching Harry's eye as he came into the withdrawing-room, she felt a pang of guilt. She was engaged to be married, and should not be forever comparing her present company with people she had met previously. It was a form of snobbery, and she disliked it in herself and in others. She set herself to making Harry laugh and succeeded tolerably well, though he, too, seemed to be in a strange mood. It was a relief when the evening was over.

The next morning her mood improved when she went riding through the Hampshire countryside with Harry. A good gallop helped to blow the cobwebs away, and when he suggested that they should walk for a while, she was happy to comply. Having tethered the horses, they walked along in silence. It was not quite as cold as the previous day, and the sun was shining. Rosanna watched the swooping flight of a sparrowhawk, then took Harry's arm.

'When are we going up to London?' she asked. 'I'm looking forward to it, aren't you?'

'Are you bored already, Rosanna?' Harry looked at her oddly. 'I usually look to spend the winter in the country.'

A faint blush touched her cheeks. 'I am a little restless. Forgive me, Harry. I need some time to settle down.'

'Yes, of course.' He squeezed her arm. 'It must seem very strange, and I know Mama's friends are too old for you. I have invited some people I think more in your style for this weekend.'

'Oh,' Rosanna looked up at him impulsively, 'you are so good to me, and I've been so ungrateful! I promise it will be better soon. It's just that everything is so different here.'

'I would do anything for you,' he said, smiling at her. 'I'm very fond of you, you know.'

'I know. I'm very fond of you, too.'

'I was afraid you might have changed your mind.'

'Oh, no.' Rosanna felt a twinge of guilt. 'No, of course not.' She flashed a smile at him. 'It was just a silly mood, but I shall be more settled now, you'll see.'

'I'm glad. I should not want you to be unhappy.'

'I am not in the least unhappy, I assure you.' She took his hand, pulling at him. 'Come, I'll race you back to the horses.'

The weekend gatherings were certainly more lively. Harry's friends were younger and had more to talk about. Rosanna enjoyed herself, deciding that marriage would not be too bad, after all. When she had her own house, she would be able to entertain whomever she pleased. Harry was a comfortable companion. They spent some time together every day, walking, riding and reading from their favourite books. Sometimes it seemed to Rosanna that they were like a couple who had been married for years. It was a pleasant relationship, but it lacked excitement. She wondered what was missing, but then she forgot in the thrill of her first visit to London.

She wrote a short note to her father's lawyer, asking him to deposit sufficient funds in her account, then set about buying a lavish trousseau. Lady Bellingham proved invaluable in seeking out the most modish seamstresses and milliners, and the pile of bandboxes in Rosanna's bedchamber grew daily.

Rosanna had no idea how wealthy she would be when her father's estate had been settled, but knew she must be a considerable heiress. Before they left England on their travels, her father had sold most of his assets and reinvested them on the advice of his friend and agent, a Mr William Martin. It had been agreed that a fixed sum should be sent out every six months to wherever Mr Whitby happened to be staying, the remainder of his profits to be ploughed back into various investments. The system had worked very well until just before Mr Whitby's death, when the money had failed to arrive. Although she had written to Mr Martin at once, his reply had not reached her by the time she set out for home. She was not, however, unduly alarmed, as the post was often erratic and letters had gone astray before. It would all be settled as soon as her father's lawyer contacted Mr Martin, telling him that she was the legal heir.

She was far too busy attending dances, dinners and musical evenings to bother her head about financial details. London was a little thin of company, most hostesses having retired to their country estates to prepare for the Christmas festivities, but there were still sufficient in town for the Bellinghams' party to be out three evenings in four. Their own ball was to be held the evening before they left for the country. It was really a celebration of Harry's engagement, and was more lavish than the dinner at Bellingham Hall.

Dressing that evening in a filmy silk gown caught beneath her breasts with a scarlet sash, revealing her slim shape in a way that was almost shameless, Rosanna's heart was pounding wildly. Her engagement was to be officially announced this evening, but why should that make her feel slightly trapped? She had a sudden urge to run away and hide, but in another moment the panic had gone. She was not being forced into anything, so it was ridiculous to think that everything was closing in about her. She held her breath and counted to one hundred; then, feeling much better, she went downstairs to stand at Harry's side and receive the guests.

Once all the more important people had arrived, Rosanna and Harry were released so that they could open the dancing, leaving Lady Bellingham to welcome the late-comers.

'You're the most beautiful girl here,' Harry whispered as they led the first dance. 'The most beautiful girl in London.'

'Only in London?' she teased, her green eyes bright with mischief. 'In Rome, you said I was the most beautiful girl in the world. At this rate, I shall be merely attractive by the time we are married, and an old hag within a year!'

'You will always be beautiful to me,' he said. 'I love you.'

'Do you?' She gazed up at him earnestly. 'Do you really?'

'Of course.' Was she imagining it, or was there just a tiny note of uncertainty in his voice? Could Harry, too, be having second thoughts? 'Why do you ask? You must know how I feel.'

'Yes.' She smiled at once. 'Why does any girl ask, Harry? I suspect that we all like to be told constantly that we are loved. It must be terribly tedious for you men.'

'What an odd girl you are,' he said, but he was laughing. 'How can you think that anything you have to say would bore me?'

'Oh, Harry,' she pouted at him, 'I don't expect you to be forever hanging on my every word! I expect you will find me very dull when I have two or three children clinging to my skirts.'

Harry smiled uncomfortably as the strains of the music died away and he led her from the floor.

After their dance, Rosanna found herself in great demand. Since this was the first real ball she had attended in London, there were many gentlemen she had not previously met, except briefly as they arrived. They were all very polite, though one or two gave her a knowing look and bemoaned the fact that Harry Bellingham had snatched an unfair advantage.

'Makes one wish one had taken the grand tour oneself, what?'

Rosanna merely smiled at the veiled hints and compliments. The more she looked about her at the available gentlemen, the more certain she became that Harry was a good choice. Most of the men seemed more concerned

with the set of their cravat than anything else! And those
who were not slavishly following fashion seemed to talk
only of hunting...

It was not until the evening was well advanced that
she became aware that she was being watched, not in a
casual way but with an intentness that she found un-
nerving. The man was of about the same height as Harry,
but broader in the shoulders and with a military look.
Although he was not in uniform, she thought he was
probably a cavalry man. With Napoleon Bonaparte
safely on the island of Elba, he would have given up his
commission to return home, and, by the expression in
his eyes, he was finding life rather dull. He had raven-
black hair, grey eyes, and a mouth that carried a hint
of steel. There was a devil-may-care manner about him
and he was almost indecently good looking, which possibly accounted for his air of arrogance. As he began to
carve his passage towards her through the crowded room,
she thought of making some excuse to leave before he
could reach her. She had seen that look before in a man's
eyes, and it always repelled her. This stranger clearly belonged to that breed who considered themselves lords of
the earth! She looked at her dance-card, relieved to see
that the next was taken, but where was the gentleman
who had written his name in the space? She glanced
round, frowning as she saw no sign of him.

'Miss Whitby?' the stranger said, inclining his head.
'Will you do me the honour of dancing with me?'

'I fear this dance is taken, sir. Besides, I do not think
we have been introduced?'

Her cool tones brought a gleam to his eyes. 'How
remiss of me. I am Justin Sawle. My uncle is Lord
Mountjoy. Perhaps you have heard of him, if not of
me?'

The hint of irony flicked her on the raw, making her
chin go up. 'Of course, Mr Sawle. I met your uncle earlier
in the evening.'

'Captain Sawle,' he corrected. 'Unfortunately I was late. Shall I ask Lady B. to introduce us?'

'Lady B.?' She glanced at him, a smile tugging at reluctant lips. 'What does the B. stand for?'

'I am far too polite to answer that, Miss Whitby, but I am sure you can supply your own solution.'

'You are not a gentleman, Captain Sawle!'

'Are you always a lady, Miss Whitby?'

'Oh, always!' Laughter made her eyes sparkle.

'If I believed you, I should be disappointed. You would then be as boring as all the others.' His scornful gaze moved round the room. 'And that would be a pity.'

'So, as I understand you, sir, I am either a liar or a bore.' She flicked her fan open, waving it provocatively. 'What refreshingly charming compliments you pay one, Captain Sawle. Your opinion of the fair sex is not overly flattering.'

'Do you want me to tell you that you are beautiful?' His brows went up. 'You are not a fool, so I presumed you must be aware of it.'

'Ah, so I am given credit for some intelligence? This grows more interesting, sir. I am not quite a hopeless case?'

'Like all women, you enjoy flattery, but you are not as foolish as most.'

'Indeed?' Green fire flashed and was met by steel. 'You almost persuaded me to dance, but alas, Captain Sawle, here comes my partner.'

'He is late, and deserves to lose his chance.' Before she could protest further, he had seized her wrist, half dragging her towards the dance-floor. 'Do not resist, Miss Whitby. You will draw attention to us.'

'Me?' she gasped indignantly. Looking round, she saw that he was right. She could not avoid dancing with him now unless she wished to make a scene. 'You are very rude, sir!' With a vague recollection of an incident at Dover, she looked at his face intently. 'Have we met before?'

'No, I would have remembered.' He quirked a brow. 'Why?'

'It does not matter. You reminded me of someone, that's all.'

'Someone who was rude to you?'

'Yes, but he was considerably older than you, I think.'

'I must protest, Miss Whitby. I may have been rude about others, but not to you, surely?'

She thought about it and was forced to admit that he spoke the truth. 'Not in actual words, but by implication. I am a female, and I think you have little respect for any of us.'

'Ah, there now you have me. I have met few females I felt able to respect.'

'There have been some, then?' She looked at him curiously. 'I am intrigued.'

'One, at least.' He smiled maddeningly. 'No, I shall not tell you. I prefer to keep you intrigued.'

'Why?'

'Because I am mad with desire for you, and if your fiancé were not watching me at this very moment, I would sweep you up on my white charger and ride off with you into the night.'

'That will teach me, won't it?' Rosanna's cheeks burned. 'Forgive me; I did not mean to pry.'

He laughed softly. 'Did you think I meant that as a set-down, Miss Whitby? On the contrary. I may not always respect your sex, but I am far from being immune to their charms. Had I seen you first, you would not soon be marrying Harry B.!'

The music had ended, and before she could think of a suitable reply, he had bowed and left her. She made her way to Harry's side, feeling slightly bemused. What had he meant by that last provocative statement? Surely not that she would be marrying *him*! A shudder of protest went through her at the very idea. Harry might be a little boring, but he was much safer than... She checked herself, angry at Captain Sawle for planting the thought in her mind. Harry was not boring! At least, only a little, now and then.

She gave him a dazzling smile to make up for the betrayal of her thoughts. 'I believe this dance belongs to you, Harry?'

He was frowning, his eyes following Justin Sawle's tall figure as he threaded his way towards the card-room. 'You seemed to find Sawle's company amusing.'

'Shouldn't I have done?' Rosanna asked, sensing his disapproval. 'He said he was Lord Mountjoy's nephew.'

'He is. His father has a huge estate. They're one of the richest families in Cornwall.' His mouth twisted with an annoyance that was almost spite. 'That's the only reason Justin is tolerated in decent society, and you would do well to steer clear of him, Rosanna. If duelling were not frowned upon these days, I know a score of husbands who would like to put a ball through that particular gentleman...'

'If they could manage it,' Rosanna murmured. She checked guiltily as he looked at her. 'You need not have warned me, Harry. Captain Sawle is amusing for a short while, but he is the type of man I particularly dislike. You will not find yourself wearing a pair of horns on his account.'

'Rosanna!' Harry looked slightly shocked, and then laughed. 'Well, I may speak frankly, then. He is not the kind of man I would ask to escort my wife home in an emergency.'

She looked at him thoughtfully. 'Is he really as bad as that?'

'One is never sure how much is true, of course, but he has quite a reputation.'

Rosanna nodded, avoiding his eyes. She had thought Captain Sawle was punishing her for her curiosity when he spoke of carrying her off. It was rather a shocking suggestion, particularly if he had been serious, and made, as it had been, to a young unmarried woman. She believed that some of the young ladies present might have swooned had he spoken so plainly to one of them. If he had expected a similar reaction from her, he must have been sadly disappointed. She smiled to herself, remembering the night the Russian count had actually tried to abduct her. She had put a ball in his arm, and then bound his wound. Poor Maximillian! He had taken it very well, though, escorting her back to her father, despite his obvious pain. Afterwards, he had become even more devoted, asking her to marry him on several occasions. Captain Sawle would have to do very much better if he wished to discomfit Thomas Whitby's daughter!

CHAPTER TWO

'IF YOU ever enter this house again, I'll have my servants thrash you, sir.' Charles Sawle looked at his son with hatred in his eyes. 'You have disgraced my name, Justin, and I've finished with you!'

'Why won't you listen to me, Father?' Justin's grey eyes had a wintry look as they met the dark gaze. 'Anne Cornwallis is lying. I'll admit I was willing enough, but she made all the running. I didn't go out of my way to seduce her. If it hadn't been me, it would have been another man. Cornwallis was asking for trouble when he married a woman so much younger than himself.'

'And you think that excuses your behaviour?' Charles felt the fury choke him. 'You bed the wife of my best friend and then shrug your shoulders! By God, sir, I'm minded to take a whip to you myself!'

'I would not advise it, Father.'

The younger man's eyes hardened to steel. He had not asked for this quarrel, just one of many since his return from Wellington's army. He had always known that his father disliked him, though it had been more apparent of late. He supposed it was because he was older now and more of a threat to Charles's authority. Sir Charles was past his prime, thickened by an excess of food and drink and prematurely aged by a choleric temperament. The colour in his cheeks was unhealthy, a sign of a blood disorder for which he stubbornly refused to be treated.

'Are you threatening me? Damn you!' he glared at his son. 'Out of my house, sir! As from today, I disown you. You'll get nothing more from me. Not one penny now—or when I die.'

For a moment Justin's face registered shock. 'The estate is entailed,' he said uncertainly. 'You can't disinherit your own son.'

'Perhaps not—' Sir Charles's eyes gleamed with hatred, '—but I can disown a bastard forced on me by that bitch I married! I took her for her fortune. The times were hard and I needed the money, but the brat she carried in her belly belonged to another. I've no child of my own, but the church shall have my estate—and make good use of it!'

There was silence as Justin stared at him. He wanted to deny it as a foul slander against the mother he had adored, but he knew it was true. Margaret Sawle had been so beautiful, too beautiful to wed a boorish country squire who was so far beneath her in every way. She had been the youngest child of Lord Mountjoy, and her father's pride. Justin remembered his maternal grandfather well; it was from him that he had inherited his long limbs and broad shoulders, and the handsome face that brought him admiring glances from every woman he met. They sent him love letters and fainted at his feet, obliging him to come to their rescue. Women! He despised every single one of them—except perhaps one he had met earlier. Anne Cornwallis had been just a way to while away a long summer afternoon, and he had long ago regretted the impulse.

'So you're throwing me out?' he said at last. 'How am I supposed to live?'

'Go back to the army,' Charles sneered. 'Or find yourself a rich heiress. I don't give a tuppenny curse what you do!'

'You know I was relying on you to cover that loan for Wheal Margaret. How can I raise the money without your support?'

'That mine is as worthless as the woman who left it to you.'

'Damn you, sir, I'll not hear another word against her!' Justin moved threateningly towards him. 'I'll leave your house tonight; nothing would keep me here now.

Break the entail, leave the money where you please. But breathe one word of this to another soul, and I'll kill you. So help me, I'll break your neck! I'll not have her memory sullied by your spite. You made your bargain with her; if you're a man, you'll keep it to the end.'

He was breathing hard, his fists clenched at his sides and a vein cording in his neck. For a moment murder lurked chillingly in his eyes, and Sir Charles took a step back, fear curdling in his stomach. He had not meant to push it this far.

'I—I'll cover the loan, of course. I gave you my word.'

'No!' Justin's refusal was like the lash of a whip, making his father recoil. 'I've eaten your bread too long, sir. I want nothing more from you.' His eyes were glittering with an anger that he could no longer control. 'I'm glad your blood is not mine. I'm cursed with your name, and for my mother's honour I'll bear it to the grave, but every night I'll give thanks that I was born of another's seed.'

'The devil carry you off!' Sir Charles stared at the man he had grudgingly acknowledged as his son all these years, the hatred surging in him. 'Get out before I set the dogs on you.'

'They'd sooner turn on you,' Justin sneered. 'But try it if you wish.'

He turned on his heel, leaving the older man gasping as his cheeks turned to the colour of puce.

Rosanna stretched and yawned, awaking to a feeling of lazy content. She had danced the night away, retiring only after the last of the guests had gone. Lady Bellingham had promised that she would be allowed to sleep on as she wished, and glancing at the ornate clock on the mantelpiece, the girl was surprised to see that it was almost eleven o'clock. She had slept the morning away! Jumping out of bed, she pulled on a loose satin wrap and began to brush her long hair. Time spent in bed was time wasted, and she had planned to visit the lending library before they left town. She had several books to return, and she meant to enquire whether they knew where she might be able to purchase a copy of a certain book she wanted as a gift for Harry.

She reached for the bell, intending to summon a maid, then changed her mind. There was cold water in the toilet jug. She would dress herself and slip out of the house without anyone realising she was awake. Lady Bellingham had insisted on accompanying her everywhere in London, and it would be a relief to go out alone for once.

Rosanna did not flinch as she washed in the icy water. It was not the first time she had had to make do with whatever was available. Travelling in Europe was not always a pleasure. She had had to contend with broken carriage-wheels on lonely roads, filthy rooms at inns little better than hovels where the sheets were crawling with lice, storms at sea and on land—and the terrifying experience of being held to ransom by brigands in the hills of Tuscany. At least it had been terrifying at the start, but their chief had been rather handsome, and in the end Rosanna had wheedled her way out of a nasty situation. He had fallen beneath her spell and eventually escorted her back to her father, unharmed and none the worse for her adventure. Everyone, except Mr Whitby, had been astonished at the ease with which she had escaped from her captors.

'You are a scheming little minx,' he had said as he embraced her. 'I'll not ask how you did it, in case there is something I ought not to know.'

Rosanna had laughed and shaken her head. 'I did not bargain with my honour, Father. I simply stood up to him and said I was surprised that such an intelligent man should waste his time in abducting people. My defiance amused him, and I discovered he had a passionate desire to study at an English university but that his knowledge of our language was not good enough. I taught him some grammar and promised him a dictionary, and that you would write him a letter of introduction to Professor Miles. You will do it, won't you?'

'How could I refuse?'

Father and daughter had then collapsed in laughter.

The prospect of walking unescorted through the streets of London was undaunting to such a girl, although she experienced a few nerves as she crept out of the house. Lady Bellingham's disapproval was far more terrifying than a brigand chief! She completed her daring escape, however, feeling a new sense of freedom as she set out in the direction of the library. With any luck, she would be back before anyone discovered she had gone. It was cold despite the bright sun, and she was glad of the new thick cloak. It had a deep edging of very expensive fur, with which the hood was also lined, and anyone glancing at her could not fail to realise that she was a very wealthy young woman.

It was more than a little unusual for a young lady of quality to be walking the streets entirely alone, so it was perhaps not surprising that Rosanna attracted attention. Much of it was from admiring young men, but also from a less desirable source. Her interest captured by her surroundings, she was not as alert as she might have been. Certainly she was not expecting the sudden push in the back as her bundle of books was snatched from her hand. She was, however, very quick to realise that she had been attacked by two rather ragged and dirty urchins, who had split and run in different directions. She gave a cry of annoyance, and set off in pursuit of the boy with the stolen books.

'Hey, you just stop that!' she cried indignantly. 'Those books don't belong to me.'

Rosanna was a healthy young woman, and she could run quite fast. She had almost caught up with the urchin when a man sprinted across the street and seized him. He caught hold of his collar, half lifting him from the ground as he cuffed his ear.

'Oh, please don't hurt him!' Rosanna cried. 'All I want are my library books. Oh, it's you, Captain Sawle...' She suddenly felt rather breathless.

Justin smiled as he saw the way her hair had come tumbling down about her face. She really is a very unusual young woman, he thought, as he gazed into those bright emerald eyes.

'What shall I do with the rascal?' he asked. 'No doubt the magistrates would hang him, given the chance.'

'No! Oh, no, you can't mean that?' Rosanna looked horrified. 'He's only a child, and I expect he's cold and hungry. Look at his face.'

Sensing a sympathetic heart, the young urchin began to cry noisily. 'I've got a sick muvver and two little 'uns to feed, sir,' he said, wiping his filthy sleeve across an even dirtier face. 'Don't let him shop me, miss? I ain't never stolen nuffin' before.'

'He is obviously a liar as well as a thief!' Justin's eyes gleamed. 'Well, what shall we do with him?'

'I have my books,' Rosanna said. 'Give him sixpence, and let him go.'

Justin laughed softly. 'Oh, Miss Whitby, what a strange idea of justice you have. The boy is clearly a villain in the making, but I bow to your judgment.' He tossed the urchin a half-guinea. 'Try not to get into trouble too soon, rascal!'

As the boy ran off with a huge grin on his face, Rosanna shook her head at him. 'I said sixpence, Captain Sawle!'

'It was all I had on me,' Justin said, his eyes narrowing as he looked at her. 'What are you doing walking without an escort, Miss Whitby? That boy was harmless, but it is not a good idea for a young lady to walk alone in town.'

Rosanna's brows went up. 'Surely you are not going to scold me, sir? I expect it from Lady Bellingham if she discovers the escapade, but not from you.'

'The more I know of you, the more you surprise me, Miss Whitby.' Justin offered her his arm. 'I happen to be going in the direction of the library; allow me to escort you there.'

'I'm perfectly capable of looking after myself, you know.' Rosanna grumbled and then took his arm. 'I should have caught the boy eventually.'

'Oh, I have no doubt of it.'

She saw the mocking smile on his lips. 'I do thank you for your help, nevertheless.'

'You overwhelm me with your gratitude.'

'Your tongue is very sharp, sir.'

'Too true. It is always getting me into trouble.'

His look told her that he was unrepentant. She wanted to say something to indicate exactly what she thought of him, but was unable to find the right words. Somehow, 'arrogant' and 'impudent' were not enough to describe the feelings his manner aroused in her. She decided that a dignified silence would be her best defence.

Glancing at her profile, Justin smothered a smile. 'Do you not think it is a little late for that, Miss Whitby? That frosty manner works only for dowagers and very correct young ladies.'

'And I am not . . .' Rosanna scowled at him, taking her hand from his arm. 'If you are imagining that I . . . Oh, I refuse to listen. I shall bid you goodbye, sir.'

She walked swiftly away, her back very straight. Justin watched her, a smile quirking the corners of his mouth. 'Goodbye, Miss Whitby,' he murmured softly.

No further incidents marred Rosanna's little adventure, but on her return to the house she found that her escape had been detected. As she entered the hall, Harry came out of a room to her left. 'Thank heaven you are safe!' he cried. 'Mama was sure you had been abducted!'

'I have been gone no more than an hour, Harry. There was no need to worry.'

His mouth thinned with disapproval. 'It was very thoughtless of you, Rosanna. I was worried, too. I thought you might have run away.'

She was immediately filled with contrition. 'I'm sorry, truly I am, Harry. I went to the library—and to buy this book. It's that copy of William Cowper's work that you wanted.' She laid her hand on his sleeve. 'I wouldn't run away; not without telling you why I was going. Not that I have any intention of leaving.'

The clouds cleared from his eyes. 'Well, you're here now, so it doesn't matter. Mr Denton from your father's solicitors called to see you while you were out. It seems to be a matter of some urgency. Mama told him we were leaving for the country this afternoon but he insisted on seeing you before you leave. I said we would call this afternoon, and we can drive down later. There's no need for Mama to wait on us. After all, we are engaged.'

'I'm quite sure I may trust you to escort me, Harry.' Rosanna's eyes twinkled, but her fiancé was serious as he replied,

'So I should hope! I believe I know how to behave as a gentlemen.'

'I'm certain of it.'

The smile left her eyes. It might be foolish, but sometimes she could not help wishing that Harry would act less circumspectly. More like . . . She dismissed the idea as unworthy. Captain Justin Sawle was an impudent rake! She could never consider marriage to a man like that. Harry might not always be exciting but she was fond of him, and love would come when they were married.

She linked her arm through his as they walked upstairs to the dining parlour. 'I wonder what can be so important that Mr Denton should come himself?' Rosanna wrinkled her brow. 'I had expected to hear from Mr Martin before this. Do you suppose that something is wrong?'

'The money you requested was placed in your account,' Harry said, 'so it can't be anything very dreadful. I expect it's just some document he wants you to sign.'

Her brow cleared. 'Yes, I'm sure you are right.' She laughed up at him. 'I had quite an adventure this morning . . .'

* * *

It was just two o'clock when Rosanna and Harry were shown into the restrained elegance of the offices of Messrs Denton, Reece and Denton, the long-established firm of solicitors who had handled Thomas Whitby's affairs for as long as Rosanna could remember.

A tall man with greying hair came to greet them. He was dressed very correctly in business grey, his thin face grave as he shook Harry's hand and then gripped Rosanna's in both his own.

'Miss Whitby, it was good of you to come.'

'I was curious, sir. Your message sounded urgent.'

'Indeed, it was of the utmost urgency.' He set a chair for her in front of his desk. 'I have received the most disturbing news—most disturbing.'

'Oh, is something wrong? My father's will was in order, was it not?'

'There is no problem there. You are your father's sole heir...' Mr Denton shook his head as if he could hardly bring himself to speak. 'As yet, I do not know the full extent of it, but I am very much afraid you have been cheated out of your fortune, Miss Whitby.'

'What do you mean?' Rosanna looked at him in surprise. 'Surely you cannot think that Mr Martin...' She saw her answer in his eyes. 'But he was a friend of Father! I can't believe he would cheat us.'

'I do not yet know the full facts,' the lawyer said. 'Mr Whitby gave Mr Martin the power of attorney over his investments. I warned him that it was not wise to place so much trust in one man, but he would not listen.'

'Father trusted Mr Martin.'

'A misplaced trust, it seems.' Mr Denton cleared his throat. 'As I said, I am not in possession of all the details, but it seems that Mr Martin turned the greater part of your father's investments into cash quite recently, and...'

'And?' Harry asked sharply.

He frowned. 'It appears that he gambled Mr Whitby's fortune away on the gaming-tables. Most of it on one particular night.'

'But that's impossible!' Harry cried. 'He must be made to repay what he has stolen from Miss Whitby.'

'Unfortunately he seems to have disappeared.' Mr Denton clasped his hands on the desk. 'A clerk from Mr Martin's office alerted me only this morning, Miss Whitby. Mr William Martin has not been seen for a week.'

'A week—and you've only just learnt of it?' Harry cried. 'This is disgraceful!'

'Mr Martin was in charge of Mr Whitby's business affairs, sir. I had no reason to suspect that he was other than honest. Indeed, until today I had thought him an excellent agent.'

'But, Mr Denton, where did the money in my bank come from?' Rosanna asked.

'That was advanced to you by my own firm,' he replied. 'Please do not be alarmed, Miss Whitby. I believe I may be able to rescue something from your father's investments. There are some small properties he did not dispose of before he left. What I need from you is a transfer of power, making me rather than Mr Martin your legal representative.'

'Yes, I suppose you are right,' Rosanna said doubtfully. 'But are you sure Mr Martin is at fault? Could the investments not simply have failed?'

'I have it on reliable authority that Mr Martin did lose a considerable sum at the tables on one particular evening—and there may have been other similar evenings.'

'It seems so unlike him. I know Father believed him to be entirely honest.'

'Many a good man's character has been wrecked at the gaming-tables, Miss Whitby.'

'Yes, of course.' Rosanna looked at him. 'Tell me frankly, am I ruined?'

'Not ruined, but you will not be wealthy. You will have an income of some kind—that is all I can tell you for the moment.'

'I see. Do I take it that you are willing to continue with my affairs? What if I cannot repay the money you have already advanced me?'

'I do not believe it will come to that.' The lawyer smiled at her. 'It is a matter of honour with me to do all I can for you. I shall make strenuous efforts on your behalf, believe me.'

'Then I must thank you, and leave my affairs in your hands, sir. I shall sign any paper you wish.' Mr Denton nodded and placed a sheet of paper before her. She read the simple document through and signed it, then got to her feet. 'In the circumstances, I think I should stay in town for a few days, don't you?'

'I shall be making enquiries. A week should put me in a better position to answer your questions, Miss Whitby.'

Rosanna nodded, turning to Harry. 'Shall we go? If we hurry, we may catch your mother before she leaves.'

Harry took her arm. He was silent until they emerged from the offices on to the street. 'Mother will naturally stay in town until this is settled.'

'Would you mind if we didn't tell your parents just yet?'

'We can't keep something like this a secret, Rosanna.'

'Please—just for a little while.'

He saw the pleading look in her eyes, and nodded. 'Well, I suppose I can think of some excuse, but they will have to know. This makes a considerable difference.'

'Yes, I can see that it does.' She looked at his anxious face. 'And I can see how shocked you are. The money means a great deal to you, doesn't it?'

'My father will have a seizure!' he replied. 'I didn't ask you to marry me just because you were an heiress, Rosanna, but, to be honest, I wouldn't have spoken if I'd known about this. We're none too full of juice ourselves at the moment, and—well, I was counting on your money to see me out of a hole. I need ten thousand pretty urgently to settle a gambling debt and my tailor's bills.'

Father swore he wouldn't pay them this time. It would
mean selling land.'

'I see. I'm sorry; this must be a blow for you.'

The sarcasm in her voice went home and he clenched
his fist, hitting it against his knee. 'We're not destitute,'
he muttered resentfully. 'Father's fortune is tied up in
land. Money is tight now and then. It's the same for
most landed families—that's why we marry money. It
infuses fresh blood...' Her silent scorn stopped him.
'Everyone expects it, Rosanna. Your father would have
understood. It was a bargain: my background for his
money.'

'Of course.' She smiled tightly. 'I'm not blaming you,
Harry, and I shall not hold you to your—your bargain.'

'Don't look at me like that,' he said. 'We'll talk about
it again when Denton has sorted it all out. It may not
be as bad as it seems.'

'So you would still be willing to marry me if I have
enough left?' She turned away, her face cold. 'Please
take me back, Harry. I'm upset. I can't talk about this
now...'

'Of course.' He looked uncomfortable as he handed
her into the carriage. 'I'm sure we can find some way
round this.'

'Are you?' She looked at a point somewhere beyond
him. 'I wish I had your confidence, Harry.'

The next few days were anxious ones for Rosanna. She
never knew just what Harry had told his parents, but
their manner towards her did not change markedly, so
she was sure he had not told them the truth. Now that
she was aware of the importance of her father's wealth
to the Bellinghams, she began to understand the significance of little things she had not noticed before, and
realised that Lady Bellingham would be much less inclined to fuss over her if she knew the truth. It was difficult for her to smile and act naturally. She had no idea
of what she would do if her father's money was all gone.
She could not marry Harry, of that she was certain. It

would not be fair to either of them. Somehow, she would have to make a new life for herself.

'If the worst comes to the worst, I can always become a governess,' she told Harry jokingly, but he did not find it amusing.

'Naturally I shall not desert you,' he said stiffly. 'We shall have to speak to my father and hope that he will help us.'

Rosanna refused to answer. Her pride had received a severe blow and she was not sure what to do. She was glad that Harry was out when the summons from Mr Denton finally came. Slipping out of the house quietly, she found a hire carriage for herself and was driven to the lawyer's office.

One look at his face told her that the news was not good. She sat down, clasping her gloved hands tightly to stop them shaking. 'Please tell me the truth, sir.'

'It is as I feared, Miss Whitby. The bulk of your fortune has gone.'

'How much will I have?'

'I can raise a few thousand pounds from the sale of some property—perhaps eight or ten thousand in all. Invested in safe securities, that will bring you an income of three hundred a year.'

Rosanna swallowed hard. It was not very much compared with what she was used to. She had often spent as much on a new ball-gown.

'My father sent many art treasures home . . .'

'All gone, I'm afraid.' Mr Denton clasped and unclasped his hands. 'I feel responsible for your loss, Miss Whitby. I should have known that something was wrong.'

'It was not your fault. Father should have listened to your advice.' She drew a deep breath. 'You must repay yourself the thousand pounds you advanced me. I fear I have spent most of it.'

'I shall do that only when I have managed to recoup some of your losses from the villain who robbed you!'

'Is there any chance of that?'

The lawyer met her clear gaze and frowned. 'To be honest, I do not know—but I intend to try.'

'Thank you. I am grateful for your help.'

'I see that your fiancé did not accompany you today. I trust this unfortunate incident has not affected your situation in that regard?'

'No, of course not,' Rosanna lied. 'I must go now, sir. Thank you again for all you have done.'

He frowned. 'I intend to approach the men to whom Mr Martin lost the bulk of your father's fortune. Since the money was not his to lose, I may be able to persuade some of them that it is not truly theirs.'

'Do you know who they were?'

'I am compiling a list now. When it is finished, I shall let you know what happens.'

'As you wish. I fear you will find it a thankless task, sir. I believe few gamblers would be prepared to return their winnings.'

'Well, we shall see . . .' As she turned away, he remembered something. 'Stay a moment, Miss Whitby. I have a letter for you. It was delivered to my office this morning.' He took an envelope from his desk and handed it to her.

She stared at the rather spidery writing. 'I do not recognize the hand. Who can it be from?'

'Please open it at once. It may contain news of Mr Martin.'

Breaking the wax seal, Rosanna scanned the message inside. She looked at the lawyer in bewilderment. 'It is from my grandfather—in Cornwall.' She shook her head in disbelief. 'He has written to ask me to stay with him.'

'Is that so very strange? He must have heard of your father's death.'

'But you don't understand . . .' She looked at the letter again, still unable to believe it. 'I thought he was dead. Father never spoke of him. There was a quarrel years ago, before I was born. I've never met Jonathan Whitby.'

'It is strange that your father should let you believe that his father was dead.' Mr Denton looked puzzled.

'But less strange that your grandfather should wish to see you.'

'Perhaps.' Rosanna tucked the letter into her beaded purse. 'I shall have to think about it. If I decide to visit, I shall let you know.'

'Very well.' He laid his hand on her arm as she turned away. 'You have enough money for the moment?'

'Oh, yes.' Rosanna smiled confidently. 'I did not spend quite all of what you advanced to me. I shall manage very well.' Stepping out into the chill of the late afternoon, she shivered. She had just ten pounds in her purse, and thought ruefully of the money she had squandered on clothes. Now what was she going to do?

'I shall look like a cad if I jilt you,' Harry said. 'No, I can't do it, Rosanna. What will people say?'

Her brittle laugh made him squirm. 'But *I'm* jilting *you*, Harry. There is no need for anyone else to know the truth. You can tell your parents that I simply changed my mind.'

He stared at her in the gloom of the mid-November afternoon. 'I can't ask that, Rosanna. You don't know what people here would say of you.'

'Since I shall not be here, it does not matter.' Her eyes were very bright as she gazed up at him. 'All I ask is that you don't tell anyone about my father's losses—not even your parents.'

'Why?' He sat on the edge of a little gilt sofa, looking perplexed. 'I don't understand, Rosanna.'

'I don't want people to laugh at my father. I know you always thought he was a bit of a fool, but he liked people and he trusted them. I'd rather everyone thought I was a heartless jilt. Please, Harry, if you ever cared for me, do this much?'

She looked so lovely, her green eyes full of a silent appeal, and his heart caught with pain. He was tempted to take her in his arms and say to hell with the money, but the thought of his father's reaction to the news that she was no longer a wealthy heiress held him back. He suddenly realised that she was offering him an easy way out. He would be the object of sympathy in Society, and his father's anger would be directed at her, not at him.

'If that's what you want,' he said at last. 'I'm sorry, Rosanna. I mean that sincerely. I'm very fond of you, you know.'

'I'm sorry, too,' she said. 'Now you had better let me go, so that I can pack. I don't want to be a burden to your parents a moment longer than necessary.'

'Where will you go?' he asked, feeling a pang of guilt. 'You have no home and no one to turn to.'

She smiled wryly as she saw his stricken face. Perhaps he did care for her a little. 'Oh, but I have,' she said softly. 'I have had a letter from my grandfather asking me to stay with him at his home in Cornwall.'

'Cornwall?' He stared at her. 'I had no idea you had a grandfather.'

'As a matter of fact, neither had I.' She wrinkled her brow. 'I have not read his letter thoroughly yet, but I know that he and Father quarrelled and did not speak to each other since. Anyway, he has asked me to stay, and I think it would be a good idea for a while. Just until I can plan my future.'

'I see...' Harry was aware of a sharp regret. 'I hope you will be happy, Rosanna.' He felt the colour rise in his cheeks as she looked at him. 'I do mean that.'

'Thank you.' She turned away, angry at his hypocrisy. She would have preferred a more honest reaction. 'I must pack now.'

'It looks as if it may snow. Will you not at least stay until the morning?'

Rosanna frowned. She longed to be away from the house, but she could not begin her journey until the morning, and she had no money to waste on a hotel.

'Very well,' she said. 'But I shall leave first thing in the morning.'

Justin Sawle wiped the fine sleet from his face as he nursed his weary horse through the muddy lanes towards the village of Sawltry. Seth Miller had sent an urgent message to London, bringing him back to Cornwall against his instincts. There was nothing here for him now—nothing but memories and wasted dreams. The thought of the empty house waiting for him was not encouraging. Seth would have seen that a girl from the village had made it habitable, but . . .

'Stop feeling sorry for yourself, man,' he muttered. 'You're lucky to have a roof over your head.'

When the mine Justin's mother had left him was in full production, the house had been built for the mine manager. It had come to her from her maternal grandfather and had not been part of her marriage settlement. Expecting to inherit a large fortune, Justin had long since spent the money bequeathed to him by his mother, most of it in trying to keep Wheal Margaret going. It had been running at a loss for the last two years, but he had been away fighting with Wellington's army and had believed that things might improve now that he was back. He was hopeful of finding a new lode soon, but that cost money. Money he could no longer hope to raise.

He had not even bothered to approach the bank after the breach with his father. Once it was noticed that his allowance had been stopped, his present loan could be called in. At the moment he had no idea how he would meet a demand from the bank—or pay the mine-workers' wages after the next month or two. He would have to close it down. The knowledge of what that would do to the people of Sawltry village brought a frown to his brow. There was no other work in the area. It would cause untold hardship, but what else could he do?

Remembering the advice given to him by his . . . No, not his father! A scowl curled his lip back as he recalled the last quarrel with Charles Sawle and the jeering remark about marrying an heiress. It was not easy to find an available heiress, even if he were prepared to seek an answer to his problems in that way. Most wealthy young ladies were fiercely guarded by their mothers, and he was seldom given a chance to get near them. Not that it had ever bothered him in the past. Marriage had been the last thing on his mind.

His eyes scanned the bleak landscape. Dusk was falling swiftly over granite tor, sweeping moorland and bare, stunted trees, cloaking all in a mantle of darkness; but at least the sleet seemed to have ceased and the wind was dropping. Thinking of his comfortable lodgings in town, he sighed. Seth's news would have to be important to make this journey worth while! He had been hoping to meet the Whitby girl again, though he knew he was wasting his time. She had made her opinion of him plain enough, both at the ball and when they met again in the street.

She was an unusual girl, he thought, remembering the way her eyes had kindled when he deliberately provoked her. She had been annoyed, but not shocked...definitely not shocked. It was a pity she was spoken for. He might otherwise have been tempted... He thrust the thought from his mind. He was not so desperate yet. A lucky win at the tables had supported him in town since he had left Sawle House, so maybe his luck would continue. He had never considered himself a true gambler, though his losses had usually been less than his winnings, but he had never needed to support himself by them. They would certainly not finance his plans for the mine. It was time he started to think about his future. He could always go back to the army, of course...

The road curved upwards and Justin felt his horse stumble as if the extra effort was almost too much. He patted its neck, sympathising. It was a foul night for man and beast.

'Not much further, old fellow,' he said. 'There's a warm stable waiting for you and a bucket of mash.'

The horse snickered, seeming to understand, its pace quickening as if it sensed that their journey was almost at an end. Justin smiled ruefully. If only his own problems could be solved as easily...

*   *   *

'You are an ungrateful, unnatural girl!' Lady Bellingham screeched. 'I don't know what your poor dear father would have said if he knew. He must be turning over in his grave.'

'My father would not wish me to marry a man I do not love,' Rosanna said defensively. 'He would understand . . .'

'Then that is more than I do! Why could you not say you had changed your mind before we gave the ball for you? So much expense, and all wasted!' She glared at the girl. 'I can see that it means nothing to you how my poor boy will suffer because of your selfishness. You have no feelings for others.'

Each word was like a stab in the girl's heart. She glanced at Harry, hoping for some word from him, but he merely avoided her eyes. 'That is not true. Harry knows I did not wish to hurt him.'

'As if it mattered to you! You are a heartless jilt.'

'No, Mother!' Harry was moved to protest at last. 'That's too strong. Rosanna has her reasons for what she's doing, and I accept them.'

'You were always too good for her.'

'Mother!'

'No, Harry,' Rosanna said quietly, 'let your mother say what she feels. I accept that she has a right to be angry.'

'I have nothing more to say to you, you ungrateful wretch!'

'Then I shall take my leave, ma'am. Despite what you think, I am grateful to you for many things.'

As she turned to leave, Harry followed her. He paused as his mother called his name. 'Yes, Mother?'

'Where are you going?'

'I have promised to take Rosanna as far as Hampshire in my carriage.'

'What nonsense is this? Let her go by the stage!'

'Lady Bellingham is right,' Rosanna murmured. 'I can manage alone.'

Harry looked down at her, a hint of shame in his eyes.
'I owe you that much, at least.'

It was on the tip of Rosanna's tongue to refuse, but
she remembered her straitened circumstances in time and
bit back the words. In future, she would have to swallow
her pride. She would have to learn to take what she could
from a hard, unforgiving world. If her grandfather did
not take to her, she would have to make her own way
from now on.

She smiled slightly, laying her fingers lightly on his
arm. 'Yes, Harry, I think perhaps you do.'

Rosanna sighed with relief as the coach pulled to a halt
at last. She felt stiff all over after so many days of non-
stop travelling. It had never been like this with her father.
They had always ridden in their own comfortable carriage, stopping whenever they pleased and continuing at
their own pace. The journey to Cornwall had been very
different. She had had to change from mail coach to
passenger coach and back again on the various stages.
The last leg of her journey had been particularly uncomfortable. Crammed inside the jolting vehicle between a plump farmer's wife and an equally stout parson,
she had closed her eyes for the past few hours, longing
for it to be over. Her grandfather's letter had stated that
she would be met in Bodmin if she sent word of her
arrival, and she was praying that he had received her
reply. Otherwise, it would mean yet another overnight
stay at an inn while she discovered some means of
transport.

It was quite dark now save for the lights of the posting
inn. Rosanna climbed down, glancing round the bustling courtyard with interest. Ostlers were unharnessing
the sweating horses while the coachman unstrapped the
baggage on the back of the coach, most of which appeared to belong to her. She had had to pay extra because there was so much of it, but she had wanted to
leave the Bellinghams' house immediately. To have asked
them to send on some of her possessions at a later date

would have been to invite a further tirade from her
former hostess—something Rosanna could well do
without.

'You've come for a long stay, miss?' The coachman
smiled and eyed her hopefully. 'Will you be needing a
room? Shall I fetch someone out to carry your bags?'

She reached into her purse for a coin, pressing it into
his expectant hand. 'I'm being met. Perhaps you would
be good enough to enquire if anyone has come to collect
Miss Whitby?'

Even as he nodded his agreement, a bulky figure
moved towards them out of the shadows. 'Would you
be Miss Rosanna Whitby?' he asked.

'Yes.' Rosanna looked up at him. He was quite a head
and shoulders above the coachman, who was by no
means short himself. It seemed that the tales told of the
giant race of Cornishmen might have some truth in them,
after all.

'I'm to take you to Rathmoor, miss. Are these yours?'
She nodded, and he shouldered two of her trunks at once,
both massive arms raised to support them. 'Please follow
me, miss. I'll fetch the rest in a moment. No one will
touch them.'

She could well believe it. Retribution would surely fall
on anyone who dared to try, and she thought that there
would be few who would dare to defy this giant. Picking
her way through the puddles, she lifted her skirts clear
of the mud, feeling relieved to see that the carriage she
was being led to was comfortable and well sprung, if a
trifle shabby.

Just as she was about to enter it, the inn door opened
and, in the sudden blaze of light, she saw a man and a
woman on the threshold. The woman was buxom, with
pale blond hair escaping from beneath the hood of her
velvet cloak, and bright blue eyes. She laughed up at the
man, lifting her face in an invitation for his kiss.

Rosanna turned away with a frown, not wanting to
see him respond to the woman's flighty behaviour. She
was sure that she had seen the man before, that it was

Captain Justin Sawle, though his back was half turned to her and she could see only his profile. Yet the sound of his laughter was familiar, and some inner instinct told her that she was right. It seemed that Harry had spoken truthfully concerning him—he was a rake! There was a gleam of gold on the woman's left hand. She was someone's wife, but not the wife of the man whose kiss she had invited. Rosanna felt sorry for her husband. She could have conducted her affair with a little more discretion!

'Make yourself comfortable, miss,' the giant said. 'Emily has put in a warm brick for your feet, and there's a rug.'

'That was very kind of Emily,' she murmured gratefully. 'What is your name, sir, and who is Emily?'

'Why, it's Benjamin, miss.' He grinned at her. 'Emily is my better half. She'll have a fire in your room and a good supper waiting on the parlour table.'

Climbing into the coach to the luxury of the warmed brick and thick rug, Rosanna relaxed with a sigh of relief. It looked as if she was going to be made very welcome at Rathmoor. She leaned back against the squabs, waiting contentedly while Benjamin collected the rest of her luggage. The inn door had closed again and the man seemed to have gone back inside. She was not sure if his companion had gone with him.

Benjamin called out to her as he returned to take up the reins. 'Shan't be long now, miss. We'll soon have you home and out of this miserable night. At least it isn't snowing. If you'd arrived two nights earlier, you'd have found the ground thick with it. Seems as if it's gone for the moment, though.'

Rosanna closed her eyes as the carriage moved forward. Her long journey was nearly over. Please let it be the last one she would need to make for a while! Surely her grandfather would allow her to stay until she had had time to decide what to do about the future? She was not sure what she wanted to do with her life now. It had been harder to leave behind her dream of becoming

Harry's wife than she had imagined, and the ordeal had not been made any easier by Lady Bellingham's behaviour, but that at least was all over now.

She tried to put the unhappy thoughts from her mind, wondering instead about the intimate scene she had witnessed at the inn. Could it really have been the man she had met in London so briefly? She rather thought it was, and felt a little sad. Despite his provoking manner, she had liked Captain Sawle. He was amusing, and it seemed a shame that a man like that should waste his life in pursuit of another man's wife. He was probably a gambler, and given to strong drink as well. No doubt he had more money than he knew what to do with. It was boredom that caused a man like that to behave so badly, of course.

Sighing, she decided to concentrate on her own future: what was she going to do now? Even if she found a home at Rathmoor, it was unlikely that she would marry. She was not prepared to set her sights lower than a gentleman, and since money was of so much importance . . . She felt a wave of bitterness. Harry had seemed so relieved when they parted!

Her eyes closed and her thoughts in turmoil, she did not know for how long the carriage rumbled on through the night. When she opened her eyes at last, she was surprised to see that the moon had come up and the rain-clouds had cleared, leaving the sky strangely light. How long was it since they had left Bodmin? She had been in a daze! She was aware that they had stopped moving, and then the door opened as Benjamin came to help her down. Stepping out, she found herself in a large courtyard, with a fountain that no longer played water over its stone dolphins, and moss-grown paving. A gasp of surprise left her lips as she looked up at the house. Why, it was beautiful! It was very old, and though she could not guess at its exact age, it looked as if it had stood there from medieval times, with its weathered timbers, long windows and stone walls that were washed to a silvery-grey by the light of the moon. Ivy trailed over its arches and roses nestled against its protecting walls, wafting their fragrance on the air, even on this winter night.

'Roses, and it's nearly Christmas!' A feeling of peace came over her as she stood staring at the house, unable to move. She had a sense of belonging, of coming home at last. It was as if the spirit of Rathmoor was welcoming her, holding out its arms to embrace her, claiming her as its own. 'I didn't know a house could be so beautiful,' she said, as Benjamin came to stand beside her.

'Ay, the old place gets to you,' he replied with a smile. 'Go on then, miss. Here's my Emily come to greet you.'

The woman in the open doorway was scarcely more than five feet tall, slim and attractive with a happy face and twinkling brown eyes. She ran down the steps as Rosanna approached. 'Well, here you are then, Miss Rosanna. Cold and hungry after your journey, I'll be bound. I hope Benjamin was there in time to meet you? You get on and fetch Miss Rosanna, I told him. Never mind your supper. "Oh, there's plenty of time," says he. He's slow, my man, but he does things in his own way, and you won't find a better or more loyal heart in all Cornwall!'

'I'm sure you're right.' Rosanna felt laughter inside her, warming her. 'He looked after me very well, and thank you for the warm brick. My feet were frozen. It was a kind thought.'

'It was nothing.' Emily beamed at her. ''Tisn't every day we have such a welcome visitor. The master's been that excited since he got your letter that I thought he would fret himself to death. He's waiting for you by the fire in the library. He'd have been at the door if I'd let him, but these cold nights don't suit him, and that's a fact. "I want to greet her at the door," he says to me, pulling a face the way he does when he's thwarted. But I had my way, miss, and I'm sure you'll agree it's for the best. We don't want him confined to his bed now that you've come, do we?'

'No, of course not.' Rosanna felt the warm glow spreading inside her as she entered the house. The hall was panelled in oak; a large rug covered the middle of the shining wood floor and a heavily carved dresser occupied the whole of one wall. Its shelves were cluttered with oddments, but a space had been cleared for a bowl of the roses she had noticed earlier, and their scent mingled with beeswax, lavender and leather. A selection of riding-crops, walking-sticks and other paraphernalia stood just behind the door.

'Don't take any notice of this clutter,' Emily said with a sniff. 'I'd have it cleared in a trice, but it's the way he likes it.'

'I like it, too. It's homely.'

Emily nodded. 'Come on then, miss.'

She led the girl through a door to their left. This was a long room facing the front courtyard; it was furnished with heavy oak pieces and looked as if it had once been used as a family room, for there were all kinds of objects piled on the tables or tucked away into odd corners, from a child's hobby-horse to a woman's embroidery frame; books, pictures, and hunting trophies, all set out in a way that suggested they somehow belonged together.

The adjoining room was a complete contrast. Small, and furnished in tones of cream and green, it was obviously a woman's retreat, with elegant little tables and sofas and exquisite china in display cabinets. It had long windows that overlooked the gardens and would be pleasant in the summer mornings, Rosanna thought. She would have liked to linger and admire its treasures, but Emily was knocking at the next door. She opened it, and gestured to her.

'Here she is, sir; and as pretty as a picture, if I may be so bold. Well, you'll be happy now, I expect—but don't keep her talking too long, for she's tired and hungry.' Emily beamed at the girl, pushing her forward into the room. 'There's your grandfather then, child. Kiss him, for 'tis what he wants.'

'Be off with you, woman, and confound your managing ways,' a man growled. 'Rosanna will do as she likes.'

'His bark is worse than his bite,' Emily whispered as she disappeared through the door.

Rosanna looked towards the fireplace at the man sitting in the tall, square-backed chair. Like the room, he was impressive; a handsome man with thick white hair, clean-cut features and brilliant blue eyes. It was clearly his domain, for the important mahogany desk, heavy, studded leather chairs and tall bookcases were all aggressively male. The walls were wood panelled to chest height and then covered with paintings of ships and the sea in every available space. Two sturdy bachelor chests stood at either end of the fireplace, the tops of both crammed with all manner of objects, some of which seemed to be no more than pebbles picked from the beach. The room had a lived-in atmosphere, and she felt it was the heart of the house. Instinctively, she knew that this was where Jonathan Whitby spent most of his time.

'Well, child, have you no greeting for me?'

'Grandfather, forgive me, I was dreaming,' she said, moving towards him. 'It's all so new to me, and so wonderful. I didn't know what to expect, but I never imagined it would be like this! I've never seen such a lovely old house!'

'Old is the word for it!' He gave a harsh laugh. 'You've seen the best of it, I'm afraid. We've kept this front wing in decent order but the rest is slowly falling into decay. Rathmoor is a liability, Rosanna. It takes all you have to give and still demands more. It has drained me and now it sucks on my dry bones, but when I die, the house will die, too.'

'You talk as if it's a person,' Rosanna said with a smile. 'If the house is so greedy, why have you stayed here?'

'Because I love it.' He lifted his bright gaze to meet hers. 'I fell in love with the place when I was a boy. I've loved it more than any woman, child or horse. Your father hated it. He ran away to escape its power. Our history is like that, Rosanna. Some of us love Rathmoor enough to die for it, others fear it. It either accepts you or it casts you out.'

She laughed and moved closer, instinctively kneeling before his chair to look up into his face. The impression of physical strength she had first received was false, she saw that now, though his spirit had not been crushed by the advancing years.

'And what is my fate?' she asked, her green eyes sparkling. 'Will this house of yours accept me, or am I to be driven out by its restless spirit?'

He chuckled deep in his throat, and his fingers strayed to the dark hair escaping in ringlets from beneath her bonnet. 'I do not believe anything or anyone could drive you away if you wished to stay, my dear. I have prayed for this day. I hoped your father would come home, though I don't blame him for staying away. He never truly belonged to Rathmoor—but I think that perhaps you do. I think perhaps you have come home...'

Rosanna sighed. 'I must be honest with you, sir. If you hope that I bring a fortune to spend on your precious house, I must disappoint you. Most of Father's money is lost.'

'That's a pity. I'll not deny I'd hoped to persuade you to spend some of your inheritance in restoring the house, but I'm glad to have you here, child.' He gazed down at her, seeing the pride and strength in her lovely face. 'You're young and strong; maybe there's hope yet. Together we might be able to keep the place alive.' He smiled wistfully. 'You've a look of Lady Caroline about you—you might even find her jewels.'

'A lost inheritance?' The girl's eyes glittered with excitement. 'Oh, do tell me more?'

Jonathan laughed loudly. 'You're a glutton for punishment, girl! The searching has driven me crazy for over fifty years. There's a fortune hidden somewhere in the house—I'd stake my life on it—but it has eluded me. The legend goes that Lady Caroline hid her jewels when the Roundheads attacked in the Civil War. Her husband was away fighting for the King, and she was left to defend the house alone. She hid the jewels and what was left of the plate, and she and her ladies bolted the doors, hiding themselves in the secret ways. When Cromwell's men came, they threatened to burn the place down unless she surrendered her treasures, so she came out into the front courtyard. She was hiding a pistol in her skirts, and rather than tell them where the jewels were hidden, she killed herself. The Roundheads were so shocked that they rode away without entering the house.'

'That's a tragic story,' Rosanna said. 'Do you think it's true?'

'It's documented in one of the family Bibles. I'll show it to you another day. Apparently she was the youngest daughter of an earl, very wild and very beautiful. She married a landed gentleman who was beneath her in every way in the eyes of society, and her father cast her off—but she brought her husband, who loved her desperately, a fortune in jewels that had been left to her by her own mother. She is wearing the emeralds in her portrait, but legend has it that she had diamonds, priceless rubies and pearls, besides lesser stones.' He grinned ruefully. 'I dare say the story has been exaggerated over the years, but the emeralds alone must be worth a fortune.'

'So, if we could find them...' Rosanna shook her head. 'You must have looked everywhere.'

'Yes. I should think there's a search at least once in every generation. The Whitbys have been looking for them since the Restoration.'

'Then we shall have to think of another way to get the money,' she said. 'There must be something we can do.'

'I'm damned if I know the answer. My revenues keep us from starving, but most of the land has been sold off over the years. I've done what I can...' He broke off as he saw that she was not really listening. 'Now what's going on in that pretty head of yours?'

'Oh, nothing,' she said. 'But I'm starving, sir! Did Emily say something about a meal?'

He nodded, amused. 'She did, and she'll have my head if I keep you from it much longer. The dining parlour is through that door and across the hall.'

'Are you not coming?'

'It's past my supper-time. Ring the bell for Benjamin.' He glanced down at his legs with a grimace of frustration. 'I need him to carry me upstairs. A riding accident left me like this last year. I fear my treasure-hunting days are over.'

'Then I'll find it for you, Grandfather.' Rosanna bent to kiss his cheek. 'Don't worry, we're not finished yet. There has to be a way of saving this lovely house, and I'll find it somehow, I promise.'

CHAPTER THREE

ROSANNA stood at the window of her bedchamber, the flickering light of the fire at her back sending dancing shadows across the wall. It was a beautiful room, though the furnishings had long since faded from the jewel bright blues, greens and golds that had once made it glorious. Yet somehow that only added to her sense of comfort and well-being. She had come home. She sensed it with every part of her being, and instinctively she knew that she would grow to love the house and its people. Sighing, she turned away to begin undressing. How she wished she still had the fortune her father had left her. She would spend it all on restoring this wonderful house. But, had she not lost her inheritance, she would be at Bellingham Hall even now.

Memories displaced her feeling of peace and she knew a surge of bitterness. No matter what Harry might say, she knew that her fortune had meant a great deal to him and his family. Anger flared in her. If men were so mercenary, they deserved to be treated with disdain. She could imagine what Lady Bellingham would have said if she had jilted her son because he was not rich! It was accepted that a man in Harry's position should marry for money, but what would people say if Rosanna did the same thing? They would call her a designing minx!

Yet why should she not do just that? A sudden surge of excitement lit her eyes. She knew herself to be attractive. During her travels in Europe, she had received several proposals of marriage, some of them from rich men, so why should she not marry a wealthy man for the sake of *his* fortune? Harry said it was accepted in polite society. His background for her money. A bargain, he had said. So why not her beauty for some rich gentle-

man's money? She could speak several languages and
was accomplished on the spinet and the harp. She would
make an excellent wife and hostess. A bargain... A little
smile curved Rosanna's mouth. All she had to do, was
to find was a man who had so much money that he did
not know what to do with it...

Justin climbed down the ladder into the long disused
mine-shaft, hearing the sound of trickling water from
somewhere ahead. It had been too wet to explore the
mine until today, the ground being waterlogged after the
snow and then the rain. It was ages since he had been
down here; this was a part of the mine that had been
worked out years before. He recalled his mother saying
how disappointed she was that the rich copper lode had
run out much sooner than expected. She had always believed that the mine had not yet given up its true riches.

Reaching the bottom rung, he frowned at Seth in the
light from his lantern. 'I thought this tunnel was under
water?'

Until this past week or so we had an exceptionally dry
year,' Seth replied. 'It has caused cracking above ground
and we've had to shore up the present workings in several
places. A couple of weeks ago I came down here out of
curiosity, and found something that I think may interest
you.'

'My mother always thought this was the richest seam.'
Justin arched his brow at him. 'Don't tell me you've
found a new lode?' He touched the walls of the shaft.
'The water is building up again now.'

'Ay, it's almost up to the lower level again; that's why
I wanted you to come down here in a hurry. I wanted
you to see it with your own eyes before the water covers
it again.'

Seth was leading the way into the narrow catacomb
of passages, the flickering light from his candle throwing
giant shadows on the walls. It was bitterly cold, and the
air was fetid. They would need to do something positive
about that if the mine was to be worked again, Justin

thought. The passage was opening out a bit, and there was a sheer drop to one side. There had once been a wooden bridge, but it had fallen into decay. Justin kicked some loose stones and counted until he heard the splash. It was a long way down.

Seth had stopped where there was only a rope ladder that he had placed in position recently. He paused at the top to glance at Justin. 'You'll have to be careful at this point. Follow me when I tell you. It's about half-way down.'

'I understand. Take care, my friend, it's a long way to the bottom.'

'I know.' Seth grinned at him. 'I've no intention of making Becky a widow just yet.'

Justin smiled, thinking of Seth's plump, pretty wife. She had two children under the age of five and was carrying her third. Her tongue was sharp, but she was a decent woman and one of the few he respected. Becky was not from Cornwall, but she had followed her man to his home with a good will, making it plain that she thought her place was beside him. Seth was lucky in his choice. He would not need to worry about coming home to find another man in his bed.

'Come down steady now.' Seth's command cut into his thoughts. He set his own lantern down on the rocky shelf and found his footing on the ladder. The walls of the shaft were covered with slime, and the stench was sickening as he hovered above the dank water. It was dangerous, but the men who worked beneath the ground took their lives in their hands daily. Beginning the slow descent, Justin took it carefully, the rope ladder swinging wildly under his weight. There was no sense in rushing it, though his pulses had begun to race and he could feel the excitement right down to his toes. If Seth were right...

'There—look to your left!' Justin turned his head obediently at the command, seeing nothing at first. 'Where the earth has crumbled. Can you see it?'

As the lantern swung out, he caught the dull gleam of something and drew a sharp breath. 'Hold the light still! Yes—Yes, I can see it. The dry summer has broken a great chunk of the earth away. They cut too low that last year.'

'I'm sure it's the start of a rich seam,' Seth said triumphantly. 'I was able to go right down when I came before, and I took some samples. I wanted you to see this first. It's high-grade copper, Justin. Enough of it to make you a rich man.'

'If we can get at it,' Justin muttered. 'It will cost a fortune to pump this damn water out, but I think you're right. I believe it's going to be worth it. I'm going back up now, Seth.'

He climbed towards the light, a fierce excitement beginning to burn inside him. The copper was there, just as Margaret Sawle had always believed. It was a vindication of her refusal to sell the property and of his own struggle to keep it going through the lean years. It would cost a great deal to get the copper out, but somehow he would raise the money. He had to, now! Everything was different. He owed it to his mother's memory, to Seth and the men who were relying on him for work—but, most of all, he owed it to himself. He was determined to succeed and to show Charles Sawle that he could stand on his own two feet. He reached the ledge and picked up his lantern, waiting for Seth to join him. They looked at each other in triumph, sensing each other's excitement.

'It's there, Justin, I promise you! I can feel it. I can almost taste it!'

'So can I.' The grey eyes glittered in the light of the lantern. 'Now all I have to do is work out how to get at it.'

Seth nodded. 'I wish I could help you...'

'You've done your part.' Justin smiled. 'It's up to me now.'

'Ay, you'll do it somehow.' Seth picked up his lantern. 'Will you come back for some supper? Becky was saying that she'd like to see you.'

'Are you sure it wouldn't be too much trouble?'

'Nothing's too much trouble for my Becky.'

'No, you're a lucky man. Sometimes I envy you.'
Justin thought of the empty house waiting for him. He
had been driven to seek company each night at the inn
at Bodmin—and some of that company could bring him
nothing but trouble. 'Thank you, Seth. I'd like that. It
will be pleasant to spend an evening with your family.'

Becky Miller's eyes strained into the darkness as she
stood at the open door of her home. Behind her were
the three rows of miners' cottages that made up the
village of Sawltry. Although a little smaller than hers,
they were much the same in construction, being built of
the same grey stone and consisting of one large room
for cooking and living, another out back for storage,
and a ladder to the tiny bedroom above. Becky's cottage
had a small parlour at the front; it was not impressive,
but enough to set the cottage apart from the others. Just
as she herself, as the foreman's wife, was apart from the
other women.

'Where are you, Seth?' she whispered, listening for
the sound of his footsteps. She was always afraid that
one day he would not come back and then she would
be alone. Except for the children. The other women were
friendly enough; they spoke to her when they passed her
door, but she was not one of them. She never would be.
She had once been in service for a time and had learnt
to read and to write her name. That was enough to make
her different, as far as the Sawltry women were
concerned.

She could see the high road from her doorway. Hearing
the sound of horses' hoofs, she frowned. That was the
coach from Bodmin. Seth was late tonight. He must have
stopped to talk with Justin Sawle. The two men were
firm friends, though Captain Sawle belonged to the
gentry and her Seth was a working man born and bred.
Yet the Captain was as at home in her tiny parlour as
in the elegant salons of London. He was a good man,
despite all that was said of him. Seth spoke highly of
him and he had always treated her with respect. Once

he had a wife, he would settle down. She had heard it said that a reformed rake made a good husband—not that Becky believed half the stories she heard. She hoped that the rumours that he was about to close the mine were not true. Seth himself had been acting strangely of late. He was up to something.

Her eyes strayed to the coach once more. It was too far away for her to see if there were any passengers, but she wondered what it would be like to travel, not just as far as Truro on fair days, but overseas. Sometimes she thought that if she had not met Seth that day... But surely that was his tall figure striding towards her through the dusk? She forgot everything but the glad surging of her blood as she ran towards him, to be caught in a crushing embrace.

'You're late...'

'I know.' He kissed her on the mouth. 'I've brought Captain Sawle home to supper, lass. Smile, and say you're glad to see him. He has some good news...'

'You're still here, then?' Jonathan Whitby looked up from his desk as Rosanna entered. 'Emily tells me you've been exploring.'

'Just enough so that I can find my way about. I haven't been in all the rooms yet—there are so many.' She wrinkled her nose. 'I asked Emily to show me Lady Caroline's portrait. Do you really think I look like her?'

'Only because of your hair and eyes. You're much prettier.'

'Flatterer!' She moved closer to the desk. 'What have you got there?'

'It's the Bible I was telling you about. I thought you might like to see it.'

She bent over his shoulder, touching the soft leather binding and silver clasp reverently. 'It's beautiful—and in wonderful condition for its age!'

'Lady Caroline's Bible is our most treasured possession,' he murmured mischievously. 'I've always thought the clue might be in here, but I haven't been able to find it. She must surely have left a message for her husband somewhere.'

'Perhaps she didn't have time. What does that writing say?'

Jonathan turned the flyleaf for her. 'It isn't easy to read, but I've deciphered most of it. Her husband wrote it in memory of her. He must have loved her very much. He says the jewels were a curse on them, and that he would give them all to have her back.' '"*Better they should burn the house and Caroline should live,*"' Rosanna read slowly. '"*Cursed are we now and for ever...*" I can't read the next bit.'

'Oh, he goes on about the family being cursed.' Jonathan traced the faded letters with his fingers. '"*Until the day she who shall once more sacrifice all for love comes... Then and only then shall the curse be lifted...*"' Jonathan frowned. 'This last piece has been obliterated later. I've never been able to make it out.'

'And what does all that mean?'

'Nothing much. I expect the poor man was out of his mind with grief. Well, there it is.' He sighed as he closed the cover. 'Perhaps the Roundheads simply made her give up the jewels and then shot her.'

'Oh, that is nowhere near as romantic,' Rosanna protested. 'I prefer the story you told me last night. Imagine that poor woman standing there alone and defenceless in the courtyard, taking her own life rather than see her beloved husband ruined.'

'It didn't give you nightmares, then? My wife thought it was a morbid tale, and so did your father.'

'I slept better than I have in weeks.' She arched her brow at him provocatively. 'Don't keep testing me, Grandfather. I have no intention of running away. I told you—I've decided to save you from ruin.'

'Very dramatic.' He frowned at her. 'The house may be going to rack and ruin; I can manage nicely. So what is this famous idea?'

'I shall marry for money.'

'Easier said than done, my girl! Neither of us can afford a season in London at the moment, though I'll grant you're pretty enough to catch a duke.'

'Oh, it wasn't a duke I had in mind,' Rosanna said innocently. 'He would probably be looking to marry money himself. I was thinking of something less ambitious. A man with money but no ancient title to protect. Someone who wouldn't look down his nose at the daughter of an ordinary country gentleman...'

'You sound as if you already have someone in mind?' He looked at her curiously, chuckling as he saw the little smile on her mouth. 'Maybe you've set your cap at him before this?'

'Oh no, it was quite the other way round. He said, if I wasn't engaged, he would sweep me up...'

'Engaged? That's the first I've heard of it!' Jonathan glared at her beneath bushy brows. 'Did the scoundrel jilt you when he discovered you were no longer an heiress?'

'No, I jilted him.' Rosanna told him. 'Forget him. It isn't worth bothering your head over. Well, what do you think of my idea?'

'It appears to be sound enough, but you haven't thought it through, child. First you have to find a wealthy man who's ready to marry you. I know you think you've found him, but you were rich when he met you. Then, even if he comes up to scratch, you have to persuade him that his money would be well spent on this ruin.'

'It isn't a ruin!' Rosanna came round and perched on the edge of his desk, giving him an innocent look. 'Don't you think I could persuade my rich husband to give me what I want?'

Jonathan's brows met in a scowl. 'You're a minx, Rosanna! I dare say you could do it if you've a mind, but don't forget that you have to live with the fellow for the rest of your life. I can't let you sacrifice yourself for my sake.'

'It isn't just for you, don't you see?' There was a sudden intensity about her that caught his attention. 'Oh,

I know I've only just come to the house, but I feel I belong here. The moment I saw it, I knew it had been calling to me all my life. I was prepared to marry Harry Bellingham because I wanted a home of my own. I thought any decent house would do, but I was wrong.' She jumped down from the desk, taking several agitated paces about the room. 'This house is a part of me. It's in my blood. I can feel it reaching out to me, imploring me to save it. Now that I understand I was meant to come here, I realise that there was a purpose in all that has happened to me. I could have married a Russian count and lived in a palace, Grandfather, but I would never have been complete.'

He looked at her anxiously. 'It's my fault. I filled your head with all this nonsense, rambling on last night about the place as if it had a soul...'

'But it has!' she cried, ceasing her pacing to look at him with wild, wide eyes. 'Don't pretend it was all non-sense, Grandfather. You've given your life to Rathmoor, so why shouldn't I? At least it would give me a sense of purpose, a reason for living...'

'A young woman like you needs a husband and babies.'

'There's no reason why I can't have them as well, but for some people that isn't enough. It wasn't for you. You had to have more.'

'That's as may be.' He moved uncomfortably under her bright gaze. 'I don't know, girl. We don't know each other yet, but I'm concerned for you. You've suffered severe blows these past few weeks, and your judgment may be impaired. I believe your happiness is more im-portant than any house.'

'But I can be happy only here!' she said, coming to kneel at his side. 'Let me do what I want, Grandfather, please? We'll give a dance. I'll invite Justin. I know I can get him to propose to me.'

'Who is this man?' he growled, weakening. 'I'm not saying I'll do it, mind. Is he of good family?'

'Harry said his family was one of the richest in Cornwall.' Rosanna laughed confidently. 'He as good as asked me to marry him at my engagement ball. His name is Justin Sawle...' She gave a little gasp as she saw the anger in his face. 'What's wrong?'

'I forbid it!' Jonathan Whitby's fist struck the table. 'You will put this idea out of your head at once! No kin of mine will marry that—that...'

'Philanderer?' Rosanna enquired sweetly. 'I know exactly what he is, Grandfather. Don't you understand? It has to be him. He is arrogant, careless and worthless; that's why I chose him. I shall use him just as he uses the women he despises. I couldn't deceive a decent, honourable man; it wouldn't be fair. No, Captain Sawle is perfect for my plans. He's so rich that it can't matter to him what he spends on his wife, and, since he is quite heartless, I can't hurt him.'

'But he could hurt you.' Jonathan shook his head. 'I won't let you do it, Rosanna.'

'He can't hurt me, because I don't love him. I don't believe I am capable of really loving any man. I wasn't truly in love with Max, my fiery Russian, though he made me quite faint with desire... Oh, don't look like that! I put a ball through him rather than let him seduce me!' She smiled as his brows rose. 'I was prepared to wed Harry, though I knew I didn't love him the way I should, but I do love Rathmoor. I think I understand men too well to love one with all my being. None of them is really worth the effort—you and Father excepted, of course. But that's different, isn't it?'

There was sadness in his eyes as he looked at her. 'You're very young to be bitter. Who hurt you so badly that you think love doesn't exist?'

'Does it?' She sighed deeply. 'I'm not bitter. I'm not even upset any more that Harry wanted my money more than he wanted me. I think it's something inside me that won't let me give my whole self to anyone. Father was a little like that, and I think perhaps you are, too?'

'Those green eyes of yours see a great deal!'

'Then let me do it, Grandfather? I have some jewellery I could sell. It might fetch a few hundred—enough for one little dance. For the New Year, perhaps?'

'If I agree—and I haven't yet—I'll pay for the wretched affair.' He scowled at her. 'Now go away and let me think about it.'

She smiled at him. 'As you wish. I thought I'd take one of the horses out. Emily says they need exercise.'

'That's true.' He sighed. 'Benjamin takes them out when he can. Be careful; there are some spirited beasts in my stable. I ought to have sold them long since, but I couldn't bring myself to do it.'

'Father always said I rode as well as most men, including him.' She dropped a kiss on the white head. 'Don't worry. I shan't do anything foolish.'

'No, you're a sensible girl. Perhaps too sensible,' he muttered. 'Go on then, wench! I'll give you my decision later.'

Jonathan Whitby might have changed his mind about her being sensible had he been privileged to see Rosanna riding hell for leather across the moors some time later. The wind stung her face, lifting the dark hair so that it streamed out like a banner behind her. It was a long time since she had been able to be free like this, and it felt so good. She was free of doubt, free of pain, at one with her horse and the stark beauty of sky, cliffs and the sea stretching as far as the eye could see.

She had not realised that the house was within half an hour's ride of the sea and she had turned this way by chance, coming on the secret cove all at once. Reining in at the top of a broad plateau, she sat looking down at the tiny sweep of golden sand enclosed by rocky cliffs on either side, listening to the surf breaking against the rocks and breathing in the tang of the salty air. It was somewhere in this region that the legends of King Arthur and his gallant knights had first taken shape, and looking about her, she could almost believe in the glory of Camelot. Her head went back and she laughed for sheer joy, feeling the life throbbing through her veins. This was her special place: she would come here again and again. She had a feeling of belonging, just as she had had at Rathmoor. It was as if she had been here before, as if she had known it all her life. Turning her horse, she raced wildly across the wide, treeless expanse of rough grass, unaware that she was being watched.

The man had climbed from the cove, reaching the top in time to hear her laughter as she wheeled her horse about. He stood staring after her, frowning. He was too far away to be certain, but something told him that she was the Whitby girl. So he *had* seen her at the inn in Bodmin—it had not been a figment of his imagination. He had been listening to something Anne Cornwallis was saying and had caught a glimpse of a girl entering a coach. She must be Jonathan Whitby's grand-daughter. He had not realised that in London. So they were neighbours, but what was she doing here? He had thought she was about to be married . . .

Shrugging, he began to walk unhurriedly in the direction of the village, which was set in a little hollow sheltered from the bitter winds. It was time he was getting back to the mine for a final discussion with Seth before he left for town. His visit to the cove had been a whim; it had been a favourite place of his mother's, where they had spent many happy hours together when he was a lad. He had meant to stay in Cornwall only a few days, knowing that his best hope of raising a loan was probably in London. He thought he might be able to raise enough to start pumping so that they could get a clearer look at the situation in the spring, and there was always his mother's family, though he would be loath to ask his uncle for help. Lord Mountjoy had always made him welcome, and he would probably agree to a loan, but there was a problem. Cousin Richard loathed him, and it would irk Justin to give him the satisfaction of knowing he was in trouble. Richard and he had enjoyed a strong dislike of each other since childhood. No, his uncle was a last resort. He would rather find himself a rich wife.

What had put that thought into his head? His thoughts strayed back to the Whitby girl. Why was she riding alone? Why had Harry Bellingham let her visit her grandfather without him, only weeks before they were due to be wed? 'I wonder...' A little smile curved his mouth. It might be worth paying a courtesy call on a certain neighbour before he left for town...

'There's a gentleman to see you, sir,' Emily said, her eyes bright with secret knowledge. 'Shall I show him in?'

'A gentleman?' Jonathan's brows went up. He caught his grand-daughter's hand as she made to leave. 'No, there's no need for you to go. It will be the Vicar or Sir Joshua. None of my other neighbours bothers to call these days...' He saw the look of triumph on his servant's face, and scowled. 'Who is it then, woman?'

'Here's his card, sir.'

He took the card, glancing at it with a frown. Saying nothing, he passed it on to Rosanna. Then, as she looked at him, he said, 'It seems you were right, miss. He must have heard that you were here.'

'Captain Justin Sawle,' she said softly, a little smile on her lips. 'How could he know? I don't understand.'

'He owns a mine not more than ten miles or so distant. He's been staying up at the house. Benjamin saw him at the Feathers Inn the night he fetched you.'

'You did not tell me!' Rosanna shook her head at him. 'You will see him, of course?'

'Since you are set on this idea of yours, I suppose I must.'

'I'll bring him in, then. He's a very handsome gentleman, I must say.' Emily gave the girl a conspiratorial look.

Jonathan turned to his grand-daughter as the servant departed. 'You're sure about this, Rosanna?'

'We discussed this last night,' she said with an admonishing smile. 'You are not going back on your word, I hope?'

'You'll have your way,' he muttered gruffly. 'I thought you might have changed your mind?'

'No.' She placed a finger to her lips. 'He's coming...'

A silence fell between them, and then Emily was announcing the visitor. 'Captain Justin Sawle, sir.'

'Come in, Captain,' Jonathan said. 'You will forgive me. I cannot get up to greet you.'

'I had heard of your accident,' Justin replied easily. 'It must be frustrating for a man as active as yourself.' He came forward to grasp the older man's hand, then his gaze turned unhurriedly to Rosanna. He smiled, and inclined his head. 'A pleasant surprise, Miss Whitby. Or is it Mrs Bellingham now?'

'Haven't you heard, Captain Sawle?' Rosanna lifted her head proudly. 'I jilted Harry. I was sure that the scandal must be all over town.'

'I have not been in town lately.' A faint smile quirked his mouth. 'My instinct is to congratulate you on a lucky escape, but you will accuse me of being rude.'

'In this instance, I believe your instincts are sound, sir.'

'Then perhaps I should feel sorry for Harry Bellingham?'

Rosanna flinched at the tone of his voice. Even though he obviously thought very little of Harry, he still believed her a heartless jilt. 'I had simply made a mistake.'

'And you were brave enough to rectify it?' Justin felt a start of surprise as he met her challenging look. There was no mistaking it! 'You have my admiration. It takes courage to bring the censure of Society on oneself.'

'I really had very little choice,' Rosanna replied honestly. 'May we offer you some refreshment? I have it on my grandfather's authority that the Madeira is quite tolerable.'

'Thank you.' He frowned as she moved to pour wine for them. There was some little mystery here, something he did not quite understand. 'Are you staying in the country for long, Miss Whitby?'

'I expect to make my home here, sir. And I am naturally eager to meet my neighbours. Your visit this morning is most opportune, for I believe my grandfather has something to ask you.'

'Yes.' Jonathan Whitby coughed, the words coming out stiffly. 'I'm giving a small dance on New Year's Eve for Rosanna—nothing very grand. It is only six months since her father died. Just a cold supper and some music for the younger ones.'

'That sounds very agreeable, sir.' Justin's assessing eyes flickered to Rosanna. 'I'm glad you have decided to brave it out and not hide from the world. You will surely discover that the gossip will last only a short while.'

'I am glad to have your approval,' Rosanna said. Her eyes gleamed with defiance. Captain Sawle would be a formidable adversary, she thought. She would enjoy the little game she planned to play with him. Despite the outrageous things he had said to her at the ball in London, it would not be easy to bring him to the point.

'I did not intend to sound patronising. I am aware that you have no need of my approval.'

'Have I not? How conceited you must think me, Captain Sawle.'

'I believe you are staying at the mine house, Captain.' Jonathan broke the small silence. 'Are you thinking of closing Wheal Margaret?'

'On the contrary; I am looking into the possibility of opening it up further. That's why I came down.'

Their conversation turned to the general problems of mining and the fluctuating prices of tin and copper. From there the two men progressed to local affairs, touching on the rumours of smuggling in the area, and politics, leaving Rosanna the leisure to listen and observe. She discovered that Captain Sawle was a free-thinker with his own definite views on the state of the country, the punitive taxes being imposed by the government and the recent war in Europe. Unlike most gentlemen she had heard speak of Napoleon Bonaparte, he was inclined to respect the defeated general, and he refused to call him a monster as so many had done.

'Napoleon was a good general and a brave man,' he said. 'I saw tears in the eyes of the Old Guard as they bade him farewell.'

'That's as may be,' Jonathan growled, 'but I'll sleep more soundly in my bed for the knowledge that he's on Elba.'

'For as long as they can hold him,' Justin murmured.

Despite their disagreement on this point, Rosanna saw that they got along tolerably well, agreeing perfectly that the tax on brandy was iniquitous. It was more than an hour before Justin rose to take his leave, having accepted an offer not only to the dance but also to dine with them on Christmas Day.

After he had gone, there was a small silence in the room as Rosanna looked at her grandfather with sparkling eyes, then she asked, 'Well, what do you think now? Will he do, sir?'

'He's not a man to be trifled with, girl.' Jonathan rubbed his chin thoughtfully. 'He's taken with you, I've no doubt of that. It was in his eyes, but I think you should go carefully. If he really cares for you, it won't matter to him that you have no money. Perhaps you should tell him the truth.'

'It cannot matter to a man as wealthy as Justin!' Rosanna cried defiantly. 'Why should I tell him?'

'Don't you think he has a right to know?'

'If he wants me enough, it won't matter. If he doesn't...' she shrugged. 'I can't force him to marry me. It will be his choice.'

'Somehow I feel you are laying up trouble for yourself, my, dear. Captain Sawle is not a weak fool who will beg to worship at your feet. If he thought you had deliberately deceived him...'

'He might fly into a rage, but what then? He would hardly divorce me; that would make him look a fool. Besides, I am sure I can persuade him to give me what I want. It shouldn't be too difficult.'

'Supposing he asks about your dowry?'

'You can say that my father's affairs are not yet settled. I do not believe he will press it further in the circumstances. He will not be marrying me for my money.'

'Are you really as hard as you sound, Rosanna?'

She flicked down her lashes, not wanting him to see that she was far less confident than she pretended. 'Father always gave me everything I wanted. He liked spending his money on me, so why should Justin be different? Rich men enjoy the pleasures their wealth provides.'

Jonathan sighed and studied the girl's face. Was she hard and calculating or a complete innocent? He did not know her well enough to judge. She had come into his life like a breath of fresh air, making the dull routine of his days exciting. Perhaps he was worrying for nothing. A girl with beauty, charm and intelligence deserved the best of everything. Many men would be only too happy to lay their fortune at her feet. If she were willing to be patient, he was sure that she could find someone who would love her enough to take her for what she was. But she was impatient and headstrong, and she had her heart set on marrying Justin Sawle.

A frown creased his brow. Had he been blind? Was there more to this than she would admit? If she were in love with the man...
He gave up the struggle to understand the workings of her mind. Her course was set, and she must follow her own destiny.

Justin frowned as he looked at the seal on the back of the letter that had just been delivered. He recognised it at once. What could his uncle want? It was unlike Lord Mountjoy to write to him.

Breaking the seal, he scanned the brief message. He had been invited to spend Christmas with his uncle, and a scrawled postscript explained why. Lord Mountjoy had been taken suddenly ill, and Richard was in France. There was little love lost between the father and son.

They argued frequently, and Richard seldom visited his home. He was a rough-tongued fellow with few manners, and his father had long despaired of him. Indeed, there was more affection between the uncle and nephew than Richard and his father, for both Justin and Lord Mountjoy shared warm memories of a woman they had dearly loved and this had made a bond between them that grew stronger as time passed. Justin had sometimes wondered if this was a part of the reason for his cousin's hatred, though it seemed to go much deeper than merely jealousy.

'Damn it!' Justin muttered as he laid the letter down. He would have to go; there was no help for it. He could not let Mountjoy down. Actually, he was very fond of the old boy. It meant he must cancel his dinner engagement with the Whitbys, and that was a nuisance. His second meeting with the girl had whetted his curiosity, and he had been looking forward to seeing her again.

Yet it might not matter too much. He was sure that he had glimpsed an invitation in Rosanna's eyes the other morning, though she had withdrawn into herself later. She was obviously a young woman with a mind of her own, and she would not fall into his hands like a ripe plum. If he wanted her, he would have to make certain of her. It would not suit *him* to be jilted! He wondered what Harry Bellingham had done to upset her. Or had she merely become bored with the idea of marrying him? Was she in fact a heartless jilt? He was not sure. Harry Bellingham had clearly had no idea how to handle her. She was a mettlesome filly, and it would need a strong man to tame her, but it might just be worth the effort— apart from the money, of course. He doubted that the rumours of the size of her fortune were true; these things were usually exaggerated, but even if she was worth only a third of what he had been told, it would be more than enough for his purpose.

'You are a cynic and a rogue, sir,' he murmured, catching sight of himself in a plain wooden-framed mirror. 'It would serve you right if this one told you to go straight to hell!'

But she would not, of course; he had not yet met a woman he could not charm into his bed if he so desired. That was it! he realised. Somehow he had to find a way of seducing her. He was certain that she was still a maiden. If he compromised... No, it would have to be the real thing with Rosanna Whitby. She would not be afraid of her reputation. He would have to make love to her, if he wanted to be quite certain that she would marry him and not change her mind at the last moment.

Justin turned away from the mirror, unable to look himself in the eyes. What he was planning to do was despicable. He had never actually planned to seduce a woman before. Damn it—he had never needed to! Many scented notes had been pressed into his hand by bored and unhappy ladies of his acquaintance. Sometimes he obliged them, sometimes he incurred their wrath by refusing their invitation as politely as he could, but the strange thing was that he seemed to be accused of adultery whether he was guilty or not. Had he seduced all the women who were credited to his account, he would have had no time for anything else!

Smiling wryly, he laid the letter down. It was a gamble he must take. If Rosanna were really attracted to him, it would make her a little anxious, a little more eager the next time they met—and if she consoled herself with someone else... He shrugged his shoulders. He was not so desperate yet. He would find the money for the mine somehow...

Rosanna opened her gift, gasping with pleasure as she saw what was inside. It was a tiny miniature of Lady Caroline painted on a thin sliver of ivory, and it had been mounted in silver so that she could wear it as either a pendant or a brooch.

'It's beautiful,' she cried, embracing her grandfather.

He smiled at her fondly. 'The miniature has lain in a drawer ever since I can remember, but you seemed so taken with her story that I got Benjamin to take it into Truro and have it made up for you. I was afraid it might not be ready in time.'

'Oh, I love it,' she said, laughing as she caught the twinkle in his eyes. 'Emily has told you that I've been searching for the jewels! I hoped I could give them to you as a Christmas gift.'

'The present you gave me was sufficient.'

She had given him a tiny silver snuff-box in the shape of a jockey's cap. It had been a favourite of her father's and she had known he would like to have it for that reason, if nothing more. Although he had not said very much about it, she felt that he had deeply regretted the breach with his only son.

'Just think how exciting it would be if I could find the lost treasure,' she said, her eyes glowing. 'I am sure Caroline hid it in the house. If she heard the Roundheads were on their way, she would hardly dare risk digging a hole in the ground. The fresh earth would have been noticed. She could simply have thrown the jewels into the well, I suppose, but they would have been found long before this if she had. Someone must have looked there?' He nodded, and she sighed. 'I expected that.'

'Is this interest in the jewels because Captain Sawle cancelled his visit today?'

Rosanna shook her head. 'He had no choice, if his uncle is ill. He sent his apologies—and the brandy for you and that play by Sheridan for me.' She thought of the boldly written inscription on the fly-leaf. There had been nothing to encourage her hopes in that brief message. 'Besides, he isn't the only wealthy man in Cornwall!'

'He's the one you've set your mind on, though.' Jonathan's eyes were thoughtful. 'Maybe he'll come to the dance. His letter promised he would if he could manage it.'

She shrugged carelessly. 'There are others, if he doesn't. Everyone else has accepted.' Her fingers played restlessly with the brooch. 'I think I'll do a little exploring until dinner. Thank you again for my beautiful gift.'

'It was nothing, girl. I wish I was a rich man and could give you the things you're used to.'

She shook her head and smiled. 'It's a pity I was never much interested in jewellery. Apart from my pearls, Father only gave me trinkets. I never wanted anything more. If I had been a little more avaricious, I might still have been a rich woman!'

'You're a strange girl, Rosanna. I don't really believe you care about money.'

'For myself? No.' She pulled a face at him. 'Don't lecture me again, Grandfather. It's Christmas Day—and I'm going treasure-hunting!'

She laughed as she made good her escape. She did not want another argument over Justin Sawle. It was so frustrating! He had seemed really taken with her in London, and she had been sure it would be easy enough to lead him into making her an offer. She had been proposed to more times than she could remember while she was travelling with her father, and though she acknowledged that many of the offers had been made her because she was an heiress, she believed some of them had been genuine. She had felt so certain that Justin really wanted her. He might not love her, but he wanted her, and he would know that her price was marriage.

Having been to the kitchens earlier to give her Christmas gifts to Emily and Benjamin, Rosanna made her way now towards Lady Caroline's bedchamber. If only she could find the missing jewels, it would not matter what Captain Sawle thought of her. She was doing this merely for the sake of this beautiful old house. Her search for the lost inheritance had led to many less pleasant discoveries; there was dry rot in part of the east wing, and some of the panelling was beginning to crumble. The plasterwork was sadly in need of repair in almost all the rooms, and the soft furnishings were faded or moth-eaten. The rotting timbers were the cause of

most concern to her, however. If work was not begun
on them soon, it might be too late.

Rosanna gazed at herself in the mirror, pouting at her
reflection in frustration. What good was it if she looked
enchanting in her soft white silk gown with its sash of
emerald green, the daringly dipped neckline, little puffed
sleeves and generous flounce? She had tried the dress on
earlier for her grandfather and 'enchanting' was his
word. She thought it gave her an innocent, ethereal look,
which was exactly what she wanted. She fastened a single
strand of pearls around her throat, and looked again.
Were they necessary? Oh, what did any of it matter if
Justin did not come? He had sent no word. It was true
that there would be two other gentlemen at the dance
who were both rich and single, but Jonathan had de-
scribed them to her in detail and she had already dismissed them as possible husbands. Only one fulfilled all
the criteria she had set for herself. He had to come this
evening. He had to!

Sighing, she picked up a delicate painted fan and went
downstairs. Jonathan was waiting for her in the long
parlour which had been cleared of furniture for dancing,
and the group of musicians were already in their place.
Emily had summoned extra help from the village, in-
dulging in an orgy of cleaning and polishing. If one did
not look closely, the faded drapes were not too noticeable, and Emily had provided a magnificent cold
supper for later in the evening. She, her sisters and nieces
had all worked very hard to make the evening a success,
and Rosanna had been down to the kitchens earlier to
thank them. If things worked out as she hoped, Emily
would soon have a large, permanent staff under her. It
was amazing the way she and Benjamin had coped for
so long.

Her muddled thoughts were thrust to one side as the
guests began to arrive. Most were close neighbours who
had driven a matter of five miles or less, though some
had come from further afield. She stood at her grand-

father's chair to greet them. The Pardoes, a family of
three girls, all slightly younger than herself, and their
parents, were the first to arrive, followed closely by Sir
Joshua Kilby, an old friend of Jonathan and the only
regular visitor since his accident. He had called several
times of late and Rosanna liked him. He was a widower,
but in much the same financial state as his close friend
and therefore not eligible as a husband.

Soon all the guests but one had arrived, and Rosanna
was obliged to leave her grandfather to gossip with Sir
Joshua, joining the younger people for the start of the
dancing. She was disappointed and annoyed at the failure
of her plan, her eyes turning again and again towards
the doorway in the hope of seeing Captain Sawle's tall
figure. When he had not arrived by supper-time, she was
obliged to accept that he was not coming.

She ate her cold chicken, ham and syllabub, listening
patiently as Lord Peter Melrose enthused about the
hunting he had had this past week. Lord Peter, a widower
in his late forties, stout, ruddy-cheeked and inclined to
be pompous, was a man of considerable wealth and
standing in the district. He had been paying Rosanna
attention all evening, and from some of his pointed remarks, she believed he was weighing her up as a possible
third wife, and mother to a brood of five children all
under the age of nine. He could certainly afford to divert
some of his wealth to the restoration of the house, but
not even for Rathmoor could she contemplate such a
marriage!

'Excuse me, Lord Peter,' she said, when she could
stand no more of it. 'I must speak to Grandfather.'

Leaving him, she made her way back to the long
parlour. A few couples had returned and were grouped
by the window. Rosanna was about to join them when
she heard voices behind her, and her heart jerked. She
turned slowly, controlling her emotions with difficulty
as she saw Justin Sawle standing by her grandfather's
chair. He had seen her, and after a moment excused
himself, walking towards her with a smile.

'Miss Whitby,' he said. 'I must ask you to forgive me for coming so late to your dance. When I arrived home earlier this evening, there was an urgent message awaiting me.'

'Since you took the trouble to come at all, you are forgiven, sir.'

'You are generous.' He lifted his brows as the music struck up again. 'May I have the honour of this dance?'

It was a waltz, still considered by many to be a little fast, but acceptable at a private party like this where everybody knew each other well—or almost everybody. Rosanna was not well acquainted with her partner, but this was not the moment to be prudish.

'Thank you,' she said, a little tingle running through her as he placed one arm about her waist. 'I hope your uncle is better?'

'I am glad to say that he is improving steadily.' Justin smiled down at her. 'He enjoys company. He did not want me to leave this morning, but he has company now. His son has come home. Probably because he was told that I was staying with his father.'

'Oh?' She glanced up at him. 'Do I detect a note of cynicism?'

'Richard and I have never been the best of friends.'

'I understand.' She pulled a face. 'I suppose I must thank your cousin for the pleasure of your company now?'

'I am gratified that it gives you pleasure.' A wicked gleam showed in his eyes. 'Yet my plans were unchanged by Richard's sudden arrival, for I intended to come this evening. What I did not expect was an urgent message from Seth.' The gleam faded, to be replaced by a frown. 'There has been a small accident at the mine. One of the men was injured.'

'I'm sorry. I hope it was not too serious?'

'Bad enough. The doctor thinks he may never walk again.'

Rosanna's face paled. 'That is awful. Is he married?'

'Yes, and they have a baby of six months. I went to see him and his wife before I came, to assure them that I would not be turning them out of the cottage, and to offer Sally work at the house so that they can pay their way. I gave them something to tide them over, but Rob is a proud man; he insisted on its being a loan.'

She looked at him curiously. 'That was a kind and thoughtful thing to do, Captain Sawle.'

His eyes held that mocking gleam once more. 'It surprises you that I am capable of an act of kindness? Surely I could do no less for the son of a family who have worked in the mine for generations?'

'I have heard of workers being turned out of their cottages in similar circumstances, but I think it is despicable. I am glad you are a considerate employer.'

'I am delighted to have your approval.'

She blushed. 'Now that was not kind, sir.'

'I am not always kind, Rosanna. Neither, I think, are you.'

'Why do you say that?'

'There is a gentleman staring at me from across the room, and I believe he would like to run his sword through me.' Justin's look challenged her. 'Have you been collecting more hearts in order to break them?'

'I do not make a habit of breaking hearts!' She looked at him defiantly. 'Harry's heart was not broken, I assure you.'

'Then I do not stand in danger of having mine crushed beneath your feet?'

A smile lurked about her mouth. 'Have you a heart to break, sir? I remember that your opinion of the female sex was of a low order—or am I mistaken?'

'Of their morals; in some cases their intelligence, and the quality of their conversation—no, you are not mistaken. I find few women tolerable companions, but they do have their charms.'

'For that remark, sir, you deserve to be hung, drawn and quartered!'

'And would be, if there were any justice.' Justin laughed. 'I did not intend any insult to you. You, of course, are not one of those silly, vapid women I find so unamusing.'

'Thank you.' Her eyes glinted. 'I suppose that was meant as a compliment—though I am not sure, since it must mean that you find me amusing?'

'But that *is* a compliment! If I did not find you interesting, I should be bored and we would not be dancing.'

'Interesting is different from amusing.'

'Ah, I see you mean to pick holes in me. I shall have to be on my guard with you.'

'No, indeed you will not. I am the mildest of creatures and would not dream of contradicting you. I only wished to be sure what you meant.'

'Rosanna, you are many things, but mild is not one of them.' He chuckled deep in his throat, intrigued by this prickly creature who seemed to invite and defend at the same time. 'I believe you know exactly what I mean. I think you have known how I felt towards you from the first. You look very lovely and very innocent, but my instincts tell me that I should be wary. You are a thing of fire and beauty—too dangerous to play games with. I believe you mean to punish me for my scorn of your sisters.'

'Captain Sawle!' She raised innocent eyes to his. 'Are you suggesting that I am inviting you to—to play games, as you put it?'

'Oh yes, you are definitely inviting me,' he murmured huskily, 'but I am not such a fool that I do not understand the rules of your games. I am not another Harry Bellingham.'

'I did not suppose that you were.'

Rosanna's heart fluttered wildly in her breast. Was he on the verge of asking her to marry him? She flicked down her lashes, not daring to look at him lest he see the excitement in her eyes.

'That is good, for you would find me less obliging. I should warn you that I have a temper when provoked, and once something belongs to me, I do not easily let it go.'

She glanced up at him then, her lips slightly parted. 'I, too, have been accused of having a temper, but I do not lose it very often. Only when I have been provoked too far.'

'I am delighted to hear that,' he murmured softly.

'That I have a temper, or that I do not often lose it?'

'Minx!' He gazed down at her. 'You tempt me, Rosanna.'

'To what, sir?' The music had ended and she curtsied to him, smiling slightly.

'That question must remain unanswered for the moment,' he said. 'Will you ride with me one morning?'

'How do you know that I can ride?'

'I saw you at the cove.'

'Meet me there, then.' Her brilliant gaze challenged him. 'On Sunday at eight.'

He held her hand a moment longer. 'Until Sunday, then.'

Rosanna stared after him as he walked away, pausing only to speak briefly to her grandfather before leaving the room. Had he ridden ten miles merely to dance with her once? It seemed that he had, for he went out without a backward glance. She was not sure whether to be gratified or piqued. Why had he not turned to smile at her from the doorway? She could not be certain of his intentions, though for one moment when they were dancing she had thought he meant to speak. If only the music had gone on a little longer!

'I believe this is my dance, m'dear?'

Rosanna turned with a smile as she heard Sir Joshua's voice behind her, giving him her hand. 'You know full well that the last dance was yours, sir. Thank you for not claiming it.'

'Young Justin would have run me through,' he returned with a harsh laugh. 'Reminds me of his mother, that young man. She was a wild one in her youth. Every man in the county wanted her, and no one could understand why she married Charles Sawle. Bit of a mystery there, if you ask me. He wasn't good enough for her.'

'Was Justin her only son?'

'Her only child. He'll inherit everything, of course. There isn't a girl in the county that hasn't set her cap at him—but he usually avoids them like the plague.' Sir Joshua winked at her. 'Come to think of it, he normally avoids little affairs like this. Quite a surprise to everyone to see him tonight. Made it plain why he came, though.'

'Did he?' Rosanna couldn't keep the sudden eagerness from her voice.

'If he'd stayed, he would have been obliged to ask one of the Pardoe girls to stand up with him. They're his nearest neighbours, don't you know?' He gave her a knowing look. 'I always thought it would take an exceptional girl to catch that rogue!'

'Sir Joshua!' Rosanna protested, pretending to look shocked.

'Don't put on those ladylike airs for me, miss! I've heard you talking to your grandfather, remember?' He grinned at her. 'I don't doubt you've hooked him. Now, all you have to do is play the line a little...'

'You are a wicked old man!'

He sighed deeply. 'Too old and too poor. Otherwise, I'd give that young scoundrel something to worry about!'

'If that were the case, there would be no contest. I should definitely marry you.'

He caught the sparkle in her eyes, and chuckled. 'I almost pity Justin. You will have him in church before he knows it.'

'Do you think so?' she asked a little wistfully.

'I'm sure.' He looked at her hard. 'That's when the sparks will start to fly. Be sure that you know what you're doing, m'dear.'

'Oh, I do.' She smiled, her eyes wide and innocent but with lurking mischief. 'I do...'

Yet later, when all the guests had gone and she sat dreaming before her dressing mirror, a picture of Justin's face came into her mind, causing her to stop brushing her hair and look at her own reflection. 'I have a temper when provoked,' he had said, 'and once something belongs to me, I do not easily let go.'

A little shiver ran down her spine. It had all seemed so simple when she had planned it, but now she was not so sure. Supposing Justin did ask her to marry him, thinking that she was an heiress, would he not be justified in losing his temper when he discovered the truth? Yet it could not really matter to him, and he was so odd that he would probably think it a huge joke! Then why not tell him now? She dared not, for fear of seeing the look she had seen in Harry's eyes. No! She was simply doing what so many others did, so where was the harm?

Picking up her brush again, she smothered her fears. Her lack of a fortune could mean little to a man as wealthy as Justin. He would settle some money on her, and he would not mind that she chose to spend it on Rathmoor...

CHAPTER FOUR

THE WIND sweeping in from the sea was bitterly cold, but once it dropped, it would rain. Rosanna looked anxiously at the sky as she rode, praying that those leaden clouds would not fulfil their promise.

She was wearing a dark green velvet riding-gown with a short jacket that fitted neatly to her slim waist. It was frogged with black braid and silver buttons, matching the tiny hat she wore perched on the back of her head, and her soft leather gloves. It was a stylish outfit similar to one she had once seen Princess Charlotte wearing in the park. Princess Charlotte was the Prince Regent's only daughter and she had been engaged to Prince William of Orange, but she had taken a dislike to him and broken it off the previous summer. The Regent was rumoured to have been incensed at her behaviour and some said he was very unkind to her. At least *she* had not been censured by her grandfather, Rosanna thought, but of course he had guessed the truth. She wondered what Captain Sawle thought of the affair. Did he consider her a heartless jilt? From some of his remarks at her dance, she rather thought he might. She could only hope it would not prevent him from speaking.

Rosanna's heart began to pound as she saw the man waiting at the head of the cliffs. He had dismounted and was standing with his back turned to her, looking out to sea in a way that made her wonder what he was thinking; but hearing her approach, he swung round, mounted his horse, and rode to meet her.

'You came, then! I thought the weather might dissuade you?'

'The prospect of a little rain does not dismay me. Where shall we ride?'

'Wherever you wish.'

'I should like to see Wheal Margaret.'

'There is little to see, and it is a good hour's ride from here.' He smiled as he saw the flash of pride in her eyes. 'Your wish is my command, but if I take you there, you must stay for luncheon at my house.'

She knew that he lived alone, and that what he was suggesting was highly improper. She saw the wicked glitter of his eyes and understood that he was testing her, discovering just how far she would flout the laws of society.

'That sounds delightful, Captain Sawle. Shall we go?'

He laughed softly. She was a bold wench, and so beautiful that he felt an ache in his loins. Her lips were moist and inviting, and he knew an urge to lie with her. It would certainly not demand too great a sacrifice to relinquish his freedom in return for all that *she* had to offer! 'I am at your service, Miss Whitby.'

The mockery in his eyes made her spur her horse forward, responding to something she did not quite understand. She sensed that they were fighting some kind of a duel, both struggling for something, but what? Supremacy? Yes, perhaps that was it. Justin was a man who would seek to dominate, and she had never been able to submit to the hand of a master. This new insight into her own character bothered her for a while, but then the mood was gone as she was caught up in the excitement of the chase.

Their horses were well matched for speed, and although Justin held his pace so that they rode side by side, she knew that he could probably outdistance her if he chose. He did not choose, however, and the thrill of riding together like this brought a glow to the girl's cheeks and a sparkle to her eyes. Thoughtful of their mounts, they slowed after a time, enjoying the fresh bite of the morning air and the tranquillity of their surroundings. There was a certain beauty in the winter-dark fields, the soil as yet unbroken by the plough, trees bare of leaves and a glowering sky.

The mine buildings had a raw ugliness that scarred the landscape, Rosanna thought. Yet there was also a feeling of rightness about them; they were in a sense the life-blood of the village, bringing prosperity to the people who worked there. Today, even though no one was working below ground, she could hear the grinding of the relentless pumps. Above that sound, the clear toll of church bells called the little community to morning service. Her eyes turned towards the house, which was set on a rise so that it overlooked the mine and the cottages. Much larger than the miners' homes, in comparison with Rathmoor it was small and squat and ugly.

Obviously Justin did not own a country house, and she thought that he must live with his father when he was not in town. It might not be too difficult to persuade him that Rathmoor was ideally situated for him in relation to the mine, and that after they were married, they would be very comfortable there if certain repairs were carried out. Her heart began to race as she turned her horse towards the house. She was risking her reputation by visiting his home. Suppose he took advantage of the situation and then refused to marry her? Yet he must be aware of the rules of this game they were playing! He would not abuse them—or would he? What did she really know of this man she was hoping to trap into marriage?

'Hopefully, Sally will have prepared a light meal for us,' Justin said as they cantered into the small yard. 'You must forgive the inadequacy of my hospitality, Miss Whitby. It suits me to stay here for the moment, but it is scarcely what you are accustomed to.' He dismounted and came to help her down. 'I could hardly let you ride so far without offering you so much as a glass of wine, could I?'

Rosanna smiled, feeling a shiver of apprehension as his hands closed possessively about her waist. She slid down into his arms, gazing up momentarily into eyes that were smoky with desire. He wanted her at this moment; she could feel it and it shook her, making her tremble. She was almost afraid of him, of the masculine strength and power of him. It was madness to think of marrying such a man! She should run from him now, before it was too late. Then he released her, and the feeling of panic receded. It was foolish to have reacted in that way. There was nothing to fear. She was in command of the situation, and could leave at any time. He had not forced her to come here and he would not prevent her from leaving.

The interior of the house was spartan with the minimum of plain, functional furnishings. Clearly no woman had ever lived here, but there was a fire burning in the grate and a spread of cold dishes on the table: beef, ham, cheeses, bread and wine. A meal intended for a man, with no sign of the little delicacies that might tempt a lady's appetite.

Justin waved her towards an oak settle, removing his riding-gloves before pouring wine into two glasses and handing her one. He smiled as she lifted it to her lips and drank with evident enjoyment. 'At least you find my wine tolerable?'

'It is very good,' she replied, feeling almost shy as his eyes went over her. 'Perhaps I could wash my hands and tidy myself before we eat?'

'Of course.' He laughed wryly. 'It must appear that I have no manners. The situation is a little strange, is it not? Come, I shall show you where you can refresh yourself.' She followed him up the stairs, their feet echoing hollowly on the wooden steps. The door he opened was to a bedroom, and since a man's personal possessions were strewn over the surface of a dressing-chest, it was obviously his. 'You will find all you need through there.'

He closed the door behind him. Left to herself, Rosanna made the necessary ablutions in the closet and returned to the bedroom itself. She paused by the dressing-chest, glancing at the assortment of objects carelessly thrown there by their owner; a few coins, combs and brushes, a diamond cravat-pin and a gold locket. Curiosity made her pick up the locket and open it. Inside was a lock of hair, woven into a plait, and it appeared to be made out of two differing shades, one of which she thought would match Justin's own hair. It was clearly a love-token, and she put it down with a guilty start as the door opened.

Justin stared at her from the threshold. 'You are ready?' He came towards her as she nodded dumbly, suddenly unable to speak or move. 'Or perhaps you are not hungry. Is this what you want, Rosanna?'

Before she realised what he meant to do, he had taken her in his arms, pressing her close to his body. Looking up at him, she saw the flame of desire leap in his eyes— and then he was kissing her. Kissing her in a way no man ever had before, with a hungry passion that set her pulses racing like the wind. Harry's kisses had not been like this, and even her Russian count had succeeded in no more than a few romantic kisses on her hand and one hasty embrace before she thrust him away. There was a force and determination in this man that she had never met before. She tried to protest, but her will to resist had somehow been sapped at the first touch of his lips and she felt close to swooning.

'You must not,' she managed at last, as his mouth released hers and she could breathe again. 'Let me go, Captain Sawle.'

'No,' he replied throatily. 'You insisted on playing with fire, Rosanna, now it is too late to change your mind.'

'What do you mean?' she whispered, her heart beating like the wings of a caged bird against the imprisoning bars. Seeing the look in his eyes, she pressed her hands to his breast, trying vainly to hold him off. 'You cannot . . . You wouldn't dare!'

He laughed harshly. 'You know there is nothing I would not dare, my lovely one! Besides, your eyes invite me to dare all if I would gain that I most desire, and I warned you that I was not a man to be trifled with.'

'But . . . it was only a game,' she breathed, transfixed by the gleam in his eyes. 'You would not . . . dishonour me?'

'That is exactly what I intend, my sweet jilt.' He smiled oddly. 'I shall bind you to me so securely that you will not dare to play your tricks on me.'

She stared at him in stunned silence. 'Y-You mean you will marry me afterwards?'

'Naturally.' His lips curled. 'I do not make a habit of ravishing maidens.'

'But this is not necessary, Justin. I would not jilt you. I give you my word.'

'You gave Harry Bellingham your word. There is no escape, Rosanna. You came here of your own free will—something no true innocent would do—and I do not intend to let you leave until you are mine.'

'No!' She felt the fear whip through her and with a tremendous effort she struggled free, backing away. 'Let me go, Justin! I promise I shall marry you.'

'What do you fear so much, my sweet?' he asked softly. 'All I am doing is anticipating our wedding night. There is nothing to fear; I give you my word. We are well suited, and I shall teach you how to be a true woman.'

'I—I demand that you let me go!' She found the bedpost at her back and knew that she could retreat no further. Looking into his face, she that saw his purpose was set. He meant to have his way, and to fight him would only make her ordeal more unbearable. Besides, he was offering what she wanted—but on his terms! She gazed up into his face, her eyes beginning to smoulder with anger. 'You will regret this, Justin.'

''Shall I?' he murmured, his lips twitching with humour. 'I do not think so. I expect to find the next few hours very enjoyable, and I see no reason why you should not also find them pleasant, Rosanna. Whether you re-alise it or not, you are a passionate woman.'

'Th—The next few hours . . .' she stammered, her knees suddenly feeling weak.

'Of course. You may not leave here until the morning.' His hand stroked the curve of her cheek. 'It will not be my fault if you are not carrying my child!'

'You devil!' She struck out at him, but he caught her wrist, holding her so easily that she was made aware of her helplessness against his superior strength. She could not escape in this way and must perforce try another. 'Please, Justin, I beg you...'

'You beg me to do what, my darling?' He encircled her waist with his free arm, catching her to him. 'Please what, Justin? Please love me? Please teach me to know myself? Is that what you beg of me? It is what your eyes say. Don't be frightened, Rosanna. I shall be gentle with you. It is not my way to hurt women—and especially the woman I want for my wife. Do not be deceived by my mockery, for it is only that. I swear I shall make you happy. Whatever I have been in the past, from this day I shall be your devoted husband.' He tipped her chin so that she was forced to look at him. 'Tell me you hate me. Tell me you don't want to marry me, and I shall let you go.'

'I...' Her mouth was dry and she was unable to form the words. It was madness, but suddenly she knew that this *was* what she wanted. Her body was dissolving with the desire to be close to his. She moistened her lips with the tip of her tongue. 'I—I cannot,' she murmured.

He gave a hoarse cry of triumph as he swept her into his arms, his mouth possessing hers fiercely. Her lips parted beneath his and she clung to him as he bore her back on to the bed. She lay trembling as his fingers unfastened the bodice of her gown and his hand slipped beneath to caress her breast. He undressed her slowly, kissing each little piece of her body that was revealed to his hot gaze. She had expected to feel some embarrassment, but when she finally lay naked beneath his hand, her shyness had somehow vanished.

'You are beautiful,' he breathed huskily, stroking the creamy silk of her skin from her high, firm breasts over the flat navel to the curve of her thigh. 'More lovely even than I imagined. I have wanted you here in my bed since the first moment I saw you. You want me too, Rosanna. I know it, but I want to hear you say it. Say you want me...'

His tongue traced the delicate contours of her ear, his breath soft and warm against her skin. A sigh escaped her as she accepted the knowledge within herself. She did want him. Her body felt strangely soft and pliant as if he had somehow robbed her of the will to resist, yet still she could not say the words. He seemed to take her silence as consent, for he eased back to a sitting position and began to unbutton his shirt.

'Your eyes tell me what your stubborn tongue will not,' he murmured. 'But I can be stubborn too.'

He was in the act of removing his shirt when a banging at the front door caused him to stop and frown. He hesitated a moment, unwilling to answer the summons, but it continued, becoming louder and more insistent. A muffled curse was on his lips as he pulled his shirt on.

'This will not take a moment. Stay where you are, Rosanna.'

His clipped tones were like a douche of cold water. She shivered, a wave of shame washing over her as he closed the door behind him. What was she doing? Jerking up, she covered her face with her hands, feeling the hot flush in her cheeks. Suddenly she was reaching for her clothes, pulling them on hastily, afraid that he might return before she was dressed. She had behaved like a wanton, responding to his touch with a shameless abandon. She must be mad! Her fingers were clumsy in their haste, and she knew that her hair was dishevelled and untidy, but she dared not stay to tidy it. She had to escape before he returned to carry out his threats—threats that had so nearly become a reality! Her heart beating rapidly, she slipped out of the bedroom and walked softly down the stairs. There were voices coming from the parlour. She paused to listen as she prepared for the final dash to the front door, knowing that Justin must see her as she passed through the hall.

'You say there has been another fall?' Justin's voice was harsh and angry. 'But that shaft was secure. I inspected it myself, Seth. There was no reason for a cave-in.'

'I know. It seems that what we suspected...' Seth's voice died away as he saw the flash of fire in his employer's eyes, realising in a moment that the look was directed not at him, but at something behind him.

Rosanna felt rather than saw his astonished gaze as she fled by him to the door. Shame burned inside her as she realised what he must think of her and knew that it was true. She pulled open the door and rushed into the yard, relieved to see her horse standing patiently where she had tethered it by the water-trough earlier. Hearing Justin call her name, she struggled to free the knot in the reins, but before she could do so, he was striding into the yard.

'Rosanna, please wait!' he commanded.

There was not time to mount before he reached her, so she stood defiantly, clutching her riding-whip as though she would use it as a weapon to defend herself.

'Touch me, and you will be sorry,' she hissed between clenched teeth.

'Don't be a little fool,' he said quietly. 'You were always free to leave if you wished. I would have seduced you if I could, but rape was never my intention.'

His words made her more aware of her own shame. 'You are a devil, and I hate you!'

'Then you need never see me again.' His mouth was hard and cold. 'Yet I think you are lying. Had Seth not come, you would even now be in my arms.' She raised her crop to strike him, but he caught her wrist. 'A small revenge, my sweet, hardly worthy of you. You should wed me, and take your revenge in other ways.'

'Marry you?' A harsh laugh escaped her. 'What choice have I? You have ruined my reputation... What must that man of yours think?'

'He might think it a little strange that you consented to enter the house of a bachelor. He knows me too well to imagine that I abducted you!' He frowned as he saw the flush in her cheeks. 'But he will say nothing.'

Rosanna stared at him, confused by the conflicting emotions raging inside her. Was he saying that he would warn his employee to hold his tongue, provided that she married him? She longed to scream her hatred at him and accuse him of being a vile blackmailer, but inside her head a little voice was cautioning her to think before she spoke. Was this not exactly what she had wanted?

'So you have won,' she said slowly. 'I must marry you or lose my reputation...'

Justin smiled without mockery, sensing her confusion. 'I'll own that this was my fault, Rosanna. I hoped to make sure of you, but perhaps I should have courted you with flowers and pretty words? Would you have had me if I had sworn eternal love on my knees?'

'Oh, don't make a fool of me!' she cried angrily. 'Let's be plain about this from the start. We both have our own reasons for wanting this marriage, so don't pretend that you love me.'

'Should I ask what your reasons are, Rosanna?' His eyes narrowed as he looked at her. 'No, perhaps not. You may keep your secrets as I keep mine. I'll ride over tomorrow and speak to Jonathan.'

She hesitated again, torn between the steadily mounting anger inside her and a desire for revenge. It would be easy to fling her defiance in his face and dare him to reveal her shame to the world, but that would not satisfy this need within her. As she gazed at him, an idea of the form that her revenge might take came to her, and she laughed. 'So it is to be a marriage of convenience, Justin? Very well. I see that it is useless to fight you. We shall be married as soon as possible, but I shall not be alone with you again until our wedding night.'

He inclined his head in assent. 'As you wish, Rosanna. But I should warn you of the consequences if you think to take your revenge by leaving me standing at the altar.'

'Oh, I shall not jilt you,' she said. 'You need have no fear of that. I have but one other condition for this marriage.'

'Indeed?' His mouth hardened again. 'Pray enlighten me, my sweet.'

She flinched at the note of sarcasm in his voice. 'I want to make my home at Rathmoor—at least when we are in the country.'

'Is that all?'

She thought he seemed as if he expected something very different, and was relieved. 'I—I love the house and—and Grandfather would miss me now...'

'If it would make you happy, I have no objection to the arrangement.' For a moment he had thought that she meant to tell him she was carrying another man's child, and he was surprised at the surge of relief. 'Indeed, it will suit me very well.' He smiled at her warmly. 'Come, if you insist on leaving, let me help you to mount.'

There was a mounting-block in the yard, and she was tempted to refuse his offer but controlled her tongue, allowing him to give her his hand and put her up in the saddle. There would be time enough to take her revenge once they were married. She looked down at him, smiling at her own thoughts.

'I shall tell Grandfather to expect you,' she said, giving the reins a little shake.

Justin stood back, watching as she rode out of the yard, his face sombre. He was not proud of himself or of what he had done. Nor could he understand why she had accepted his offer. What had changed her mind so suddenly? Surely she had not really believed that Seth would gossip about what he had seen? It would not even occur to the man, but of course she could not know that. Yet somehow he felt that Rosanna had capitulated for reasons of her own. There was a sour taste in his mouth as he turned and walked into the house. It would be his own fault if she left him standing at the altar after the way he had behaved!

Unaware of the thoughts of the man she had left
behind, Rosanna urged her horse to a gallop. It was good
to feel the wind in her face, cooling the heat of her cheeks
and blowing the shameful memories from her mind. As
she rode, shame turned to anger against the man who
had sought to trap her. She blocked out the knowledge
that she had walked willingly into his lair, thereby encouraging him to believe that she might not be averse
to his advances, might even enjoy them. As she had!
The traitorous thought was swiftly crushed. No
gentleman would have behaved as he had. She had not
really wanted his lovemaking. He had cast some kind of
a spell over her, dominating her by his superior will. He
was a master in the art of seduction, a vile, despicable
brute, and she hated him! Then why had she agreed to
marry him? There were other rich men who might wish
to make her their wife, so why not choose one of them?
But then she would lose her chance of revenge... A revenge so sweet that it made her laugh out loud just to
think about it.

Absorbed in her own thoughts, Rosanna did not at
first see the coach with the broken wheel lying on its
side at the bend of the road. Only when the two men
suddenly came out from behind it to stand in her path
did she check her pace, swerving hastily on to the
greensward in an effort to avoid them, mud from her
horse's hooves spattering over them as she swept past.
Hearing one of them curse furiously, she glanced back,
something stirring briefly in her mind as she saw his
angry face. It was not enough, however, to disturb the
pattern of her thoughts, and only much later, when she
was on the point of falling asleep in her bed, did she
remember where she had seen him before.

'Why, you look a treat, Miss Rosanna!' Emily dabbed
at her eyes, then blew her nose hard. 'I'll tell Benjamin
you're ready, shall I? Sir Joshua and the master are
waiting for you downstairs.'

'Give me five minutes, Emily.'

Rosanna sighed as the woman went out, glancing at her reflection in the mirror. She was wearing a gown of straw satin, its full skirts caught with silk roses and yellow ribbons. It was not what she had planned to wear as Harry's bride—that was a romantic white lace dress, quite inappropriate for this wedding. She had made the decision days ago, as soon as the arrangements had been settled, but now she was not sure it had been the right one. She looked well enough, but the white dress would have been special. However, it was too late to change her mind.

She picked up her nosegay of snowdrops, and smiled. They were the first of the year and grew only in one sheltered spot in the garden, where Emily had gathered them earlier. Everyone was so excited over the wedding; Sir Joshua insisting that, as her grandfather could not walk down the nave with her, he would give her away himself. Jonathan Whitby would be in the church to witness her marriage, though. Benjamin would see to that, carrying him from the coach to the special chair with wheels that he had made for his master himself.

A pang of guilt made Rosanna close her eyes for a moment. Even her grandfather was pleased about the wedding now. Only last night he had told her that, in his opinion, Justin was a decent man and nowhere near as black as he had been painted. Emily had been happily preparing for a week, ably assisted by a score of relatives she had dragooned into her service. Messages of goodwill and presents had been arriving daily. No one guessed that it was all a sham.

She had seen Justin several times since that day at his house, though never alone. He had dined with her and Jonathan, visiting on most days and going out of his way to be charming. Anyone would think that he really cared for her and that their marriage was a love match. Unless, like her, they knew him for what he truly was. Now it was her wedding day and she was so nervous that she felt like running away. For a moment she felt dizzy and the room seemed to whirl. She could not do it. She

could not marry Justin. Then, as her mind cleared, she
controlled her nerves. There was nothing to be frightened
of, since she knew exactly what she was doing. With any
luck, she would have had her revenge by the end of the
day, and the money she needed so sorely for Rathmoor
would be within her grasp. Lifting her chin a fraction
higher, she left her room and went downstairs to greet
the little group of servants and friends who were waiting.
She smiled at Emily and Benjamin, moving as if in a
dream towards Sir Joshua and her grandfather.

'Beautiful,' Sir Joshua said. 'You should be proud of
your girl, Jonathan Whitby.'

'I am. She's a fine lass.'

Tears misted Rosanna's eyes, but she blinked them
away. Everything was vaguely unreal as she took Sir
Joshua's arm after first bending to kiss her grandfather's cheek. Then Benjamin came to carry his master
out to one of the waiting carriages, and they all followed.

It was a cold morning, the ground hard with frost
beneath the horses' feet, and little clouds of white
forming about their nostrils as they pawed the ground
restlessly. Yet she was hardly aware of the cold or the
glistening beauty of the moor stretching far away into
the distance, shimmering with thousands of tiny crystals
that made the landscape glow with light. She was numbed
in body and mind, wrapped in a strange silence that
nothing seemed to penetrate, though she answered when
spoken to, but from a distance with a separate part of
her mind.

The church stood in the centre of the village, and despite the cold the inhabitants had turned out to watch
the Squire's grand-daughter's wedding. Jonathan Whitby
was well liked and respected in the area, and there was
a rippling cheer as he was carried to his chair and pushed
into the church. A burst of clapping greeted the bride's
arrival from those who had waited so patiently outside,
and as she went inside, she was aware of many more
who had crowded into the back pews behind the guests.

Rosanna's face was almost as pale as the snowdrops she carried as she walked down the nave towards the two men standing at the end. Justin had told her that a friend of his would be supporting him, but both their faces were a blur as they turned to look at her. She took her place at Justin's side, glancing at him briefly without really seeing him.

'You look beautiful,' he whispered.

Rosanna heard him, and a tingle ran down her spine. She kept her gaze fastened on the altar, suddenly very much aware of what was happening and of the man at her side. Every word of the service made its impression on her and she was stabbed by guilt as she made her vows. This was wrong, terribly wrong! Marriage was sacred, and this was a mockery of all that it stood for. She heard Justin's strong, clear voice as he repeated his vows, and her hand trembled when he slipped a plain gold band on to her finger.

'You may kiss the bride, sir.' The Vicar smiled down on them.

Rosanna lifted her face, expecting Justin to kiss her briefly on the cheek, but instead he took her into his arms, holding her close as his lips took possession of hers in a long, passionate kiss. She stiffened, fighting the surging in her blood and the sudden foolish desire to respond with all her being. She saw the question in his eyes as he released her, and dropped her lashes to cover her own confusion. Then she laid her hand on his arm, and they walked out of the church together to the clamour of bells pealing out joyfully. A child ran to press a straw love-token tied with ribbons into her hands.

Tears were burning behind her eyes as Justin helped her into the coach. She sensed his gaze and fought the turmoil raging inside her, her restless fingers pleating the satin of her gown as the wheels of the carriage began to turn. They had decided to dispense with a wedding trip, preferring to begin their new life at Rathmoor. It had surprised Rosanna that Justin had made no mention of a visit to his home, and she knew that he had declined to invite his father to the wedding. His uncle had been unable to attend because of ill-health, but he had sent them a handsome gift of two silver candelabra. Her husband's own gift to her had been a beautiful diamond brooch.

Although Justin glanced at her from time to time as they drove, he did not speak until he handed her down at Rathmoor. 'I know this has been something of an ordeal, Rosanna, but there is no need to look as if you were facing a death sentence. We shall suit one another as well as most husband and wives. I meant what I said to you that day at my house. You need not fear that I shall be an unfaithful husband.'

She swallowed hard, not daring to look at him. 'I am glad to hear it, Justin,' she murmured. 'I think you may change your mind when you hear what I have to say later, but I thank you for the thought.'

'What do you mean?' he asked, his gaze narrowing suspiciously.

She saw a flash of anger in his eyes and a tremor ran through her. 'I cannot tell you now,' she said, her mouth suddenly dry. 'Our guests are arriving.'

There was a conflict of emotion in him. Taking advantage of his momentary indecision, she brushed past him and walked into the house. Justin followed her into the long parlour, where a splendid buffet had been laid out in readiness. He caught her arm and swung her round to face him.

'I want to know what you were hinting at, Rosanna. Why should I change my mind?'

'Justin, I...' She was saved from replying by the arrival of Sir Joshua, closely followed by her grandfather and Benjamin. 'I'll tell you later—when we are alone.'

Leaving him, she went to kiss and be kissed by the new arrivals. Justin frowned as he watched, but he did not follow her nor did he pursue his interrogation when she came back to stand at his side to receive their guests. Glancing at his profile, she sensed that he was very angry. He was polite enough, answering the good wishes of their neighbours with a smile, but there was a tiny pulse beating at his temple, a sure sign of his inner turmoil.

The reception was not a long-drawn-out affair, because the inclement weather made everyone leave for home long before dusk fell. By the time the candles were lit, only Sir Joshua remained, retiring to the library to nod over a glass of brandy with his old friend.

As the last of the guests departed, Justin turned to his wife, his eyes glinting. 'Now, Rosanna,' he commanded icily, 'I want the truth. Are you carrying another man's brat in your belly? Is that why you agreed so readily to this marriage?'

'How dare you?' Her hand snaked out, slapping him across the face. 'How dare you insult me like that? Just because I almost... Oh, you are despicable!'

Her blow had taken him by surprise. He stood staring, as she turned and ran from the room, then he was stirred into action. 'Rosanna, I mean to have an answer. You won't escape so easily!'

He followed her out into the hall, sighing with exasperation as he saw her disappearing up the stairs. She was being even more difficult than he had expected. He knew he was at fault for behaving so badly the day she visited his house, but he had hoped she would put the incident behind them once they were married. Obviously he had misunderstood what she had said earlier, but the thought had lingered unpleasantly in his mind for days. Why else should she have agreed to marry him after making it so plain that she despised him? Walking at a slower pace up the stairs, he reached the top in time to see her disappear into a bedroom—but not the one he had been shown a few days previously and which he understood they were to share. What game was she playing now? Did she mean to lock him out on their wedding night?

Expecting the door to be barred, he was surprised when it opened easily. Rosanna was standing by the window, her back towards him. He hesitated just inside the door, not knowing quite what to say.

'I'm sorry if I misjudged you,' he said hesitantly. 'I jumped to conclusions because of what you said.' The words of apology died away as she turned to face him, her eyes glittering like ice. She looked as if she hated him. 'What is it?'

'Stay where you are,' she said. 'I have something to say.'

'Indeed.' Once again he was plagued with doubts. 'Then I suggest you begin, madam.'

'I have a proposition to put to you.'

'I'm afraid I do not understand. We were married just a few hours...'

'I am your wife, but you will never share my bed. It shall be a marriage in name only.'

'What nonsense is this?' He took a step towards her but something in her look made him pause. 'Perhaps you would care to explain?'

'It is my revenge for the way you behaved when you had me at your mercy. You humiliated me—and I do not care to be treated in that way again.'

'I'm damned if I'll agree to that condition!' he muttered.

'You have no choice, unless you mean to use force.'

'Why the hell did you marry me?'

She drew a deep breath, knowing that what she was about to say was outrageous. 'I need money to restore Rathmoor. If you want an annulment, I'll agree to it for a reasonable settlement—shall we say twenty thousand pounds?'

'You married me for my money?' He was astonished. 'But you're an heiress!'

'I *was* an heiress. My father's agent cheated him out of most of his fortune.' Rosanna swallowed hard. 'I decided to marry for money, and I knew you—you wanted me. I intended it to be a true marriage until...'

'Your father lost everything?' Justin was reeling from the shock. She had no money. She had married him, knowing that he believed she was an heiress—and now she was refusing to be a true wife, demanding a huge sum as the price of an annulment. Fury surged through him. She was a cheat and a liar, and he wanted to take that slender white throat in his hands and break it. 'You little...'

Rosanna felt a thrill of fear as she saw his rage. 'It can make no difference to you,' she said defensively. 'I have only done what many others do. A man takes a bride for her dowry and everyone congratulates him. If you had not behaved so badly, I should have been a good wife to you, but now I shall never...' Her voice trailed to a whisper as she saw the strange expression on his face.

'Makes no difference?' He gave a harsh laugh. 'My God, it would be amusing if it were not so tragic! You little fool, you have ruined us both!'

'What do you mean?'

'I have no money—save for a few pounds I won at the card-tables.'

The shock wiped the colour from her cheeks. 'You have no... You are lying! You think to deceive me!'

'Me—deceive you?' he echoed incredulously. 'I believed you to be an heiress. Why else do you imagine I tried to seduce you? I need a loan from my bank to open up the mines. On the strength of our marriage, I have already agreed terms.'

She stared at him in disbelief. 'You married me for my money? But—But Harry said your father was one of the richest landowners in Cornwall...'

'My father and I have quarrelled. He has disowned me, and I can expect nothing more from him.' Justin frowned. 'I only wanted security from you. There is a rich lode waiting to be mined if I can raise the money.'

'A likely story!' Rosanna said scornfully. 'I suppose you have gambling debts to settle. Men are such liars! Even if I had the money, I would not give it to you for such a purpose.'

The scorn in her eyes made the fury boil inside him. 'By heaven, I ought to kill you!'

'That should be quite easy,' she said. 'As you see, I am unarmed. I should have had my pistol ready—but I imagined you to be a gentleman.'

'As you are a lady?' She shrank from him, and as he saw the fear in her face, he gave a cry of disgust. 'You need not fear for your maidenhood. It would give me more pleasure to bed any drab from the streets than to lie with you. You're not worth the effort!'

With that parting thrust, he turned and strode out of the room, leaving her staring after him with stricken eyes. She put a hand to her head, swaying dizzily. What had she done? She tried to tell herself that Justin was lying in order to cheat her of the price she had demanded for his freedom, but she had seen the shock in his face. He had no money. She had married him for a fortune he did not possess. He had believed her an heiress. Like Harry, he had wanted her not for herself but for her father's money... It would have been funny had it not been so tragic—he was right! She felt like laughing wildly, hysterically, but then the tears began to slide down her cheeks. Suddenly she was overwhelmed by grief. The tears she had kept inside when Harry deserted her were falling now, and she was sobbing as the pain ran through her. She fell to her knees and then to the floor, her whole body shaking with the storm of emotion that swept through her.

She had been blinded by her pride and her desire for revenge, and now she had lost everything.

Justin pushed his horse hard, heedless of the biting wind that drove into his face and caught his breath. He was conscious only of the anger inside him and the need to put some distance between himself and the woman he wanted to kill. If he had stayed in the house, he might have done something he would live to regret.

'The bitch!' he cursed aloud. 'The lying, cheating bitch!'

'You will never share my bed,' she had said, her eyes full of disdain as she looked at him. 'I shall agree to an annulment, for a reasonable settlement...'

His laughter rang out harshly as the bitter humour of the situation struck him. She must really hate him to have planned such a cruel revenge. How she must be regretting it now! She had risked everything on the throw of the dice, and she had lost. His laughter ceased abruptly as he remembered that he, too, was caught in the web of lies she had woven.

The impulse that had made him ride wildly into the night was suddenly stilled. He slowed his pace, then dismounted, tethering his horse at the head of the cliffs so that it should not stray in the darkness. He knew why he had come here. He needed to be alone so that he could think. There were so many memories here for him. Memories of a time when he had played on the sands as a child, under the watchful eye of the only woman he had ever truly loved. Margaret Sawle had been so beautiful, so warm and tender. He had adored her blindly to the day of her death, and no other woman had ever been able to stand comparison with his memory of her. All the rest were pale imitations, liars or cheats... like the woman he had married.

Climbing down to the cove, Justin felt the bitterness twist inside him. Even his adored mother had not been perfect. The knowledge hurt him more than the fact that he was a bastard—a penniless bastard. His mouth curved in a rueful smile as his anger died, becoming a muted ache. Was he not as much to blame for what had happened tonight as Rosanna? He had married her for the sake of the fortune she was supposed to have inherited. They were both equally guilty of deception, and each caught in the trap they had set for the other.

The sand crunched beneath his feet as he walked deep in thought. Perhaps an annulment would be the best way out. He had no wish to go on with the marriage now. Or had he? Remembering the thrill he had felt watching his lovely bride walk towards him in church, he wondered at himself. Had he married her simply because of his financial difficulties, or had there been another, deeper reason? The money had certainly been a very pleasant prospect. With a fortune behind him, he knew the bank would have been willing—eager, indeed—to lend him the money he needed to get the mine into full production.

If only Rosanna had not deceived him! She had never actually mentioned her inheritance, but he had assumed—as everyone else had assumed. Everyone still believed her to be wealthy. If that belief were sustained, it might be possible to secure his loan from the bank . . . Providing that he stayed married to Rosanna . . .

Supposing he did just that? It would mean agreeing to her terms—at least for the moment. She was angry with him. In his heart he could not blame her after his behaviour at the mine house. Now that his own anger had passed, he could think more rationally. If she had behaved outrageously, so had he. He grinned as he recalled the way she had out-manoeuvred him. He had fallen neatly into her trap.

'The little schemer,' he murmured, his sense of humour restored. It had taken courage to face him with her demands. No wonder she had looked terrified all through the service. He had suspected another reason entirely for her odd behaviour. Suddenly he realised that he would rather have it this way than discover that she had married him because she needed a father for another man's bastard. Nothing could have hurt him quite as much as that.

She had insisted at the start that she had intended it to be a true marriage, and the little scene after their wedding had been revenge for his attempt at seduction. Something had upset her deeply that day at the mine, though he did not really understand why. At the time, he had been certain that she wanted him to make love to her, at least after her initial protest. She had responded so sweetly to his kisses. If Seth had not interrupted, she would have been his, he was certain, so why...

Justin bent to pluck a flat pebble from the beach, sending it skimming across the silver surface of a calm sea. There was a strange reluctance in him to let her go without a fight. She had so nearly been his. Damn it, she was his! There was no way she could get an annulment without his consent—and he would never give it. His decision made, he retraced his steps to the foot of the cliffs. He had taken her for richer or poorer—what irony there was in those vows now!—and he would keep her. She belonged to him, whether she liked it or not, and he intended to make sure that they stayed bound together.

Rosanna pressed the cold, wet cloth to her cheeks, glancing anxiously at her reflection in the mirror. She could not face anyone until some of the redness had gone from beneath her eyes. No one must guess that she had cried herself to sleep, though Emily would know something was wrong when she went to make up the bed in the room that had been intended as the bridal chamber.

Taking another look at herself, she decided that she looked reasonably presentable. Everyone would soon have to know that she had spent her wedding night alone. When Justin demanded an annulment, it would all come out. She bit her lip, realising how very unpleasant that would be, for her and her grandfather. It would cause quite a scandal—and all for nothing. Oh, why had she not listened to Jonathan's advice?... Her thoughts were suddenly suspended as someone knocked at her door.

'Yes, who is it?'

'May I come in? I want to talk to you, Rosanna.'

Her heart thudded as she heard Justin's voice. For a moment she wanted to run and hide, but she knew that this moment had to be faced. She had taken her revenge, and now she must pay for it.

'The door is not locked,' she said, clenching her hands into tight fists. 'Come in if you wish.'

She turned away as the door opened, pretending to be occupied with a hairbrush. There was silence for a moment, a silence that sent a prickle of apprehension down her spine.

'We have to talk, Rosanna.'

'Why?' She did not twist her head to look at him. 'It was all a terrible mistake, and the sooner it is over, the better it will be for both of us. I shall not contest your application for an annulment.'

'I do not intend to ask for one.'

Her whole body jerked round at that, her eyes flying to his in alarm. 'But you must.'

'Why?' he asked the question now, looking at her calmly. 'I have given the situation some thought, and I have decided it will suit me to remain your husband.'

'You will never be my husband in anything other than name!'

He inclined his head slightly. 'I understand that, Rosanna. It will not be a true marriage. Even so, it may serve my purpose.'

She stared at him uncertainly, so sure that he would demand his freedom immediately. What could he gain from the marriage now? 'How? I told you that I have no money.'

'Who else is aware of that? It does not seem to be commonly known.'

'My father's solicitor, Harry—not his parents, though—and my grandfather.' She sighed. 'What difference does it make?'

'It could be important. As I told you, I have already arranged a loan. Provided the bank does not discover that you have no money, they will be happy to finance me.'

The tiny spark of hope inside her died. He did not want her for herself, but even now, was trying to use her for his own ends. Like all men, he was quick to turn any advantage to his own use. She wanted to scream at him, to tell him that she despised him, but she could not summon up enough energy. Her night of weeping had left her drained emotionally. What did it matter? What did any of it matter now?

'My father's affairs were very complicated. They have not yet been settled. It may be that something will be salvaged in the end.' Why had she told him that? She had not intended to.

'I hope for your sake that that will be the case,' Justin said. 'I am interested only in securing a loan. I think the bank will be satisfied if I tell them that my wife's fortune is tied up in assets abroad. Once the mine begins to pay for itself, it will not matter.'

Rosanna turned her head aside, tapping with her hairbrush. 'You will be entitled to any money I may eventually have.'

'You may keep it for the house. It must mean a great deal to you, since you were willing to sacrifice so much for it.'

She could not look at him. 'Perhaps I shall find Lady Caroline's jewels.'

'Jonathan did mention them.' Justin laughed softly. 'Perhaps I should help you to look? It could solve all our problems.' He took a step towards her. 'I'm sorry, Rosanna, I haven't exactly played fair with you...'

She jumped to her feet, moving away from him. 'If I agree to this—this sham arrangement so that you can secure your loan, it ends there, Justin. I meant what I said last night.'

He shrugged his shoulders carelessly. 'That is your choice, Rosanna. I own I thought it would be pleasant to share your bed, but it does not matter. I give you my word that I shall never force you to do anything you dislike, so you need not shrink every time I come near you. If you have no wish for my attentions, there are others who are more accommodating.'

'I am sure of it,' she said bitterly, 'but you will please be a little more discreet in future, sir. An inn is not the best place to meet your mistress.'

'So you saw me in Bodmin.' A smile flickered at the corners of his mouth. She was not quite as indifferent as she made out. 'I shall be more careful in future, I promise. Now, my dear, shall we go down to breakfast together? I think I ought to spend at least one or two days in your company before I attend to business. We don't want to give our neighbours reason to gossip just yet, do we?'

Rosanna glared at him. Why did he look so pleased with himself? She had expected him to storm out of the house in a temper, leaving his lawyers to sort out the muddle. His behaviour was surprising—and a little un-nerving. He was being so reasonable that she could do nothing less then comply with his request, unless she wished to make a fool of herself.

'I do not wish to detain you from your business, sir.'

'Oh, I think I can spare you a few days of my time.' Justin gave her a deceptively bland look. 'I presume that you intend to carry out the less intimate duties of a wife? You will see to it that my cravats are starched and my meals served as I like them?'

'Of course.' She had the feeling that he was laughing at her. 'I shall try to make you a good wife in every way—except one.'

'Then I suggest we get to know one another a little better.' He smiled and offered her his arm. 'Perhaps you will show me the house after we have eaten? We might even look for your ancestor's jewels...'

CHAPTER FIVE

ROSANNA pulled her work-basket towards her to sort through the coloured threads. She had found some unfinished tapestries, and realising that there was sufficient material to re-cover all the chairs in the dining-room, she had undertaken the task.

Justin had gone into Truro to see the bank manager about the loan he had arranged. It was three weeks since their wedding, and the atmosphere between them continued to be tense. At the beginning, he had tried to bridge the gap, taking pains to make conversation and discover what interests they might have in common. Rosanna had rebuffed every attempt with icy coldness, determined to make him suffer. This had led to quarrels, the most recent one before he had left that morning.

'Since my presence is obviously distasteful to you, I may as well go into town,' he had snapped. 'I'm not certain how long I shall be—I may not be home for dinner.'

'You are free to do as you please.'

'You have made your feelings perfectly clear, madam.' Then he had left without a backward glance.

After he had gone, Rosanna was surprised to find that she missed him. She spent the morning with her grandfather, but he always rested in the afternoons and she had turned to her needlework out of frustration, annoyed with herself because she could not prevent herself listening for Justin's footsteps in the hall.

On hearing his voice, her heart jerked and she pricked her finger. When she looked up as he entered, she was very much aware of the male vitality of him as he seemed to dominate her little room. How very handsome he was! An involuntary smile lit her eyes and she thrust her

needlework aside, jumping to her feet. Justin crossed
the floor, taking her in his arms to kiss her lightly on
the mouth.

'Forgive me? I did not mean to quarrel.'

She was trembling as he let her go. 'You must be
hungry. I shall speak to Emily...'

'Emily knows I am back.' He caught at her wrist.
'Don't go.'

She glanced at him uncertainly. 'Justin, I...'

'I'm not asking you to share my bed. I know you are
still angry, but I would like to earn your respect if I can.
Can we not try to live comfortably with one another?'

She swallowed hard, fighting the temptation to give
in. 'I think that might be possible, but will you be satisfied with such an arrangement?'

'I am willing to try—if you are?'

'I—I am not angry any more, Justin, neither am I in
love with you...' She gave him a tentative smile. 'But I
think we might be tolerable companions.'

'Then we are agreed. We shall be companions, and in
time we may become friends.' He sat down, looking
about him. 'This house is beginning to look better
already. All it needed was a woman's care.'

She looked at him suspiciously. He was behaving as
if they had been married for years, and she did not quite
believe in this new, mild Justin. However, it was better
than the armed truce that had existed between them since
their marriage, and she did not know what else to do.
They could not go on quarrelling for ever. She picked
up her embroidery but was unable to concentrate.

'Was your journey successful?' Why did she suddenly
feel so much more alive now that he was home? 'Were
you able to secure the loan you wanted?'

'I explained that funds would become available in a
few months, and they were eager to help.'

'So you will be able to open new workings at the
mine?' She frowned. 'How long before you know
whether or not there is sufficient copper to make it worth
while?'

'That remains to be seen. So long as the bank believes me to be married to an heiress, there will be no hurry to repay the loan.'

'I see no reason why they should ever learn otherwise.'

'We must hope that nothing happens to arouse their suspicions.'

'My father's solicitor told me that I will have some money when everything is settled.'

'Then you will be able to realise your dream of restoring the house.' He smiled. 'I believe it means a great deal to you?'

'Yes. I love it.' Her face lit up as she glanced round. 'After my mother died, I was sent to boarding-school and Father sold our home. I had to stay with friends during the holidays. Then, when I was seventeen, I persuaded Father to take me with him. We were abroad for three years. Coming to Rathmoor was like coming home.'

'I begin to understand. It is too beautiful a house to be allowed to crumble into a ruin. I am sorry I do not possess the fortune you believed me to have, but perhaps one day I shall be able to oblige you. If the mine is as profitable as I hope, I shall eventually be able to give my wife anything she desires.'

Rosanna could not look at him. This was terrible. She felt so ashamed. He was being so considerate, so reasonable. She could not bear it. In another moment she would start to cry! She got quickly to her feet. 'Excuse me, I must speak to Emily.'

As she rushed from the room, Justin's eyes glinted with humour. So the citadel was not impregnable after all! He would have to go carefully, but it should not be long before she capitulated. Unfortunately, patience was something he had never learned to cultivate. He wanted her *now*. Every time he looked at her he could feel the hot grinding in his loins, and it needed all his will-power to keep him from taking her in his arms and holding her until she admitted that she, too, felt this strong physical attraction. She had so nearly been his... But he was afraid to act precipitately, lest he damage the frail relationship that was beginning to build between them . . .

'Won't you sit down, Mrs Sawle?' Becky Miller set a chair for her guest in the tiny parlour. 'Perhaps you would care for a glass of wine? It's elderberry, and I make it myself every year.'

Rosanna smiled and thanked her. Justin had suggested that she visit Seth's wife while he was at the mine to supervise the installation of new machinery, and now she was glad that she had come. Becky's two dark-eyed children were peeping at her from behind their mother's skirts.

'You must be very proud of your children,' she said. 'How old are they?'

'Simeon is four and a half, and Mary is three next week.' Becky looked fondly at her little ones as she poured the wine and then sat down opposite her guest. 'They keep me busy, I can tell you! I'll have my hands full once the baby comes. Still, Seth says I can have some help if things go well at the mine. Sally Rush will be glad of a job. She doesn't like taking charity from Captain Sawle now that there's no work up at the house.'

'Sally Rush?' Rosanna repeated. 'Wasn't it her husband who was injured in an accident just after Christmas?'

'Ay, that's right. The Captain has been good to them, but they would both rather earn a living. Now that he has pulled through the worst of it, Rob has started to carve wooden love-spoons. He was always good with his hands. Sally takes them into town to sell. It helps, but it isn't enough, of course.'

'Carved spoons?' Rosanna nodded thoughtfully. 'Do you think we could visit Sally before we go? I've had an idea, but I would need to talk it over with her first.'

'I'm sure she would love to see you, Mrs Sawle. The poor lass can't get out much these days.'

While they had been talking, little Mary had sidled towards Rosanna. She stood quietly, sucking her thumb, her big, dark eyes looking up at the lady in the pretty dress. Then she reached out solemnly to touch Rosanna's gown, stroking the velvet and smiling suddenly as she felt its softness.

'Do you like that?' Rosanna asked, feeling an odd tug at her heart as the child held out her arms. She lifted Mary on to her lap, enjoying the fresh, clean smell and the warmth of her tiny body as she nestled against her breast. 'Would you like a dress like this for your birthday?'

'Oh, you mustn't spoil her, Mrs Sawle!' Becky exclaimed.

'Why not? I have plenty of material I can make up.'

'You're a born mother,' Becky said with a smile. 'She doesn't take to everyone like that. You'll be wanting a large family yourself, I expect?'

Rosanna felt her cheeks burn. 'I . . . We haven't really decided yet.'

Becky laughed good-naturedly. 'Bless you! You don't decide things like that; babies come when they're ready. With a fine man like Captain Sawle as a husband, though, you've no need to worry. You'll be breeding before you know it.'

Mary had decided she wanted to get down, and Rosanna was able to hide her confusion as she assisted the child. She had been married barely two months, but already people were beginning to look at her as if they expected to see her slim waist thickening. What would they think as the months passed and she showed no signs of motherhood?

'I think we should go and see Sally now, don't you?' She stood up. 'I believe I may be able to provide work for both her and her husband—when he is well enough.'

Becky stared at her in surprise. 'That would be a marvellous thing,' she said. 'But how is it to be done?'

'I'll tell you on the way,' Rosanna replied, taking the little girl's hand. 'It's only an idea, but I think it might work.'

They went outside, the children clustering at Becky's skirts as they walked down the rough path to the other cottages. It was a bright, breezy day, and several of the miners' wives were standing at their doors, talking. They stared at Rosanna hard, eyeing her gown enviously. A dress like that would buy food for a year or more! There was, however, no real hostility in them. She was Captain Sawle's wife, and he was a good master. They all knew that the mine had been losing money for months. Many a man would have shut it down long ago, regardless of what that would mean for the folk hereabouts. A less compassionate master would not have cared if the closure meant starvation for the mining families. So, though they envied his wife's gown, they bore her no real malice.

Sally Rush's cottage was right at the end of the row. It had a neat garden with flowers at the front, and bright curtains at the windows. Inside, it was spotlessly clean, and there was the tantalising smell of baking. Sally blushed as she saw her visitors, hurrying to set a stool for the Captain's wife. 'I wish I'd known you were coming,' she said. 'Everything is awry...'

'It all looks perfectly tidy,' Becky said. 'How's your man today, then?'

'Not too bad. He had a better night.'

'Well, maybe there's some good news for you,' Becky said. 'Fetch one of Rob's spoons and show Mrs Sawle.'

'Rob's spoons?' Sally looked bewildered, but she did as Becky asked, bringing a selection for her visitors to see.

Rosanna felt a thrill of excitement as she looked at the exquisite work. She smiled at Sally. 'I have an idea— but you must tell me if you dislike it,' she said.

'Is there anything else you want, Mrs Sawle? Only I'd like to call in to see Rob and feed the baby before I help Emily with the dinner.'

Rosanna shook her head. 'No, you can go now, Sally. How is your husband today?'

'The pain was worse this morning, but he's fine in himself. He has almost finished carving that panel you gave him to copy.'

'Already? I wasn't expecting it so quickly. You mustn't let him tire himself.'

'You try telling him!' Sally laughed, the lines of strain leaving her pale, pretty face. 'He's that proud of his work—and grateful to you for giving him the chance to do a real job.'

'When I saw those wonderful spoons, I knew he could manage so many of the little jobs that need doing at Rathmoor. Benjamin does his best, but he hasn't Rob's flair. Together they will be able to repair furniture, wood panels and picture frames.'

'That chair Benjamin made for him has eased his back. If he could only stand on his feet, he'd be able to do so much more. He was saying only last night what a shame it is to see it all going to ruin for the want of a little work. He's taken a liking to the place.'

'Perhaps he will walk again, Sally. You mustn't give up hope yet.'

'A month ago, I thought he'd be dead before the year was out. He had no pride left in him. Then you came to see us, and it was like an answer to my prayers. I'll never be able to thank you enough for what you've done, ma'am: giving us work and letting us live in this beautiful house.'

'Rathmoor is big enough for all of us. It needs people and life. You had better go now, Sally. The baby will be waking and crying for her feed.'

Rosanna sighed as the girl went out. She liked having Sally and her husband in the house; it helped Emily and it had not been simply charity on her part. Rob's carving was exquisite, and he had already begun to earn his keep, even though he could not move from his chair without assistance. Fortunately, he seemed to accept Benjamin's help without bitterness, perhaps because he was not the only invalid in the house, but also because he had regained his pride. He could see with his own eyes that there was much he could do to help improve the house, though it would be a long, slow job. What Rosanna had not anticipated was her own reaction to hearing a child crying in the house. It had made her realise how difficult it would become for her over the years. She was not desperate for a child yet, but she had hoped for a family. Perhaps, in time . . .

No! No, it was impossible. She thrust the thought from her quickly. She would never be able to bring herself to accept that kind of a relationship with Justin. They were comfortable enough with each other these days, though sometimes, when he left her alone in the evenings, she could hardly control her indignation. She guessed that he went to meet someone, and that that someone was probably the woman she had seen with him in Bodmin. One night she had watched for him to come in, going down to the library on the pretext of wanting a book. There had been a strong smell of wine on his breath as he lurched past her a trifle unsteadily in the hall. At breakfast the next morning she had refrained from making any comment about his drinking, knowing that she had no right to censure his behaviour. Her bargain with him did not allow her to complain if he found his pleasures elsewhere. No one was allowed to guess that she was hiding her hurt deep within herself. There was so much to occupy her time that she managed to push her doubts to the back of her mind, except when she lay alone in her bed.

If she suspected the cause of her heartache, she would not admit it to herself. Her pride would not let her go to Justin and admit that she had made a mistake. Besides, she did not believe it would make any difference if she did. He seemed quite content with his life as it was. They breakfasted together most mornings before he left for the mine. Sometimes she rode over with him to visit Becky and the children, but more often he went alone, returning in time for dinner, or simply to change his clothes before going out again. During the evenings when he stayed at home, they played cards in the library with Jonathan, unless he had retired earlier. Occasionally, Rosanna played the spinet in the front parlour while Justin relaxed by the fire with a glass of wine.

Now and then he would come and stand beside her, perhaps touching her shoulder briefly when he leaned over to look at the music, then moving away again. Once, she had glanced up at him, surprising a look in his eyes that made her heart leap, and for a moment she had thought he would take her in his arms, but then he yawned.

'I'm damned tired. Think I'll turn in now, Rosanna, if you'll excuse me? Must be all these late nights...'

Rosanna watched as he walked away from her, stung by his attitude. Obviously he found her company so boring that he preferred to seek his bed at nine in the evening. Yet, when he went out to meet his mistress, it was often past midnight when he returned! What made that plump fair-haired woman so fascinating? Such thoughts were ruthlessly crushed. She was not jealous of his mistress. It was nothing to her if he chose to waste his time with a woman who had neither real beauty nor intelligence... It could not matter to her who shared his bed, since she herself had no wish to, so why should it hurt when she heard him return to his room in the early hours of the morning?

Realising suddenly that it was almost time for dinner, Rosanna closed her work-basket and hastened up to her room. Justin had said that he might be home for dinner, and she did not want to keep him waiting. She had just finished changing her gown and was fastening her pearls when there was a knock at her door.

'Come in,' she called, knowing it would be Justin. He often came to her room at about this time so that they could go down together. It was a little ceremony that she looked forward to. When he entered, however, she was a little surprised to see that he was only half dressed. Although wearing his breeches, his feet were bare and his shirt was open to the waist. He appeared to be struggling with a pearl button at his wristband.

'Could you fasten this for me, Rosanna?' he asked. 'The wretched thing seems to be stuck.'

She was very conscious of the spicy scent that seemed to waft from his warm skin as he held out his wrist for her to fasten the button that had somehow become entangled in his lace ruffle. His skin had a deep olive sheen, and she felt a sharp tingling sensation as her arm brushed against his bare chest. For some unaccountable reason, she was breathless as she fumbled with the button, succeeding in fastening it only after several nerve-racking seconds.

'Thank you,' Justin said. 'Just couldn't seem to manage it myself. You look very elegant this evening, my dear. Are you expecting guests?'

'No...' She fought for calmness. 'I—I thought you might be staying in this evening, Justin. It would be pleasant to dine together for once.'

He arched one brow, looking faintly surprised. 'If I'd known how you felt, I would have cancelled my dinner engagement with Major Burrows. It seems that the rumours are true. Napoleon has escaped from Elba and landed in France. Apparently he is marching on Paris, and Louis has fled. If that is true, it will mean another war with the French.'

'But *you* would not need to go,' Rosanna said, her heart jerking with fright. 'You resigned your commission only last year.'

'If there is a war, Wellington will need all his officers.' Justin grimaced. 'You might be lucky enough to be widowed, Rosanna; then you would be free to find yourself a rich husband.'

She felt the hot tears stinging behind her eyes and turned aside so that he should not see how much he had hurt her. 'Please go away, Justin. Go to your dinner appointment or your mistress; I don't care which.'

Justin frowned as he saw the tension in her stiff shoulders. He had not meant to lash out so cruelly, but his nerves were tightly strung and for once he had let down his guard. The touch of her hands had sent his blood surging, but she had remained as cool as ever. The frustration built in him as he realised that despite all his efforts to tantalise and tease her into some response, the citadel remained unbreached, and he was suddenly very angry.

'Then you won't bother to wait up for me, I presume? Very wise, as I expect to be late. Goodnight, my sweet wife. I wish you pleasant dreams in your chaste bed.'

Rosanna kept her back turned until she heard the door slam behind him. The tears were slipping beneath her lashes and the pain in her breast hurt so much that she could hardly breathe. How could he say such terrible things? Did he think her so cold-hearted that she would welcome his death simply because it would allow her to marry again? How much he must hate her if he could think that! It was a while before she could calm herself sufficiently to go downstairs. Her grandfather's shrewd eyes went over her face, but he made no comment. She knew that he was aware of the tension between her and Justin, but he had never said one word. There was no need for him to reproach her, since she was only too conscious that she had brought this distressing situation on herself. Hiding her unhappiness as best she could, she kissed the old man's cheek.

'How are you tonight, dearest?'

'I'm well enough, child. I take it Justin won't be dining with us this evening?'

'No. He has a dinner engagement with Major Burrows, that friend of his from Bodmin. You remember he came to our wedding?'

'Of course I remember—a tall chap with whiskers. I'm not in my dotage yet, girl.'

'I wouldn't dream of suggesting it!' She smiled fondly. 'Justin seems to think there may be another war in France.'

'Bound to be, with that monster on the loose. I warned him how it would be. I suppose he will want to be off again? At least you'll know where he is.'

Rosanna saw his frown. 'I know where he is tonight. Please don't upset yourself, Grandfather. You know I'm not in love with him. He has every right to do as he pleases—it was part of our bargain.'

'And what do you get out of it all? No, don't look like that, child. I'm sorry. I shouldn't have said anything. It's not my affair.'

She knelt at the side of his chair, looking up at him. 'If I'm unhappy, it's my own fault. Justin intended to be straight with me. It was I who—who refused to be a true wife to him. I—I can't explain why.'

'You've no need. I know you too well, my girl. It's your pride that stands between you.' He stroked the dark hair. 'Do you think I haven't seen the way he looks at you? You could end this nonsense tomorrow if you had a mind to it. If you'll take my advice, you'll swallow your pride and make it up with him before it's too late.'

Emily came in then to announce that dinner was ready, and Rosanna was saved from replying. She wheeled her grandfather's chair into the dining-room and took her seat. A third place had been set at the end, but she averted her eyes from it. There was no sense in being silly just because her husband was dining with Major Burrows. If he *was* with his friend and not with his mistress . . .

As usual, Emily had prepared an excellent dinner consisting of several courses: pigeons in red wine, a fat capon, a dish of baked parsnips in butter, a meat pie and pastries, but Rosanna could manage only a little of the chicken and a glass of white wine. After dinner, she played a hand of cards with her grandfather, then wished him goodnight as Benjamin came to carry him up to his room. It was still only eight o'clock. The house seemed empty and silent as she took out her work-basket and then pushed it away in frustration, getting up to pace about the little sitting-room. She was too bored and restless to stand yet another long evening alone. She wanted someone to talk to—someone who could make her laugh. She wanted Justin. Even if he only sat by the fire drinking his wine, it would be better than this. Yet, remembering the first few days of their marriage when he had gone out of his way to please her, she knew that it could be so much better.

The silence was almost unbearable. She went into the long parlour and sat down at her spinet. For a while the music eased her loneliness, but when she finished playing, it swept over her again. How could she bear this empty life? She could fill the house with dinner guests, but in her heart she knew that she would still be alone. She would be alone until she had a real and loving relationship with her husband. But how could she tell Justin what was in her mind? He did not love her. She was not even sure that he wanted her physically any more—and should he reject her offer, it would break her.

Sighing, she closed the lid of the spinet and stood up. She would go to bed and try to sleep. Perhaps, then, she could forget this dull ache about her heart for a little while . . .

'You surely don't mean to enlist?' Major Paul Burrows gave his magnificent dark whiskers a twirl as he eyed the glowering face of his friend. 'Even if old Boney is on the loose again, you can't mean to risk everything just for the sake of some sport?'

Justin stared gloomily into his wine-glass and then at a picture on the wall of Paul's library. He must have looked at that damned portrait a thousand times over these past few weeks, and each time he felt like hurling something at it. It was the look in the woman's eyes that reminded him of Rosanna, making him feel vaguely guilty. Damn it—and her—to hell!

'What have I to lose?' he muttered morosely.

'For a man who has recently been married to a wealthy heiress, who also happens to be one of the prettiest women I've ever laid eyes on, that is a singularly foolish question!'

Justin grunted, his mouth twisting. He wondered what his friend would say if he guessed the true state of affairs. Paul had made no secret of the fact that he thought Rosanna a fine catch, and considered him a fool for leaving her alone so often to spend his evenings drinking in Paul's library. While not doubting the truth of this, Justin knew he had no alternative. He had to get away from her or go mad with frustration. He had expected to find his little game of cat and mouse amusing, and he was disgusted at his own lack of will-power. Rosanna had not given an inch, while he was on the verge... He thrust the thought from him swiftly, applying himself to the matter in hand.

'Boney has to be beaten once and for all,' he said. 'You know I've always admired the man, but he can't be allowed to go rampaging all over Europe again. Wellington will fight, and I want to be there.'

'Well, I wouldn't want to miss the show myself,' Paul admitted. 'I'm not married, of course. Tell you what, old fellow, you talk it over with Rosanna tomorrow. If you're still set on it, we'll go together.'

Justin drained his glass, reaching automatically for the crystal decanter. Talk to Rosanna, after the way she had acted earlier this evening? She had shown that she did not care one way or the other and practically wished him to the devil! There was little point in inflicting more humiliation on himself, since she had made her feelings so clear, but he supposed he would have to try. Seth could take charge of the mine in his absence, but there were certain things that needed to be discussed in case he was killed. Pushing the decanter away from him resolutely, he stood up.

'I think I'll get a good night's sleep. I want to be up early in the morning.' He smiled a little self-consciously. 'I'll let you know my decision by the end of the week.'

'I shan't blame you if you change your mind,' Paul said with a grin. 'I know what I'd do if I were lucky enough to be in your shoes!'

Justin chuckled, his sense of humour stirred, despite himself. 'Maybe you're right,' he murmured, more to himself than his friend. 'Maybe I've been all kinds of a fool—but tomorrow I intend to find out.'

Rosanna smoothed back a wisp of hair from her face, looking at the dark shadows beneath her eyes. Were they very noticeable? She had slept hardly at all, hearing Justin come in well before eleven o'clock. For a long time afterwards she had lain wakeful, fighting the temptation to go to his room and demand an apology for the terrible things he had said to her before he went out. She was tired of the pretence that this ridiculous marriage was a satisfactory state of affairs. It could not go on like this. It would be better to end it, each of them going their separate ways.

Going downstairs, she made up her mind to speak to Justin before he left for the mine. She could not go on hiding this hurt inside her. However, the smile he gave her as she entered the breakfast parlour made her heart jerk painfully. He was helping himself to thick slices of a large honey-roasted ham, and he gestured towards it with the knife.

'This is very good. May I cut some for you?'

'Yes, please.' She sat down at the table, watching him carve the thin slices just as she liked them, and smiling as he set the plate before her. 'Justin, I have been wanting to talk to you...'

'Indeed?' He sat opposite her, helping himself to various preserves. 'Then it is fortunate that I have no engagements today, isn't it? We could go riding this morning, if you wish?'

Rosanna swallowed a piece of the delicious ham and sipped the hot, fragrant liquid in her dainty cup. She had no liking for the sweet chocolate that many ladies took in the mornings, preferring the slightly bitter taste of coffee. 'I should enjoy that,' she said. 'But aren't you going to the mine today?'

'There is no need for me to go every day now that the new pumps are installed. Seth is in charge of the day-to-day running of the mine. A visit now and then should suffice.' Justin looked at her across the table. 'It occurs to me that we have seen little of our neighbours since the wedding. They are obviously reluctant to intrude, so perhaps we should give a dinner party to show that we are ready to receive visitors?'

'That would be pleasant.' Rosanna swallowed nervously. 'Does that mean you intend to be at home more often in future?'

'Perhaps. It rather depends on you, my dear.'

'Wh—What do you mean?'

'I was not sure that my company would be welcome. It's as simple as that.'

'Oh . . .' She looked down at the table. 'It—It would suit me very well if you were to dine at home more often.'

'Then I shall make a point of it.' He pushed away his empty plate and stood up. 'If you will excuse me, I shall have the horses made ready. Perhaps you will join me when you have finished?'

'I've finished now.' She had swallowed only a morsel or two, but her stomach was churning, making it impossible for her to eat. 'I shall not keep you for more than ten minutes or so while I change my gown.'

'There is no hurry. I can wait.'

'Thank you.' She smiled shyly, her heart fluttering as she saw his look. He could be very agreeable, when he chose. 'I'll join you in the courtyard.'

Her pulses were pounding as she hurried upstairs. Was she imagining it, or had there been a new warmth in Justin's eyes as he looked at her just now? He had obviously decided that a change was needed—might it not lead to a new beginning between them? Yet how could things change when he did not love her?

Dressing quickly in a riding-gown of green velvet, she set a saucy little hat on the back of her head and picked up a pair of soft leather gloves. She was aware that she

looked rather rakish, and that excitement had lent a new
sparkle to her eyes, but would Justin notice it?

He was waiting with the horses in the courtyard, and
as he came to help her into the saddle, she saw something in his face that made her heart jerk. He had not
looked at her like that since before their wedding day.
So he did still find her attractive! She trembled as his
hands encircled her waist, almost giving into the temptation to arch towards him so that he was forced to embrace her; but then she found herself in the saddle,
looking down on him, and the moment had passed. A
faint blush stained her cheeks. What a fool she was! He
had only to look at her, and she was ready to fall into
his arms, like any of those other silly women he so despised. She repressed the surge of longing she had experienced, determined that he should speak first and
forgetting the long hours of loneliness she had endured.
If he wanted to change things between them, *he* must
make the first move. She had not deserted him night
after night to seek a lover!

That, of course, must end if he wished for a new relationship with his wife. She had not complained before
this, realising that she could not expect a man like Justin
to live the life of a monk. She would, however, require
an undertaking that he would break with his mistress
before she could consent to... Was she really contemplating that kind of relationship with the man who had
so humiliated her at his house? He had planned to seduce
her as a way of making certain that she would not jilt
him. Could she really have come so far that she was on
the verge of capitulating?

Urging her horse to a quick trot, Rosanna wrestled
with the disturbing thoughts whirling in her mind. Pride
had made her refuse to be a true wife to Justin in the
first place. Pride, and the fear of being dominated by a
stronger will than her own. That day at his house had
shown her how dangerous it would be to surrender to
such a masterful man. She would never again be entirely
her own mistress: a part of her would irrevocably belong

to him. Was she prepared to surrender her independence? Supposing Justin used his power over her to make her his slave?

Glancing sideways, she saw the serious expression on her husband's face and realised that he had been watching her. What is he thinking? she wondered. He was obviously not satisfied with their present situation, or he would not have spoken as he had this morning. Yet he had spoken, and perhaps there was a chance for them, after all. Suddenly her doubts fell away. She gave him a provocative glance, urging her horse to a gallop, and laughing as he instantly took up the challenge. The sun had broken through the clouds, taking the chill of the March winds from the morning. It lifted her mood, making her feel better than she had for weeks.

'I'll race you to the cove,' she cried, her eyes bright with mischief. 'Beat me if you can...'

It had been a wonderful day, Rosanna thought, as she dressed for dinner in a gown of burgundy silk. For once, she and Justin had not quarrelled the whole time they were together. After their ride, they had eaten a light meal, and then spent the afternoon exploring the house. Justin had light-heartedly suggested that they look for Lady Caroline's jewels, and they had actually found a secret passage leading from her ancestor's bedchamber to the long parlour. Justin had discovered it by accidentally pressing a knob in the carved panel behind the bed.

When the panel slid back to reveal a dark aperture, Rosanna had given a squeal of delight. 'You've found it!' she cried, feeling sure that they would discover the treasure somewhere within the passage. 'Oh, let me see what's in there, Justin?'

He had smiled at her indulgently, lighting a candle and warning her to stay close behind him. 'Be careful,' he said, 'the steps are very steep.'

They had discovered that the passage ended rather disappointingly behind a tapestry in the long parlour. It was just a passage, with no little chambers or anywhere that could contain a hiding-place for the jewels. Seeing her chagrin, Justin had laughed.

'If it was so easy, my sweet, the jewels would have been found long ago. I am sure that there are other passages connecting with this one, but we simply haven't found them yet.'

Jonathan confirmed his theory over dinner. He had known that such a passage existed, though he had never managed to find it himself.

'It was mentioned in the diary of Lady Caroline's grandson,' he said. 'Charles Whitby seems to have been one of the most thorough of the treasure-hunters. He found the passage when he was a child, and he spoke of others, but he never admitted to finding the jewels. I've read his account a hundred times, but the secret of how to open the panel eluded me. At least you've managed to do something I never could!'

'You must have many family documents relating to the legend,' Justin said thoughtfully. 'I'd like to examine them, if I may? If the jewels really did exist, the chances are that they are still hidden in the house.'

'I'm sure of it,' Rosanna said, her eyes sparkling. 'If only we could find them!'

'You're welcome to make use of what you like. Most of the Bibles and accounts are in the library, but there's a trunk full of stuff in the cellar.' The old man's eyes narrowed. 'I expected you to be off to France with Wellington.'

'I haven't yet made up my mind.'

Justin's gaze turned to Rosanna. She flicked down her lashes, remembering their quarrel the previous evening. Why was he looking at her like that? She had enjoyed his company today, but he had given her no sign of his intentions. Did he expect her to beg him to stay at home? Much as she longed to begin a new relationship, she could not bring herself to go that far. He must make his own feelings plain before she admitted what was in her own mind.

Justin seemed to be waiting for her to speak, but when she remained silent, he turned back to Jonathan, beginning a discussion of the repeal of the apprenticeship and wages act that had taken place the previous year—a conversation she could neither enter nor comment on. She sensed that he was deliberately excluding her, and realised that she had made him angry.

Jonathan retired to bed soon after dinner, leaving them to amuse each other. Rosanna suggested a game of chess, believing that Justin preferred it to cards, but he refused, taking up his usual position by the fireplace. His mood had changed, and the easy companionship they had shared earlier was marred by tension.

'Why don't you play something?' he asked, pouring himself another glass of wine.

'My playing seems to irk you,' she replied with a frown. Was it going to turn into another of those times when he sank into a morose mood, leaving her before the evening was out? 'You usually retire to your room soon after I begin. I thought we might do something different tonight?'

'And what had you in mind, my sweet? We could sing a duet—a romantic ballad, perhaps?' He arched his brow as she stiffened. 'Or would that be too much to ask? What kind of a woman are you, Rosanna? Are you as cold as you seem, or is it that you really hate me?'

'Why must you always torment me?' she cried, pressing her nails deep into the palms of her hands. 'I do not hate you. You are my husband . . .' Her voice died away to a whisper as she saw the sudden gleam in his eyes.

'Would that I were,' he murmured. 'Your husband, Rosanna—when I have never lain in your bed? What kind of a life is it when we share nothing more than a few words in passing?' He had risen from his chair and was moving towards her. 'Don't you feel the waste of it? My God! Don't you feel anything?'

His hands were gripping her shoulders, digging into her flesh. He was hurting her, and there was a wildness in his eyes that frightened her. He seemed so very masculine, so dominant, that her instinct was to defend herself.

'Let me go, Justin,' she cried. 'You are hurting me!'

'So you can feel pain,' he muttered, the anger pouring out of him as if he had lost control. 'Sometimes I have doubted it. Do you know how often I have wanted to hurt you, to wring some response, even if I had to shake it out of you?'

'How should I respond?' she asked bitterly, the unfairness of his attack beginning to make her angry. 'Should I have nagged you because you stayed out all night and came home drunk and stinking of brandy? Should I have made a scene when you left me to go to your mistress night after night?'

'My mistress?' A startled expression came over his face, and then he laughed. 'Damn it! I think you're jealous, Rosanna.' He caught her chin, forcing her to look up at him, smiling in satisfaction as he saw the slow flush in her cheeks. 'That's it, isn't it? You're jealous of my mistress...'

She felt as if he had slapped her. How could he humiliate her like this? She had believed that he might have come to care for her a little, but now he was showing his contempt, mocking her because she had been betrayed into letting her guard down for one instant.

'You are cruel, and I hate you!' she cried, wrenching away from him. 'You despise all women and seek to use them for your pleasure. Well, I shall not be used by you—neither shall I stay here to be humiliated...' Giving a little cry of despair, she rushed past him and out of the room.

'Humiliated?' he echoed in astonishment. 'What the hell do you mean by that?'

For a moment he was too stunned to move, then he followed her with swift strides, catching her at the top of the stairs. She glared at him as he grabbed her wrist.

'Let me go, Justin. I'm warning you...'

'You are warning me?' His eyes glinted with temper. 'By heaven, madam, I have had enough of this! You speak of humiliation—when you have clearly shown your contempt on numerous occasions! I have borne with you long enough, Rosanna, but no more. I may have treated you badly once, but you have taken your revenge a thousand times.'

He had begun to drag her with him as he spoke, and she struggled as she guessed where he was taking her. 'No! You devil, let go of me. I won't! I won't...'

Justin ignored her protests, keeping a firm grip on her wrist as he marched her down the hall and then thrust her inside the bedchamber they were to have shared on their wedding night. Only then did he release his grasp, turning to lock the door behind them and placing the key in his waistcoat pocket.

Rosanna rubbed her wrist, looking at him accusingly. He had not really hurt her, but she was not going to admit it. 'You vile brute,' she muttered. 'I don't know why you've brought me here, but...'

'Do you really not know?' he asked mockingly, a cold glint in his eyes. 'You are not as stupid as that, my sweet. I have brought you here to do what I should have done on our wedding night. You are a cheat and a liar, Rosanna, but you are also my wife. I may be all kinds of a fool, but I want you. I have wanted you from the first moment I saw you—and now I intend to have you.'

Rosanna felt a shiver of fear run through her as she sensed the anger in him. 'No, Justin!' she cried, holding up her hand to ward him off. 'Not like this, please!'

'No?' His brows rose disbelievingly. 'I have waited for a sign from you, but you give nothing. How long do you expect me to wait, my love? I was wrong to agree to this unnatural arrangement. It cannot go on.'

'I know that,' she said stiffly. 'I—I too have thought that it might be best to—to end it.'

'You think that I shall give you up now?' he asked, a dangerous note in his voice. 'I warned you at the start that I do not let go once something belongs to me. You may as well accept your duty, Rosanna, for I shall not be thwarted again.'

'No,' she whispered, beginning to tremble. 'Please, Justin...'

'What is it you fear?' he asked, coming towards her. 'Is it physical violence? Surely you know that I would never hurt you?'

She ran the tip of her tongue over dry lips, knowing that her fear was not really of him but of something deep within herself. 'Will you not let me go?' she begged.

'No. It is for the best, Rosanna. Admit it, and make it easier for yourself. I do not want to force you, but I mean to have you one way or the other.'

'Then I have no choice,' she said, lifting her head defiantly. 'But I shall not easily forgive you.'

'I am sorry you feel like that,' he muttered, his breath coming faster now. 'I would rather have had you willingly, but I shall not be denied.'

It was useless to fight him any longer. In her heart, Rosanna knew that she would melt at the first touch of his lips, just as she had the first time he had tried to make love to her, and this time no one would come to disturb them.

'You are stronger than I,' she said chokingly. 'Do what you must. I shall not fight you.'

'Then let me love you, Rosanna,' he said huskily, his arms going round her. 'Let me show you that there is nothing to fear.'

He bent his head, his lips brushing hers with a sweet tenderness that set her body trembling. Her head went back as she ceased to resist either mentally or physically, her body arching against his instinctively. She gasped as his lips touched her throat, and her hands moved up over his shoulders, clasping the soft velvet of his coat as she felt the dizzy sensation sweep through her. Her pulses were throbbing with something that she dimly recognised as desire, and she knew that she wanted this. She had wanted him from the first, just as he had wanted her. Only her stupid pride had kept her from confessing it.

Justin bent to sweep her up in his arms, carrying her towards the bed. She lay looking up at him as he began to undress her, her lips parting as she found it more difficult to breathe. She neither helped nor hindered him as he unfastened her bodice, touching his lips to the palpitating swell of her breasts. He lifted her hips to ease off the layers of petticoats, his hand moving caressingly over the smooth flatness of her stomach. For a moment he looked at her, and then left her as he quickly removed his own clothing.

Rosanna's heart was beating wildly as he returned. She stiffened as he lay down beside her, feeling the burn of his flesh against her as he pulled her to him. Then, as his kisses set the blood flowing hotly in her veins once more, she relaxed and opened her lips beneath his. His tongue flicked between her breasts, his mouth moving to tease and caress the rose-pink tips. She gave a little cry of pleasure as his lips travelled downwards, sending tremors of desire shooting through her. She moved her head on the pillow restlessly, losing all restraint as he sought and found the warm, secret place between her thighs. At first she was shocked by the touch of his hand, but then she began to moan softly with the pleasure of it, her legs parting willingly as he moved to cover her with his own body. She felt a sharp, tearing pain as he thrust into her, and her nails dug into his shoulders. Her cry was stifled beneath his kiss, and in a moment she had forgotten the pain as he moved rythmically inside her, slowly but surely bringing her towards a climax of such intensity that her body shook and she cried out again and again.

He did not leave her immediately afterwards, rolling over on his side to hold her while she wept against his chest. The deep, painful sobs shook her, and he stroked her hair, comforting her as if she were a child.

'Forgive me,' he whispered against her ear. 'Don't cry, my love. Everything shall be as you wish, I promise. Go to sleep now.'

She tried to find the words to explain how she felt, but they stuck in her throat. All she could do was to bury her face in the salty warmth of his shoulder as the stupid tears ran uncontrollably down her cheeks. At last the storm of emotion left her, eased by his gentleness. She curled trustingly into the curve of his body, exhausted and drained, sleeping like a babe in his arms.

In the darkness, Justin's face was sombre. He had had his way, but at what cost to her? She was his, but he had taken her without her true consent, and her tears were a recrimination he found hard to bear. He was aware of something within him he had never experienced before: a desire to protect and cherish the woman he had earlier sought to dominate. He had broken down all her defences, and now he was afraid that she might hate him for it. He might be able to command her obedience in their bed, but supposing she withheld all the rest? What an empty victory it would then be . . .

CHAPTER SIX

ROSANNA stretched and yawned. She felt different this morning: more relaxed, happier. Opening her eyes, she registered the unfamiliar surroundings and suddenly the memories came flooding back, making her body tingle.

She was alone in Justin's bed, and judging by the bright spring sunshine streaming in, the morning was well advanced. Throwing back the bedcovers, she retrieved the clothes she had been wearing the previous evening, wanting to escape before her husband returned. She supposed she ought to feel angry about the ruthless way he had taken her, but she did not. There was a spring of happiness bubbling up inside her.

Glancing at her reflection in the mirror, she saw a new brightness in her eyes, and began to laugh. She was not angry with Justin. She was glad that he had broken down the barriers between them! She was in love with him. She could admit it to herself at last. She had fallen for his charm the first time they danced, but she had resisted so fiercely that her mind had invented all manner of excuses for the way he made her feel whenever he touched her. It was true that she loved Rathmoor, but she had never even considered marrying anyone but Justin. She knew now that all her talk of marrying for money had been merely a smoke-screen to blind herself to the truth. Justin was the one man she had been waiting for all her life!

'What an idiot I am!' she whispered, as the sparkle suddenly left her eyes.

She was behaving like a very silly woman. Nothing had really changed, except that he had broken down her resistance. Had she told him she loved him while she lay in his arms? No, she did not think so. She had wanted to tell him, but the words had stuck in her throat and she had wept instead. Thankfully, she had been saved from the final humiliation. Dressing quickly, she hurried to her own room, locking the door behind her. She needed time to think, time to decide how she would behave when she next saw her husband.

As it happened, Justin did not return to the house until well into the afternoon. Busy in the still-room, Rosanna was not even aware of his presence in the house until she went upstairs to change for dinner. He was emerging from his own room, cloaked and booted as if for a journey. He stared at her strangely, as if he had wished to avoid this meeting and was embarrassed by it.

'Are you going out?' she asked, feeling a coldness inside. She had hoped that there might be some sign of a change, but clearly the previous night had meant little or nothing to him.

'I'm going away for a while, Rosanna. I have spoken to Jonathan. Everything is in order. I left a letter in your room.'

'A letter?' She felt as if the ground had given way beneath her. 'You were going without saying goodbye to me?'

He avoided her eyes. 'I thought you might prefer it that way. I believe it is best that I go.'

'You intend to join Wellington?'

'Yes.'

'Then there is no more to be said.'

'No. I'm sorry.'

He walked on past her. There was a great ball of misery in her, clawing at her breast. He was going away—leaving her! She found it impossible to speak, but then as he reached the top of the stairs, she turned quickly.

'Take care, Justin. I do not wish to be a widow,' she called, then, before he could answer, she ran down the hall and disappeared into her own room.

She leaned against the door, her heart beating wildly. Would he follow her? Would he demand an explanation of what she had just said? For a few seconds, her expectation was high, but then she realised he was not coming. Her pulses slowed as the excitement drained away. He was not coming. He had either not heard or not understood what she said—or perhaps he just did not care?

His letter lay on her dressing-chest. She stared at it for several minutes before she could bring herself to reach for it. Opening the seal with shaking fingers, she saw that it was brief and to the point. He apologised for his behaviour the previous night, going on to say that he thought it best if they were apart for a while.

> Should I be killed, Rosanna, I have made arrangements for my affairs to be settled. I have nothing to leave you but the mine, which I hope will be profitable within a year or two. If I am fortunate enough to see you again, I shall hope that you will have learned to forgive me.
>
> Justin.

Forgive him? Why should he think he needed forgiveness, when all he had done was to show her the truth? Suddenly, she tore open the door, running along the hall. He must not leave without knowing that she loved him!

She was breathless when she reached the entrance hall, her pulses racing. Emily was busy polishing as she rushed past her out into the courtyard, to see Justin's horse carrying him beneath the arched gateway. She screamed after him, 'Justin, don't go! I have to talk to you—I have to...' She was too late. He had gone, perhaps never to return. The pain swept through her, beating at her temples. 'Don't go,' she whispered. 'I love you...'

The pressure of her grief was too much to bear. It seemed as if the earth was spinning, faster and faster, until she was whirled into space.

Benjamin saw her fall. He ran to catch her up in his arms, and calling for Emily, he carried her back into the house.

*   *   *

There had been another small cave-in at the mine. With the other wives, Becky hurried to the entrance as they began to bring the men out, their faces blackened with grime. From all around her she heard cries of relief as the women saw that their men were safe, but where was Seth? She murmured a prayer of thanks as she saw him bringing up the rear. It was so like him to make sure that everyone else was out first. She ran towards him, prepared to throw herself into his arms, stopping in shock as she saw the blood seeping through his shirt just below his left shoulder.

'Oh, Seth,' she choked, 'you've been hurt!'

'It's not bad, lass,' he said, seeing the alarm in her face. 'I was caught by the rock-fall. Fortunately there were no bad injuries this time.'

Becky walked at his side as they turned in the direction of the village, glancing at his grim face. With Justin away, everything fell to Seth. It was a big responsibility, and she knew it worried him. She had been heating water for the washing before the bell warned of the accident up at the mine. The big wooden tub was still full of clean, soapy water. She gestured towards it with a nod of her head.

'Take off your clothes and into that tub with you, Seth. It will ease the pain and I can wash away the blood. You're covered in it.'

Seth did as she said, sighing as he sat down in the warm water. 'This is a treat, Becky love,' he said. 'Wash my back for me, will you?'

As she bent over him, he caught her and brought her head down so that he could kiss her lips.

'Away with you,' she cried laughing. 'Let me bathe your shoulder.'

'I'd rather have you in the tub with me.'

'Seth Miller! You should be ashamed of yourself.'

'I mind the time you wouldn't have said no.'

Becky coloured and shook her head at him. 'The children could come in...'

Seth laughed, and let her go. 'I'll not risk your modesty, sweetheart.'

Becky smiled and began to sponge the blood from her husband's body. Once most of it was washed away, she saw that it was only a small cut, though there was massive bruising on his back and shoulder.

'You're going to be sore for a few days,' she said, patting his back dry and smoothing some cream into his flesh. 'What happened this time?'

'We were exploring a new tunnel when some of the shoring gave way. I think it had been tampered with.'

'Are you going to send a message to Mrs Sawle?'

'Why? There's nothing she can do about it. I shall have to keep my eyes open, that's all.'

'It's a pity Captain Sawle felt he had to rejoin his regiment. Things are bad hereabouts, Seth. The price of bread is soaring since they brought that law in about foreign corn.'

'It's not just here. Justin told me that there were riots in London over those damned corn laws.' Seth smiled grimly. 'He's determined to keep the mine going, whatever happens. Let's hope Wellington puts a stop to Boney quickly so that he can come home again...'

There were many influences at work when Napoleon Bonaparte left Elba to return to France. Perhaps the accusations of cowardice, the taunting of old enemies or the urging of his mother; it might merely have been boredom that made him break his word. Yet surely it had been inevitable that such a restless spirit would seek a larger stage on which to play out the remaining acts of his life?

Whatever lay behind the decision, it was taken and acted on with all the old brilliance and courage shown in former years. While the English Commissioner was away on a visit to Italy, Napoleon ordered his only warship to be provisioned for a voyage. On 28th February 1815, the Commissioner returned to Elba to find that Napoleon and his faithful Guard had sailed two days previously. It was too late for the English ships to catch the *Inconstant*, and at least three French vessels had failed to realise the significance of her voyage. By the first day of March, Napoleon had landed at Antibes.

The great general had less than a thousand men, but he firmly believed that the people would rally to his standard. It was at Grenoble that his belief was first put to the test. Meeting an infantry regiment on the road, he advanced alone, shouting, 'Kill your Emperor if you wish!' It was brave, reckless and typical of the man who had once held all Europe in the palm of his hand. One musket-shot could have ended his mad adventure there. Instead, the soldiers broke ranks, cheering and surrounding him with cries of *'Vive l'Empereur!'* The garrison at Grenoble went over to him. Before then he had been merely a gambler, but after his rapturous reception there, he was the Emperor again.

When news of his landing reached Paris, Marshal Ney promised to bring him back in an iron cage, but the troops were sullen and disinclined to move against the man they had worshipped. Louis XVIII was no more popular than his Bourbon predecessor. The people had warm memories of Napoleon, and Ney was shaken by a letter from his old friend, reminding him of his former loyalty. He changed his allegiance, announcing to the world that the Bourbon cause was lost.

The King left Paris on 19th March, and on the following day Napoleon was carried triumphantly up the steps of the Tuileries by an excited crowd. His first acts were to assure everyone that he was not interested in war. He had renounced his idea of a great empire and would apply himself only to conserving the happiness and prosperity of his people. The other nations of Europe had not forgiven him, however. At the Congress of Vienna, the allies had proclaimed him an outlaw, and since he could not be trusted to keep his word, he must be defeated once and for all. The allied forces of the English, Dutch, Belgians and Hanoverians under Wellington, and the Prussians under Blücher, would join with the Russians and Austrians to crush this rebellious general for ever.

It was a warm June morning when Rosanna rode into the courtyard to find Seth Miller waiting for her. She had been to the cove, and the ride had lifted her spirits, bringing a fresh colour to her cheeks. Seth came to help her to dismount, giving her an anxious look as Benjamin led the horse away.

'Forgive me for coming, Mrs Sawle,' he said. 'Justin stressed that I wasn't to trouble you with problems at the mine, but I had no choice.'

She nodded and smiled at him, stripping off her gloves. 'Come into the house and tell me about it, Seth. I hope it isn't about Becky or the children?'

'No, they're well. Becky was hoping you might ride over to visit one day if you're not too busy?'

'Yes, I'm sorry I haven't been over more often. My grandfather hasn't been well this past month, and I haven't wanted to leave him for too long.'

'I'm sorry to hear that.' Seth frowned. 'Perhaps I shouldn't have come?'

'Don't apologise, Seth. I know you wouldn't have come if it wasn't important.' She led him into the long parlour. 'Shall I ring for Emily? Will you take some refreshment with me?'

'No, thank you, ma'am. I'll be away as soon as we've spoken.'

She nodded, understanding his impatience. She had already kept him waiting, and he must have much to do. 'There's some trouble at the mine, I take it? Not another accident, I trust?'

'No, not lately, thank God! It's the bank, Mrs Sawle. I went to draw the men's wages in Bodmin and they refused me. Said it was orders from London. No more money until the Captain arranges some security.'

'That's ridiculous!' Rosanna cried. 'Justin had negotiated a fresh loan. Something has to be wrong.'

'I argued with them for over an hour, but they refused to give me a penny until they have fresh orders. The men will work for a while without pay, I know, out of loyalty to Captain Sawle, but most of them will need to look for alternative employment within a matter of days.'

'Yes, I understand,' Rosanna said, her eyes thoughtful. 'Since there's nothing Justin can do for the moment, it is obviously up to me. I shall go to London myself and speak to Mr Denton. Don't worry, Seth, I'll get some money for you somehow.'

Seth's face cleared. 'I know I shouldn't have troubled you, but Becky told me you'd help us. Captain Sawle had such high hopes before he left. I'd feel I'd failed him if we had to shut down while he was away.' He hesitated, then said, 'It looks pretty certain that there'll be a war, doesn't it?'

'Yes, I'm afraid so. As I understand it, Wellington's army is spread out along the Belgian frontier, waiting for a confrontation. At least, that's what Sir Joshua has told me.' She bit her lip. 'I had a brief note from Justin before he left England, but I've heard nothing since.'

'Well, I expect it's difficult with things the way they are. Perhaps it will all come to nothing, and the Captain will be home before you know it.'

'Yes.' Rosanna turned away for a moment to compose herself. She was not sure that Justin would come back to her even if war did not break out. 'I must not keep you, Seth. I know you want to get back to the mine. I shall see what can be done immediately. I think I can find you enough to carry on for the moment.' She had some jewellery she could sell in Truro. It would not amount to much, but it should pay the wages for a while.

'Thank you.' Seth turned to leave. 'I hope Mr Whitby will soon be himself again.'

'He was a little better this morning. I shall not like leaving him, but I know he will understand in the circumstances. I'll send you word as soon as I return.'

After he had gone, Rosanna rang for Sally. She would need a female companion on her journey, and the baby was weaned at last. Besides, she could not deprive her grandfather of Emily's services. Nor of Benjamin, she realised. Even so, she had no intention of travelling by the mail coach this time. Sir Joshua would be only too pleased to lend her his comfortable carriage. He might even be persuaded to accompany her himself...

The news that Napoleon had succeeded in bringing the bulk of the French army across the Sambre had reached Wellington in Brussels. He at once dispatched orders to the various camps to break up and concentrate on Quatre-Bras.

'The sly old fox!' Paul Burrows exclaimed as word of the French attack on the Prussians at Ligny began to circulate amongst the officers. 'Damn it! Boney could crush Blücher and leave us high and dry.'

'It certainly looks as if Wellington's been caught with his pants down this time,' Justin agreed. 'We must hope that Blücher avoids a stand-up fight until we can muster in sufficient strength.' He grinned at his friend. 'At least there's a ray of light in all this—it will put paid to the Duchess of Richmond's ball!'

'Yes, that's a point,' Paul agreed.

In assuming this, they were both wrong, however. The officers invited were ordered to attend as though nothing unusual was happening, but to leave quietly at ten o'clock and report to their various divisions. Unwillingly, but forced to obey his commander's order, Justin accompanied Major Burrows to the ball. He stood near the balcony, intending to slip away as soon as he could. In this aim he was thwarted, however, having caught Wellington's eye and been drawn into his net. It was while he was still in conversation with the Duke that he heard a familiar female voice.

'Why, Captain Sawle, I thought it must be you.'

Turning to see Anne Cornwallis, Justin glowered. 'Madam, I am surprised to see you here. Is your husband with you?'

'Of course,' she trilled, fluttering her fan. 'Henry came to support his nephew. It's the boy's first campaign. What a delightful coincidence. You are going to dance with me, of course?'

'Go on, sir.' Wellington nodded approval. 'My officers must always do their duty.'

He could not refuse Anne without offending everyone. Bowing, he offered her his arm and led her on to the floor. 'You are flirting with danger, Anne. You know your husband suspected us of having an affair.'

'But that was before you were married.' She smiled up at him. 'We were in town before we left England, and I was introduced to your wife at a dance. Such a delightful creature! I wonder you could bear to leave her.'

Ignoring her taunt, Justin looked down at her. 'You must be mistaken, Anne. Rosanna is at home in Cornwall.'

'Not when I saw her. She was at Lady Carmichael's evening party. She came in with an elderly gentleman, but she was dancing with Harry Bellingham for most of the evening. Lady Carmichael introduced us later at my request.'

'Indeed?' Justin's face was frozen. 'For what purpose, may I ask?'

Anne raised mocking eyes to his. 'Oh, not to tell her that we had been lovers. I would never be as indiscreet as that. Surely you did not think it?'

'It would do you little good, Anne. I should be an uncomfortable enemy.'

'Oh, your little secret is quite safe.' She fluttered her lashes at him. 'You must know you can trust me.'

'I would sooner trust a serpent.'

'Wicked man!' Anne pouted prettily. 'You were not always so unkind, sir.'

'I was tempted, and I fell.' He scowled. 'I thought I had made it clear that our affair was over.'

'It could always begin again.'

'No, it could not.' Justin stopped dancing, releasing her. 'Excuse me, madam, I must leave you.' He walked away, leaving her staring after him in annoyance.

'So you see, Mr Denton, I must have a capital sum, even if it means selling the property at a loss.'

'I could not advise you to do that, Mrs Sawle. If you have patience, it should provide you with a reasonable income. Perhaps as much as five hundred a year.'

'I am grateful for your advice, sir, but I must have the money at once.'

'I need more time. You should have six or seven thousand pounds when my negotiations are completed.'

'I understand that, but the bank are insisting that at least five thousand pounds is paid into my husband's account. Apparently they have heard some rumours concerning my father's estate.'

'I fear that may be my fault, Mrs Sawle. I have been trying to recover some of the money Mr Martin stole from your father. I do actually have five hundred pounds from that source, but so far I have not been able to convince the other gentlemen that they should repay the money.'

'Five hundred pounds will be very useful, sir, but I must have the rest quickly.'

'If you insist, I can find a buyer for your property tomorrow, but you will lose at least a thousand pounds by it. You realise that this would leave you with nothing if your husband's mine were to fail?'

'I understand the consequences, sir. However, I am prepared to take the risk. Wheal Margaret means a great deal to my husband, and I trust his judgement.'

'So you are ready to risk everything for his sake? He is indeed a fortunate man. Very well, Mrs Sawle, I can only advise you. If you wish to sell, despite my warnings, I shall do my very best, and I shall continue with my search for the elusive Mr Martin.'

'Thank you. I know I can rely on you.' She smiled, and got to her feet. 'No, don't bother to see me out. I am returning to Cornwall tomorrow. I know you will see that everything is done as quickly as possible. Sir Joshua will advise my husband's bank that the money will be with them within the month.'

'As you wish.'

The solicitor walked with her to the door. Once she had gone, he shook his head. She was as headstrong as her father had been. If Thomas Whitby had listened to his advice, she would still be a wealthy young woman. He had hoped to obtain the best price for her property, but now he would have to take what he could get.

'I hope that young scoundrel appreciates what you've done for him, m'dear,' Sir Joshua said, glancing at Rosanna as he handed her into the carriage. 'If you'll take my advice, you'll put that five hundred pounds Denton gave you in a safe place.'

'I had thought of using it for the house,' she said, 'but perhaps you are right. If things do not go well at the mine, Justin may need it.'

'That was not what I meant, and you know it—but I suppose you will do as you please. You're a stubborn wench, Rosanna. I dare say you would have come to town on your own, if I had let you.'

'If necessary,' she agreed with a naughty glance. 'But it was very much more comfortable with you as my escort—and Sally, of course.' She smiled at the girl sitting opposite. 'It was very wicked of you, Sir Joshua, to tell Lady Carmichael that I was your niece.'

'We couldn't have everyone thinking you were my light o' love, m'dear! With your husband away, I was concerned for your reputation. Not that it would bother you in the least, you minx. If I were Justin, I should very likely put you over my knee! As to the ball—well, that's another matter.' He smiled at her fondly. 'I didn't see why you shouldn't have a little fun while we were in town. Sophia is an old friend and you can always rely on her to give a decent affair. If Justin had any sense, he'd be here with you himself. Then you could dance with him instead of half of London.'

'I only danced with five or six gentlemen,' Rosanna objected. 'And mostly it was with Harry, so that doesn't count.'

'The man you were once engaged to?' Sir Joshua's brows rose. 'If I were Justin, Harry Bellingham would be the last man I wanted near you.'

'Harry's name has been linked with several heiresses, so I've heard.' Rosanna retorted. 'I don't think Justin has any need to worry about him. Besides, he will probably never know that I was in London.'

The air was full of smoke as the cannon fired repeatedly. Napoleon had begun his attack on Blücher on 16th June. By 8 pm, he had partially routed the Prussians, who had lost some sixteen thousand men during the day. Had it not been for a muddled and countermanded order diverting a reserve corps, it might have been a resounding victory for the French. On the morning of 17th June, Napoleon's force started to pursue the Prussians with thirty-three thousand men, and he ordered the Guard to move to Quatre-Bras. By the time Napoleon himself joined Ney there, however, Wellington had returned to Waterloo. All this time and during the night, it rained continuously.

Forced to retreat with the English army, Justin had heard the complaints of the men. Struggling through the mud and rain, they had grumbled among themselves, hating the idea of a retreat. It had been a long, cold night. Now it was the afternoon of 18th June, and Wellington's troops were under fire on the field of Waterloo. Two miles beyond the village of Waterloo, and a mile from the hamlet of Mont-St-Jean, a ridge stretched across the Charleroi road. It was on this ridge that the Duke had posted his army, extending to the left and to the right, uniting behind Mont-St-Jean and the farm of the same name. To the right, in the valley, lay the Hougoumont château and woods. It was here that the action had begun between eleven and twelve that morning.

The fierce fighting continued throughout the afternoon, but the English troops were holding out, though suffering appalling casualties. The French, in turn, came under fierce fire from the English while advancing through the woods. Smoke and flames billowed up from buildings ignited by the French shells, but the English soldiers maintained their ground, stubbornly refusing to give way. Napoleon threw his men forward against the English squares, but they were met with lethal volleys of musket-fire as the English held, and fell back, dying in their hundreds.

Justin was in the cavalry, which took the brunt of a furious charge from the cuirassiers, who fought until the English cavalry pushed them back. The French infantry, having routed the Belgians, were turned on with renewed venom by the English cavalry and broke, leaving their eagles lying on the ground in the stampede to escape.

'We've routed them, lads!' Justin cried triumphantly. He turned to wave his sword at Paul, who was a few yards to his right. The smile on his friend's face was the last thing he saw before the musket exploded in front of him and he was thrown from his horse to the ground. The last thought he had was of Rosanna and Harry Bellingham dancing...

'Have you heard the news, Rosanna?' Jonathan smiled at his grand-daughter as she bent to kiss his cheek. 'Wellington's done it, girl! He's beaten the monster.' He began to cough, but shook his head when she offered a glass of water.

Trying to hide her anxiety, she turned to the man she knew must have brought the news. 'Is it certain that Napoleon is beaten, Sir Joshua?'

'His army was routed at... What was the name of the confounded place?' He scratched his head. 'Ah yes, Waterloo, that's it! A terrible battle by all accounts, on

18th June. Wellington's dispatches speak of awful losses on both sides.'

'June the 18th—why, that's nearly two weeks ago,' Rosanna cried.

'I heard rumours in Bodmin some days ago,' Sir Joshua said, nodding, 'but I did not want to say anything until I was sure of me facts. Rumours can sometimes be misleading.'

'Yes, I know.' She forced a smile to her stiff lips. 'We are so much out of the way here that I am sure we should never hear anything if it were not for you.'

'You know I'm always eager to pass on any news I can,' he said. Noticing her anxious look, he cleared his throat nervously. 'I shouldn't start worrying yet, m'dear. Even though Boney's routed, it will be some time before Justin can leave the army. The monster will have to be dealt with more severely, this time. It could be weeks or months before the army is disbanded.'

'Yes, I realise that.' She avoided his sympathetic gaze, twisting her hands in the folds of her skirt. 'You would tell me if you heard... I mean, if Justin's name was on the list of casualties?'

'Of course, m'dear.' Sir Joshua's fist hit the table in front of him. 'The young scoundrel had no business going off like...' He stopped suddenly as a strange, strangled cry broke from Jonathan Whitby's lips. 'My God! You'd best fetch Benjamin, girl. I think we should get him to his bed.' As Rosanna hesitated, he barked at her. 'Do as I tell you! You're not needed here. And tell my man to go for the doctor!'

Sensing that Sir Joshua had taken charge of the situation, Rosanna fled. The dreadful sound of choking followed her.

The only light was from one small candle, its flickering flame throwing shadows into the corners of the bedroom. Jonathan was sleeping now. He had come through the earlier crisis, but was very weak. The doctor thought it could only be a matter of days, perhaps hours. Sitting by the bed, Rosanna was fighting her tears. She had known her grandfather for only a few short months, but in that time she had come to love him dearly. He was old, and it was not a terrible tragedy that his life should end this way, peacefully, without pain, yet she knew that she would miss him terribly. She felt a tear trickle down her cheek, and brushed it away.

'You should be in bed, child.'

The voice was barely a whisper. She leaned closer so that she could hear him. 'I wanted to be with you, dearest. How are you feeling?'

'I'm comfortable enough for a dying man.'

'Grandfather, please...'

'Give me your hand, girl, and stop crying over what must be. We're neither of us fools, and I haven't much time.'

She took his hand, holding it gently. His fingers closed over hers. 'You should rest, dearest.'

'Time enough for that when I'm in my grave. I want you to know that everything I have will be yours. Yours, not your husband's. I've seen to that. I may not have much to leave, but if you're sensible, you won't starve.'

Rosanna blinked hard. 'I wanted so much to find the jewels for you. I promise I'll find a way to restore Rathmoor one day.'

'Don't make rash promises to me or to yourself, girl. I know you love the place, but I want you to live your life for yourself, not for this old ruin. If Justin doesn't come back, you must sell it. Use the money to find happiness... Don't stay here to wither away into an old woman. And if he does come home, tell him you love him. Life's too short to waste it, girl.'

'Oh, Grandfather,' she murmured, bending over to kiss his wasted cheek, 'why didn't I know you years ago? I do love you so very much.'

His fingers tightened round hers. 'Don't cry for the moon, Rosanna. Always remember to take what you can from life. You gave me many precious hours, and I'm grateful for them. I wish I could have lived to see your first child born, but it was not to be.'

'If ever I have a son, I shall call him Jonathan.'

'Your husband may have something to say to that.' He smiled and sighed, closing his eyes. 'I'm tired, child. Leave me now, and let me rest. I shan't sleep, knowing I'm keeping you from your bed.'

'You're a stubborn man,' she said, kissing him again before she released his hand. 'I'll go now. God bless you, my dearest. I'll see you in the morning.'

Tears were running silently down her cheeks as she left, knowing that this was probably the last time she would see him alive.

Justin stirred, putting his hand to the source of the pain. There was a thick bandage round his head. He could feel a sticky patch where the blood had soaked through, and he felt as if he had been kicked by a horse—but he was alive. He thanked God for it, letting his eyes wander round the room. It was a large room, possibly in a château, and he was not alone. There were rows of wounded men on either side, and in the middle. He was aware now of the groans, the stifling heat and the stench of sickness. It made him want to retch. He tried to sit up, but fell back as dizziness swept over him.

'Don't try to rise,' a voice said. She came towards him from out of the sunlight streaming through a long window. 'You have been badly wounded, sir. You must lie still.'

She was young, her white habit telling him that she was a novice who had not yet taken her final vows. Her face was not pretty, but she had a gentle smile and her voice was soothing. He lay back, as her cool hand stroked his brow.

'How long have I been here?'

'A few days. Since the battle. You were hit by musket-fire, but you were lucky. You have only the one wound to your head. It will heal, now that the fever has broken.'

'Fever?' Justin passed a hand across his brow. 'I don't remember... How did I get here?'

'A friend brought you. You were lucky that he saw you fall. Had you lain unattended all night, you might have bled to death.'

'Paul? Was it Paul?'

'I do not know. I was not here when you were brought in.' She looked at him thoughtfully. 'You have spoken sometimes in your fever, but Paul was not the name you cried. It was Rosanna, I think, and someone called Harry.'

'Harry Bellingham.' Justin's eyes closed. 'I see I have told you all my secrets, sister.'

'I remember nothing,' she said, 'and I am not yet a bride of Christ. You may call me Maria. Is there anything I can bring you?'

'Could I have some water, please? Oh, sister—Maria—can you tell me if Wellington won?'

'I was wondering when you would ask. It is usually the first question.' She smiled at him a little sadly. 'For me, there are no winners or losers in a war, only the sick and injured. But yes, your Duke won his battle.'

'Thank you,' he said, lying back with his eyes closed as she went away.

So he had talked of Rosanna and Harry Bellingham in his fever. Well, it was not surprising; he had thought of little else since Anne Cornwallis had taunted him with it at the Duchess of Richmond's ball. It had not taken his wife long to find a new lover after he left, he thought bitterly. Yet it was to the man she had jilted that she had returned. But why? Why to Harry? He had never asked why she had jilted Bellingham; it had not seemed to matter. Now he thought he understood. She had done it out of pique or pride, realising her mistake too late. She was in love with Harry. That was why she had refused to honour her marriage vows until he had forced her to capitulate.

A little cry of pain left his lips as he remembered that fateful night. At first, he had thought her surrender meant that she loved him, but his triumph had turned to ashes as she sobbed afterwards. A few tears might have been taken as natural, but her body had been shaken by the depth of her grief. He had left her sleeping, riding off in the early hours of the morning to shout his frustration at the empty moors. It had dawned on him then that he had no choice but to go away for a while. If he had stayed... Another groan broke from him as a thought came unbidden into his mind, and he saw his wife lying in Harry Bellingham's arms.

'Are you in pain?'

Justin became aware of the young novice bending over him. He thrust the bitter thoughts to the back of his mind, accepting the cup of water with a grateful smile.

'No, I am not in pain,' he said. 'No more than before...'

'It's a long time since you've been over,' Becky said, smiling as she drew her visitor into the little parlour. 'I was sorry to hear about Mr Whitby.'

'Thank you.' Rosanna stroked Mary's head as the little girl peeped from behind her mother's skirts. 'He did not suffer a great deal at the end, but I miss him terribly.' She blinked hard. 'I wanted to come sooner. You received the clothes I sent for the baby? May I see him?'

'Of course you can. He's sleeping now, but he'll wake for his feed soon enough. Come and look at him.'

The child was in a cot by the kitchen fire, sound asleep, his fair lashes curled on his cheek. The sight of him gave Rosanna a strange ache inside. She looked at him longingly, wanting to hold him in her arms. If only he was her baby—hers and Justin's. Turning back to Becky, she was unaware of the naked longing in her eyes.

'He's beautiful, Becky. You're so lucky!'

Becky felt a surge of sympathy. Seth had told her how the Captain's wife had saved the mine from closure. It wasn't right that she should be suffering as she obviously was.

'Maybe the Captain will come home soon,' she said. 'You should write and tell him he's wanted here.'

'Is there some trouble at the mine?'

'No, it's you I'm thinking of, lass. I don't like to see you wasting away for lack of your man.'

Rosanna turned aside, hiding her emotion. She had had only one brief letter from Justin, telling her that he was alive. He had decided to stay in London for a while. He had not mentioned when or if he was coming home.

'I can't write to him, Becky,' Rosanna said, feeling a crushing sensation in her chest. 'He will come home if he wants to.'

'So you'll let your pride stand in the way, will you?' Becky asked belligerently, her arms akimbo. 'You need not look at me like that... Do you think I don't know things haven't been right for you from the start? I don't know what's wrong, and I'm not asking, but I do know that you love the Captain and that you're unhappy. Tell me to mind my own business if you want to, but don't hide from the truth. You need a man of your own, same as the rest of us.'

Tears stung Rosanna's eyes. 'He doesn't want me, Becky.'

'That's something I'll not be believing,' Becky said with a shake of her head. 'I've seen the way he looks at you when you're not aware of it, and I'd stake my life that he's mad for you. Take my advice, and get him back here before it's too late.'

'Supposing he doesn't want to come?'

'Then find a way to make him realise what he's missing. You're a clever enough woman to know how that's to be done, I'll be bound. 'Sides, half a loaf's better than none.'

'Grandfather said something similar to me before he died,' Rosanna said. 'Perhaps it would be better to have an unsatisfactory marriage than nothing at all.'

'All marriages have their good and bad times, lass. Even me and Seth take on against each other now and then, yet I wouldn't change him for the world.'

'Then you think I should write to Justin?'

'If you want him.'

'I do... Oh, I do!' Rosanna said. 'But I don't think I'll write to him. I'll go to London and speak to him myself.'

'Go to London on your own?' Becky stared at her. 'You're never thinking of it?'

'Why don't you come with me?' Rosanna said. 'You've often said you would like to see something of the world.'

'Me?' Becky echoed. 'Go all the way to London? I couldn't! What about Seth and the children?'

'You could take the children with you,' Rosanna said, a sparkle in her eyes now. 'We could employ a nurse for them so that you could accompany me when I walk in the park. I'm sure Seth wouldn't mind, for a little while. He could get one of the village women in to clean and cook. You ask him, Becky, and see what he says.'

'Me go to London as a proper lady's maid?' Becky said wonderingly.

'No, as my companion,' Rosanna said. 'We're friends, Becky. You would be my companion.'

'That wouldn't be right; but I'd like to be your maid for a time.'

'Then you'll speak to Seth about it?'

'I'll think about it,' Becky said. 'What about Sally, though? Didn't she go with you the last time?'

'I don't think she would consider leaving Rob at the moment; he's been acting a little strangely recently. I shall ask her, of course. If I go, I shall take a house for three months, and it will have to be staffed. I would take Emily and Benjamin, but they don't hold with foreign parts.'

'Most folk around here would agree with them,' Becky said. 'I've always wanted to see a bit of the world. I'll speak to Seth then, and see what he says.'

Justin glanced up as the door opened and Paul came into the suite of rooms they were sharing. He poured himself another glass of brandy, indicating the crystal decanter on the tray.

'May I pour you one?'

'Not for the moment.' Paul frowned at him. 'Have you had another of your headaches?'

'No, they stopped some weeks ago.'

'Then why the hell are you wasting your time drinking alone? It's time you stopped feeling sorry for yourself. You're lucky to be alive, man!'

'And I owe my life to you—and the nuns.'

Paul sat down, crossing his long legs in front of him. He had not been sure whether to tell Justin what he had discovered, but now he thought that a sharp shock might be exactly what his friend needed. 'I suppose you know that Rosanna is in town?' he asked casually, perfectly aware that Justin had no idea.

'Rosanna?' Justin's head came up at that. 'Are you certain?'

'I saw her going into a house in Great Queen Street, and very fetching she looked, too...' Paul hesitated before delivering the *coup de grâce*. 'She was carrying a baby in her arms.'

Justin's face went white. He had no need to count the months; he knew almost to the hour how long it was since he had seen her. A year and two days. Plenty of time... Yet how could he be sure that the child was his and not Harry Bellingham's? Pushing back his chair with a scrape, he got to his feet.

'You will please furnish me with the number of the house in Great Queen Street, Paul.'

'I'm not sure that I should give it to you.'

'You will do so, however, unless you wish me to break your damned neck!'

'Such gratitude,' Paul said mockingly. 'You will find her at number ten, Justin. She has been there for a week; I made a few enquiries.'

Justin laughed harshly. 'I suppose the whole of London knows, except me. I shall pay my wife a little visit, since she did not bother to inform me.'

CHAPTER SEVEN

JUSTIN was seething with anger as he walked through Lincoln's Inn Fields and turned into the adjacent Great Queen Street. The houses here were built of fine red brick, with heavy wooden eaves and white cornices, and fronted in the Italian style. Perhaps a less fashionable area than it had been a hundred years before, it was still pleasant enough, and it must have cost Rosanna a pretty penny to take the house for the season. She might have at least had the decency to inform him of her intention to spend the summer in town!

He rang the front-door bell, frowning as an elderly footman opened the door. Rosanna was obviously living in some style. It was late in the day for an informal call, and he was aware of the speculation in the servant's eyes.

'Is Mrs Sawle at home?' he asked, 'I should like to speak with her immediately.'

'Indeed, sir?' The footman seemed to look down his long nose, as if wondering whether Justin was a fit person to invite into the house. 'I am not sure if Madam is at home, sir. Perhaps you would care to wait while I enquire? What name shall I give?'

'You may tell my wife that her husband is here, and I shall wait in the parlour.' Annoyance glinted in his eyes. 'Well, how much longer do you intend to keep me standing on the step?'

Something in his manner seemed to convince the footman that it would be dangerous to deny him. 'Yes, sir,' he said stiffly, stepping back reluctantly so that Justin could enter. 'If you would care to wait in the parlour to your right, I shall enquire if Madam is in.'

'Thank you. You may tell Madam that I intend to wait until she *is* in—however long that may be.'

The footman inclined his head, beating a dignified retreat into the upper reaches of the house, leaving Justin to pace the small but elegant parlour in frustration. He wondered where Rosanna had obtained the money to establish herself in such style. Was she being kept by a lover? The thought made him burn with anguish, and he clenched his fists at his sides. By heaven, if... At a light step in the hall, he spun round, his heart catching at the sight of her. She was wearing a light muslin gown that clung provocatively to her figure, and he thought that she was lovelier than ever. The year they had spent apart had not changed her, except perhaps to give her the added lustre of maturity. She had become a woman, and a beautiful woman. A woman he found very desirable.

'Justin!' she cried, coming towards him with hands outstretched. 'How good of you to call.'

He took her hands, kissing the cheek she offered and feeling bewildered. 'Rosanna? You did not tell me you were coming to town.'

'It was an impulse. I meant to tell you, once I was properly established,' she said lightly, her eyes going over his face and noticing the deep scar at his temple. 'Sir Joshua is with me. He has been very helpful since Grandfather died. I suppose you did get my letter?'

'Yes, I was sorry to hear of his death, Rosanna. It was too late for me to be of help when I read of it.' He stared at her, wondering why he felt as if he should apologise. He had come here in anger, but now he was suddenly at a loss. 'It was fortunate that you had a friend to help you.'

'Yes.' She gazed up at him. 'You did not tell me in your letter that you had been wounded.'

He touched the scar awkwardly. His wound had kept him tied to his mattress for several weeks, and afterwards he had suffered severe headaches. 'I was lucky. Paul saw me fall, and got two of his men to take me to the nuns. Had it not been for them, I might have died.

This is past history, however...I think there is something of more importance that you should tell me.'

'Do you mean about the mine? There have been problems, but...'

'I meant the child.' Justin felt his anger return. 'Is it mine, Rosanna? Or Harry Bellingham's?'

A shock ran through her as she saw the fury in his eyes. What on earth was he talking about? It was a moment or two before she realised that someone must have seen her with Becky's child in her arms. He had heard gossip concerning her, and now he was practically accusing her of betraying him. Anger boiled inside her. How dared he accuse her of adultery—he, who had gone to his mistress in the first weeks of their marriage!

'I can see that you have already decided I am guilty,' she said, raising her chilling gaze to his. 'Who told you that I had a child?'

'Someone saw you with a babe in your arms.' Justin felt a knot of sickness in his stomach. He had hoped that she would deny it at once. 'I know you've been seeing Harry Bellingham, Rosanna.'

'Do you, indeed? I do not know who your spy is, Justin, but he or she is wrong!'

'You were dancing with him all evening.'

Rosanna glared at him angrily. 'I only wish I had married Harry! At least then I would have had a proper marriage instead of this mockery. Harry would not have spent the past five months in town, while his wife...' She gasped as Justin moved threateningly towards her. 'Yes, use your strength to subdue me—that's all you know, isn't it?'

The accusation in her eyes flayed him like a lash. He recalled the night he had held her in his arms; his joy when he had possessed her, and then the bitterness of her tears. Now, he felt, she hated him. His fingers relaxed their grip on her wrist, and he let her go.

'I should not have come here. You have chosen your path—and I have chosen mine.' He brushed past her and went out of the door.

Rosanna stared after him, her emotions bruised and torn. She knew she ought not to have let him go, still believing that she had had a child by Harry, but she was hurt and angry. She would tell him the truth soon, but it would not harm him to suffer for a while. His careless behaviour had brought her so much pain that she wondered if it was worth while going on with this empty life. He was so cruel. How could she love a man who could hurt her like this? And yet she did. It was as if she was bound to him by an invisible chain that chafed at her flesh, rubbed raw by the bitterness that lay between them.

Tears stung her eyes, but she blinked them away. No matter what he said to her, she would always love him. Suddenly she understood her own heart better than ever before. It had been hard for her to make the necessary commitment to love, but now that she had, it would last for the rest of her life. Although Justin had hardened his heart against her, she would win him back.

Lady Carmichael's ball was the biggest crush of the season so far. Rosanna paused on the threshold of the ballroom, her hand resting lightly on Sir Joshua's arm. It was a magnificent scene beneath the glittering chandeliers; jewels flashed from the throats and fingers of the ladies, their gowns a sea of bright, whirling colour reflected a thousand times in the sparkling mirrors. The floor was highly polished so that the dancers' feet glided effortlessly as they performed their elegant twists and turns. Rosanna's toe tapped in time to the music and her spirits lifted a little. She knew that Justin had been invited this evening: surely he would come!

She had attended several musical evenings and card parties, in vain looking for his tall figure among the guests. It was almost as if he were deliberately avoiding any house where he might meet her. But with the lure of the card-tables and the promise of high stakes at the first large event of the season, he must be at least tempted to put in an appearance.

It was at once clear that she would not lack for partners, whatever her husband might decide to do. Her lack of a sharp-eyed guardian had not gone unnoticed, and she was continually sought out by hopeful gentlemen, some of whom surrounded her the moment Sir Joshua left her side. The fact that none of them had so far received any indication that she might be thinking of taking a lover did not seem to deter them, and her dance-card was soon filled. Apart from one space that she had crossed out just in case Justin arrived late in the evening, as he had once before.

'Mrs Sawle?' The voice at her elbow stirred a vague chord in her memory. 'Am I too late to reserve a dance with you?'

Turning, Rosanna looked up into the hard face of the tall, heavily-built man who towered over her. She had a feeling that she had seen him before, but could not immediately recall where or when.

'Let me introduce myself,' he said, smiling wolfishly. 'I am Justin's cousin Richard.'

'Lord Mountjoy's son?' she murmured, remembering in that moment where she had first seen him. Once on the wharf at Dover, and again when his carriage had run off the road on the day she had first visited the mine house. So he was Justin's cousin! No wonder she had seen a similarity in their features. 'Justin has spoken of you, and I have had the pleasure of meeting your father. Unhappily, I must tell you that my dance-card is full.'

'A pity.' His eyes raked her with a familiarity that she found disturbing. 'Perhaps we shall meet again another night, madam.'

Rosanna nodded, turning to greet her first partner with a feeling of relief. She was glad that she had been unable to grant Richard a dance. She had disliked him at their first meeting when he was so rude, and even now, when he was being polite, her instinct was to distrust him. Justin had spoken of him without warmth, and she knew that they had never been friends. It was a little strange that he should bother to seek her out in the circumstances.

Dancing with partner after partner, she soon forgot the small incident. It was towards supper-time that she first noticed Justin, who was standing at the far end of the room and appeared to be watching her. Her heart skipped a beat, and she laughed nervously up at her partner.

'So, Harry,' she said mischievously. 'Miss Bransen is to be the lucky girl. When is your engagement to be announced?'

'Perhaps next month,' Harry replied gloomily. 'Nothing has been settled yet. She's an excellent girl, and my mother likes her—but she isn't you, Rosanna. I can't seem to make up my mind to it.' He sighed heavily. 'I should have married you when I had the chance, and said hang to the money!'

'Poor Harry,' Rosanna teased. 'My five thousand wouldn't have paid your tailor's bills, let alone your horses and your gambling debts. No, you will be far better off with Miss Bransen. She's very pretty—and her father is worth a fortune. A good, solid fortune in land.'

'Perhaps you're right—but I'm still in love with you...' Harry faltered as he felt a heavy tap on his shoulder. Turning to find himself staring into the furious eyes of Rosanna's husband, he felt hot beneath the high neck of his lace cravat.

'Excuse me for interrupting,' Justin said through frozen lips, 'but I wish to dance with my wife. She is still my wife, you know. Or had you forgotten?'

Harry felt the lance of his eyes, and dropped his gaze. 'No, of course not. Excuse me.' He stepped aside to allow the exchange.

Rosanna shivered as Justin put his hand on her waist. 'There was no need to speak to Harry so rudely.'

'Indeed? I think perhaps there is a need for much more.'

Her cheeks felt hot as she looked into his furious eyes. 'You are being very foolish, Justin.'

'I do not care for being made a cuckold, madam.'

'And I do not care for your tone, sir. If I had betrayed you, it would be your own fault...'

'If... Are you trying to tell me that the child is mine?'

'Oh, you impossible man!' Rosanna cried angrily. 'The child is neither yours nor Harry's...'

The music had stopped, and she walked from the floor, leaving Justin staring after her, but in a moment he had recovered enough to follow. Catching up, he took hold of her wrist, turning her to face him.

'Are you telling me that you have another lover?'

'People are staring, Justin. Keep your voice down.'

'To hell with them!' Justin muttered. 'I demand an answer now, Rosanna. Just who is the father of your child?'

'I have no child, Justin. If you had made a few enquiries instead of leaping to conclusions, you would have discovered that the only children in my house belong to Becky Miller.'

'*Becky's* children... Becky is with you?' Justin frowned. 'Why did you not tell me that the other evening?'

'Because you made me angry.' Her eyes flashed. 'You so clearly thought that I had betrayed you. I decided to punish you a little.'

'You expect me to believe that Harry Bellingham has not been your lover—when I heard him telling you he was still in love with you only a moment ago?'

'You may believe whatever you wish.' Rosanna glared at him. 'Excuse me, I have to go upstairs to tidy myself.'

She walked away, her back straight and stiff.

Justin watched her go, his thoughts confused. If what she had just said was true, he had made a complete fool of himself, yet how could he believe her? He turned away towards the card-room, his face angry. What did any of it matter, anyway? She had made her feelings towards him plain enough.

Rosanna was still smarting from the quarrel when she came back downstairs after tidying her gown and hair.

Justin was as arrogant as ever, and she had been a fool to imagine that they could ever be friends. Lost in her own thoughts, she did not see the man at the foot of the stairs until he spoke to her.

'You are not dancing, Mrs Sawle. Perhaps I could take you in to supper?'

She looked at Richard Mountjoy with a feeling of distaste. There was a strong smell of brandy on his breath. 'No, I think not, sir. I am meeting someone.'

'Not your husband, I trust? That would be too dull. Why don't you dance with me instead?'

'I'm sorry, I cannot.' Rosanna felt a tingle of annoyance as he continued to block the narrow hall. 'Please let me pass.'

He smiled mockingly, placing one booted foot against the wall. 'And if I do not choose to let you go?'

'Then I should think you very rude. And I might be forced to call for assistance.'

'Do you imagine Harry Bellingham would come to your rescue?' Richard leered at her. 'My cousin is a fool to neglect you, Rosanna. Everyone is talking of it. Anyone can see that a woman like you needs the attention of a red-blooded man. Perhaps I should call on you myself. Would you like that, sweet cousin?'

'You, sir, are drunk,' Rosanna retorted angrily. 'I shall not receive you if you call. Now please stand aside!'

'You would be wise to do as she asks, Richard.'

Justin's cool voice behind made Rosanna swing round. 'Thank goodness you've come, Justin!'

For a moment the two men stared at one another, then Richard's eyes dropped. 'I appear to have made a mistake. Justin, excuse me. Madam, I beg your pardon.'

As Richard walked past them, Justin's cold eyes flicked to his wife. 'I should have thought you would know better than to encourage the attentions of a man who is clearly drunk!'

'I was not encouraging him,' she replied. 'I do not like your cousin, Justin. He was rude to me the very first time we met, and tonight his behaviour was insulting—as yours is.'

He looked at her face, seeing the pride and anger there. 'Well, perhaps I was a trifle hasty...'

'You were more than that. Now, if you will let me pass, I think we have no more to say to one another.'

'I came in search of you to—to apologise. If I was wrong to accuse you of taking a lover, I'm sorry.'

'*If* you were wrong?' Her eyes flashed with anger.

'That was clumsy.' He gave her a rueful grin. 'I should have said that I was sorry for suspecting you in the first place.'

'So I should imagine!' She felt her heart flutter. Did he know that he could melt her with just one smile? It would serve him right if she sent him away, but she could not. 'I may forgive you, but only if you take me in to supper. I am starving!'

The tension was broken, and he laughed, offering her his arm. 'Your wish is my command, as always.'

Her smile became a little fixed. 'If only you meant that! I have missed you, Justin.'

'Have you, my dear?' His voice was light, unconcerned. 'If I had known that, I might have come home sooner.'

'Would you?' She stopped and looked up into his face, her pulses racing. 'You could not have thought I wanted you to go away when you did?'

'Could I not?' He inclined his head to a gentleman they passed in the hall. 'It was an awkward situation. I had behaved badly, and I believed you might be happier if I never returned to Rathmoor.'

'I have not been happy, Justin.'

'Have you not, my dear?' He gazed down into her lovely face. If only he could believe she meant what she said—but he had seen the way she laughed up at Harry Bellingham. 'I thought I had caused you enough grief.'

'Come home,' she said, her voice throbbing with sudden passion. 'And, this time, let it be a true marriage. I want a husband and children. I am tired of this lonely, sterile life.'

His look was penetrating. 'Has it truly been so for you? I had thought perhaps you had found consolation elsewhere.'

'You mean with Harry, I suppose?' She sighed. Why could he not believe her? 'Harry will soon be announcing his marriage to an heiress. Anything that was between us is over. I swear I have not been unfaithful to you.'

'Have you not?' he asked lightly. 'Then perhaps it is my duty to come home. We shall talk again another day, more privately. For the moment, perhaps you will allow me to serve you some supper? What may I bring you? Some ham, perhaps, cut thin as you like it? Or the chicken and green peas? A little champagne...'

'I don't understand you, man,' Paul complained as Justin stared moodily out of the window. 'Rosanna has asked you to go back. What more do you want? Most men in your situation would be overjoyed at being given a second chance.'

Justin remained at the window, watching a tiny bird diving beneath the eaves. 'It's a husband she wants, and children—not me. Harry Bellingham is the man she truly loves, but she can't have him. I'm merely a substitute.'

'You can't be sure of that.'

'I feel it, Paul. I saw the way she smiled at him. She was happy with him. I've given her nothing but heartache.'

'Then it's time you thought about what she wants, Justin. Good God, man, she's your wife! If children will make her happy, do your duty by her. You can come back to town once she's in an interesting condition.'

'I don't want to waste my life drinking and gambling as I have been doing these past months.' Justin was smiling ruefully as he turned round. 'You may think me all kinds of a fool, Paul, but I'm in love with her. I think

I fell in love with her the first time I saw her. I didn't know it, then. I didn't understand until it was too late.'

Paul twirled his moustache to hide his embarrassment. 'Then I don't see your problem, old fellow.'

'I want her to love me,' Justin said with a strange twist of his lips. 'I have this thing inside me, this devil that drives me. I can never settle for second best. I have decided to go back to Rathmoor, but it won't be easy. I don't want to hurt her, but this monster inside me will never rest. I shall never be satisfied until I can be sure that she is all mine: mind, body and soul.'

Paul looked at him uncomfortably. 'Can anyone ever have all that? Couldn't you just settle for a decent, amiable relationship? It seems to me that you create trouble for yourself by wanting too much, Justin.'

Justin laughed harshly. 'Living with Rosanna, having her in my bed and in my arms will probably be like living in hell. I'll hurt her a thousand times without meaning to, but not as often or as deeply as she'll hurt me. Oh yes, it will be hell. But a living hell is better than a slow death—and I have been slowly dying inside since I left her...'

Rosanna looked across the carriage at Becky, and smiled. They were on their way back to Rathmoor at last. Sir Joshua had gone home a few days previously, leaving Justin to close the house and attend to the details of their return to Cornwall.

'You'll be in good hands now, m'dear,' he had said gruffly. 'I've had a word with the rascal, and he intends to do right by you.'

'Yes, I know.' She had kissed his cheek. 'Thank you, my best of friends. I couldn't have done it without you.'

'You'd have managed somehow, I dare say,' he growled, but his look was full of warm affection.

After their talk, Justin had moved into the house, and into the master bedroom, which had a dressing-room connecting with hers. She had been a little shy when he came to her that first night, feeling that they were almost meeting as strangers after so long apart, but when he took her in his arms, the old longing came surging back and she responded to his kisses without restraint. Her pride held back the words of love that rose to her lips, but she nestled contentedly against his shoulder afterwards. She had woken while it was still dark to feel the bed cold and empty beside her, and a little of the warm glow had gone. He had not stayed, preferring to seek his own bed. She had hoped that they might find a kind of companionship in the aftermath of passion, bridging the gap that still lay between them in spite of the meeting of their bodies in the act of love. She had a part of what she wanted, and she must try to be content. She did not want to drive him away again.

Now they were on their way home, Justin riding beside the carriage, leaving more room inside for the women and children. Mary had crawled on to Rosanna's lap, nestling against the softness of her velvet gown. A gentle smile curved her lips as she looked down and stroked the little girl's shining curls. God willing, it would not be too long before she had a child of her own. Perhaps, then, this ache in her heart would go away. She would have her child to love, and it might ease this longing for something she might never have.

As if sensing her thoughts, Becky smiled and nodded. 'Give it time, lass,' she said. 'You've had your way. Don't expect too much too soon. A man has his pride—and your man more than most. It will come right, you'll see. You'll see . . .'

'Are you sure you won't stay the night, Becky?' Rosanna asked, as the carriage lurched to a halt in the courtyard. 'We've been travelling for six days, and for five hours today.'

'I'd rather get home, if you don't mind,' Becky said. 'Seth will be glad to see me back, I dare say.'

'But you'll come in for some refreshment while fresh horses are harnessed?'

'That would be . . . Well, I never!' Becky cried. 'Lord love us, it's a miracle! I never thought I'd see the day . . .'

Rosanna, following the direction of Becky's gaze, saw something that amazed and delighted her. Justin had dismounted and was talking animatedly to a man who had just walked unaided down the front steps—unaided except for a crutch he had fixed under his right armpit.

'I don't believe it!' she cried, jumping out of the coach and running across to the two men. As she reached them, Sally came hurrying out of the house. 'Sally! Rob! This is wonderful. When did it happen? How? Oh, I can't tell you how happy I am!'

Sally brushed a tear from her cheek as Rosanna embraced her. 'It had started before you went away. Rob felt the movement coming back in his toes first, and he's been secretly building up his strength to surprise you. He first felt it months ago, but he wanted to get on his feet before he told anyone.'

'So that's why he was acting so strangely,' Rosanna said, her throat tight with emotion. 'It's a miracle! I couldn't have asked for a nicer homecoming.'

Becky had come up with the children and their nurse, and Emily was standing in the doorway with Benjamin behind her. They were all beaming, their faces wreathed in smiles of pleasure. Blinking back her tears, Rosanna bent to pick up the smallest child, her eyes flicking to her husband for a moment. He was standing a little apart from the crowd, watching her with a strange expression. There was amusement in his eyes, but also something else she could not quite read. In the midst of all her friends, she felt her love flow out to him. Surely he must know that he was the rock on which her happiness today was built?

Yet, as she looked at him, his smile faded and he turned away, striding towards the stables.

Seth was checking the ledger in the mine office when the shadow passed across the window. Looking up, he saw Zeb Tolly come in and stand awkwardly in the

doorway, staring in that sullen way of his without
speaking.

'What is it, Zeb?' he asked. 'Is something wrong?'

'Ay, you could say that.'

'Well, are you going to stand there all day?'

'The men aren't happy, sir, and that's the truth.'

Seth nodded. He had been aware of a dissatisfaction
among the men for some time. The copper was not
coming out as fast as he had expected, and they had had
some trouble: nothing that he could put his finger on,
but several minor accidents. Things disappeared.
Wooden shoring gave way for no reason—and there were
too many absentees. He believed some of the men had
started to look for work further afield.

'So what do you want me to do about it, Zeb? I know
things have been difficult recently.'

'The men think the mine is cursed.'

'That's nonsense!' Seth cried. 'We've had a run of
bad luck, that's all. We should soon be through to the
best copper.'

'If there's any there.' Zeb scowled at him. 'When is
Captain Sawle coming home?'

Seth had been wondering the same thing for months.
The war was over long ago. If Justin cared about the
mine, he ought to be here, sorting out the problems.
Seth was doing his best, but there were some details that
only Justin could solve.

'I don't know, Zeb,' he replied honestly. 'I hope it will
be quite soon now.'

'I reckon it'ull have to be,' Zeb said sourly. 'Otherwise the men will leave.'

As Zeb went out, Seth closed his ledgers and stood
up. He yawned and stretched, feeling that he had had
enough for the day. The thought of his empty cottage
was not appealing. He had let Becky go on her trip to
town, knowing it was a wonderful chance for her, but
he missed her more than he would admit to himself. He
was not sure what he would do if she did not come back.

He could find himself another woman, but there would never be another quite like his Becky.

Seth stopped to fill his long clay pipe with tobacco, and drew a deep breath, tasting the sharp, hot smoke on his tongue. He did not often indulge himself, though it was said to be good for the health to smoke a pipe a day. It helped to clear his thoughts as he wended his way slowly homeward. If he did not hear from Justin soon, he would have to write him a letter.

Pausing at the top of the hill, he noticed smoke coming from his chimney. For a moment he was puzzled, then he saw the door open and a woman come to look out. She waved her hand as she saw him, calling his name.

'Becky!' he cried, suddenly beginning to run. 'Becky, lass, you've come home!'

She had seen him and was running to meet him, scrambling up the incline in her haste. He increased his pace, swooping on her in delight.

'Seth!' she cried. 'Did you miss me?'

'Ay,' he replied with a smile, 'you could say that, lass. Come away into the house and tell me all about it, then...'

Their loving seemed to Rosanna to have a new dimension that night. Was it her imagination, or did Justin give more of his inner self? His lovemaking had always been skilled, bringing her steadily to a passionate climax that made her cry out with pleasure, but now his kisses had a new tenderness that seemed to draw her very soul from her body. There was surely a new protectiveness in the way he held her to him when their passion was spent. As usual, he said very little, his hand moving over her smooth back with strong, firm caresses that made her almost purr with content.

'It's good to be home, isn't it, Justin?' she murmured, tasting the salt of his sweat on her lips.

'Yes, it's good to be back,' he said, a faint smile playing about the corners of his mouth in the darkness. 'You belong here, Rosanna. Rathmoor was waiting for

you. Your people were waiting for you. You have us all
in thrall, haven't you?'

'What do you mean?' she asked sleepily.

'Nothing. It is but foolish talk, my love. Go to sleep.'

She had slept then, and waking later, found him still
beside her. It was the first time that he had stayed with
her all through the night.

Justin breathed deeply as he emerged into the fresh air.
He was feeling pleased with his inspection below ground.
The work was going well, and the copper being ex-
tracted was of a reasonable quality. As Seth followed
him out, he jerked his head towards the house.

'We'll have some wine while we talk—away from this
noise.'

Seth grinned and pointed towards the house. He was
used to the constant noise of the pumps, hardly aware
now of the grinding or the smoke from the tall chimneys.
Justin had forgotten the reality of it all in the past year.

They passed a tributer on his way to work; it was
almost time for the change-over, and men were strag-
gling towards the pithead. Young boys of ten and eleven,
too, helping their fathers by barrowing the raw material
away to be washed and sorted. Children under the age
of ten were not employed below ground at Wheal
Margaret, though at other mines in the area they were
not always so particular. Children were often easier to
come by than ponies, and cheaper to feed.

'How are the pumps standing up to all that water?'
Justin asked as they reached the relative quiet of the
mine house. 'There seems to be a lot of it now.'

'Yes, it's been increasing recently,' Seth replied with
a frown. 'We had trouble with the pump in No. Three
last week, but it's working again now. The men like the
water; they say it's a sign there's a lode of good-quality
ore somewhere.'

'Let's hope they find it soon, then,' Justin said. 'I was
shocked when you showed me the balances, Seth. The
price of copper has been bad this past month or so. We're

holding our own, but only just. I don't want to go to the bank again unless I'm forced.'

'You'll need a new guarantee. The five thousand pounds Mrs Sawle deposited has kept us going, but we'll need more soon. Especially if you want to push further in No. Five.'

'Five thousand pounds Rosanna deposited?' Justin stared at him. 'What are you talking about? This is the first I've heard of it.'

'It's in the books,' Seth said gruffly. 'I thought she would have told you. It was while you were in the army. The bank refused to advance me a penny, even for wages. I had to go to Mrs Sawle.'

'But I negotiated a loan before I left. I assumed you were working on credit?'

'No. It is Mrs Sawle's money that's kept us afloat. If it hadn't been for that, we'd have ground to a halt long ago,' Seth said. 'I hope as I did right?'

'I don't see what else you could have done.' Justin frowned. 'Still, I wish you had told me, Seth.'

'I'm sorry. I expected Mrs Sawle would tell you herself.'

'Do you know where she got the money?'

'From a Mr Denton in London. She went up especially to arrange it all. It was just before the war started, as I recall.'

'That explains something that has bothered me.'

'I apologise if I did wrong.'

'No, you did what you had to do, but this makes it all the more important that we should make the mine pay. That money was all Rosanna had, and I have to be able to reimburse her one day.'

'We should make a break-through soon, Justin, but we could do with some more tackle. We've had too many breakages. The men are getting restive. There was some talk of there being a curse on us, but I've managed to smooth things out for a while.'

'We can't afford any more of these accidents, Seth. When did you say they started again?'

'About a month ago. It's queer, that. There was none at all for almost a year, then they started happening again.'

'You think someone is trying to cause trouble, do you?' Justin sighed as he nodded. 'I agree with you—but who would want to make things bad for us? Not the other mine-owners. I've seen them from time to time in Bodmin or Truro; there are no hard feelings between us. Who could it be?'

'If I knew that, I'd make damn sure it didn't happen again! I think one of the men is involved, for there's been no one hurt since Rob was caught in that rockfall—and that could have been a genuine accident. It's the tackle that takes the brunt of it. It's as if you have an enemy who knows you're working on a thin string. It's *you* he wants to ruin, Justin.'

'You mean someone outside the mine is paying one of our men to bring the work to a standstill, knowing that each setback brings us a little closer to closure?' Justin ran his fingers through his hair. 'I wish to God I knew who it was! Keep an eye out, Seth, and talk to a few of the men you most trust. Somehow we've got to stop this before someone gets killed!'

Rosanna put down her embroidery as Justin came in, looking at him in surprise.

'You're home early. Emily hasn't started dinner yet.'

'I may not be in this evening. I thought I might ride over to dine with Paul.'

'I see. I'll tell Emily.' She felt a coldness inside, and it showed in her face.

'I'm going to see Paul, Rosanna, that's all. I have some business I want to discuss with him.'

'I did not say I doubted you.' But she had; she had!

'No, I saw it in your eyes. Believe me, I have no wish for another woman's company.' She had got to her feet, but he pressed her gently back into her chair. 'No, don't go. I want to ask you something.'

She had hoped that they were growing closer together, but she could sense the restlessness in him tonight. 'What was it you wanted to ask?'

'Why did you give Seth the money, Rosanna, and where did you get it?'

She looked up as relief surged. 'Mr Denton sold some property for me. He was able to get the five thousand pounds the bank demanded as a deposit.'

'But why did you do it? That was your money for the house.'

Rosanna looked away. 'I had another five hundred, most of which I spent in London. Rob and Benjamin are doing what they can. I do not believe we are in danger of the walls collapsing about our ears.'

'That is not the point, and you know it.'

'Oh, don't fuss so, Justin.' She glanced up at him. 'You were not here, so I did what I thought was right. I couldn't see all those men out of a job.'

'Was that your only reason?'

'What other reason could I have?' She glanced up at him blandly. 'Do you perhaps have an enemy who wishes you harm? Sir Joshua went to the bank on my behalf, and they told him they had received information about my fortune which would suggest that you had lied. That's why they stopped your credit.'

She had successfully changed the subject. Justin looked at her thoughtfully. 'You are the second person to suggest that today, Rosanna. The accidents have started at the mine again. It's as though someone knows we're only just hanging on—as if whoever it is is out to ruin me.'

'But who would want to do that?'

'I have no idea, I've racked my brain, but I can't think of anyone who hates me that much. Unless...'

'Have you thought of someone?'

He shook his head. 'There was someone who might have thought he had cause, but it was all so long ago.'

'Have you considered your cousin?' Rosanna gazed up at him. 'You have never been friends, I think?'

'Richard?' Justin wrinkled his brow. 'He hates me, but why should he bother? We're old enemies. Why do this now?'

'I don't know, but . . .' She hesitated, then said, 'You remember the—the day I came to the mine before we were married?'

He nodded, his eyes as bright as a hawk's. 'Yes, how could I forget? What has this to do with Richard?'

'When I left you that day, I almost rode into two men. They came out suddenly from behind a carriage that had overturned. One of them was Richard. I did not know who he was then, but I recognised him because we had met once before.' She explained the circumstances, and Justin frowned. 'You remember, when we first met, I told you that you reminded me of someone? There are faint resemblances in your features, though his are far coarser.'

'Richard was between here and the mine?' Justin seemed almost disbelieving. 'You didn't recognise the second man? Could it have been his driver—or someone from Wheal Margaret?'

'I don't know. It might have been his coachman—though it was a light phaeton; something he could have been driving himself.'

'Richard often drives his own cattle, and it sounds like him to have overturned it. He has the worst hands of any man I know! It was a quarrel over a horse he had ruined that began the trouble between us years ago . . . But I cannot believe that he would go to so much bother to ruin me. What could he gain from it?'

'Satisfaction?' Rosanna suggested. 'You said he was jealous of your relationship with his father.'

'Yes, but surely . . .'

'It may be only a coincidence, but I thought you should know.' She stood up again. 'Now, if you will excuse me, I shall tell Emily that you will not be at home for dinner.'

'No...' Justin caught her wrist. 'I've changed my mind. I can ride over to see Paul in the morning. Perhaps you would like to come with me? We could go into Bodmin.'

'Yes.' The tension went out of her. 'Yes, I would like that.'

It was fair day in Bodmin. Justin glanced at Rosanna apologetically. 'I'm sorry, I had forgotten how crowded it would be.'

'I don't mind,' she said, smiling at him. 'It's fun, isn't it?'

The streets leading into the little town were crowded with people, some on horseback, many more on foot, but all dressed in their Sunday best. Women carried baskets of pies and cakes they had baked and were hoping to sell. Horses and cattle had been brought for barter, and there was an excited atmosphere that showed in the faces of men, women and children alike. Piles of produce were heaped at the front of the covered stalls; men crowded round several large barrels of cider that had been hauled in on a wagon—much to the annoyance of the local innkeepers. There were all kinds of attractions, from pedlars with trays of cheap trinkets to silk-merchants with rolls of beautiful material spilling from their superior stalls. Cries of 'Hot gingerbread' were to be heard, and the squeals of excited children as they bought a penny cake that burned their lips as they tried to bite it. A team of jugglers was entertaining the crowd at one end of the street, while an ancient gypsy fiddled for coins at the other, and a wrestling-match was going on in the centre, noisily supported by a score of on-lookers—several of whom seemed to have visited the cider-wagon a little too often.

Justin helped Rosanna to dismount, giving their horses into the care of an ostler at the Feathers Inn. Seeing the sparkle in his wife's eyes, he realised that she was at-tracted by the fair and took her arm, accepting her un-spoken wish to mingle with the happy crowd.

'You've never been to a fair like this, have you?'

'No.' She laughed up at him. 'It wasn't considered proper for Madame Belvoir's young ladies—and Father always steered well clear of them when we were travelling. He thought it was an invitation to beggars and thieves.'

'He was probably right. I dare say there's a fair sprinkling of pickpockets and rogues here today!'

'Since I haven't any money for them to steal, it doesn't really bother me,' Rosanna said. 'Oh, look, Justin! That man is actually burning his own skin. Now he's going to swallow the fire-stick. Ugh! How can he do that?'

'I don't suppose he's in any real danger of burning himself: it's all a trick.' He glanced down at her in amusement. She was almost like a child, fascinated by all that she saw. 'Do you want to view the bearded lady or the man with two heads?' He gestured towards some brightly-coloured tents. 'Or would you rather have a tooth drawn?'

'Wretch!' She pouted at him. 'I don't believe there's a man with... Oh, Justin, look across the street! The man next to the toffee-apple stall. He's the one I saw with Richard. The man I was telling you about last night.'

Justin looked at the scruffy-looking figure she had pointed out. 'Are you sure, Rosanna? It was a long time ago.'

'I know, but I've a good memory for faces, and they were both so angry because I spattered them with mud. That man shook his fist at me.'

'I'm not surprised! He's one of the rogues I was speaking about just now. His name is Nick Tregear; he and his brother are mixed up in all kinds of unsavoury things. When an exciseman was killed about two years ago over at Boscastle, it was whispered that Nick was the one who fired the shot, but it couldn't be proved. The "gentlemen" are a close-mouthed lot.'

'Smugglers, you mean?' Rosanna shivered. 'Do you think Nick Tregear is behind the accidents?'

Justin hesitated, and then shook his head. 'No, I don't. Seth wouldn't harbour his sort in the mine, neither would most of the men. Smuggling is looked upon as a bit of a lark by many hereabouts—but murder is something else. Nick is not liked at Sawltry, and if he were seen skulking about the engine-house or anywhere on my land, it would be reported.'

'What was Richard doing with a man like that?'

'I'm not sure, though I have a good idea. There's many a landed family in these parts with cellars full of good French brandy that's never seen a penny paid in tax.' Justin took her arm. 'If you've had enough of this, we'll bespeak a decent meal at the inn—unless you've seen something you want to buy? Some silk for a new gown, perhaps?'

'No, not today, Justin. I think I have enough clothes to last me for a while. I spent a fortune on my trousseau before I realised that most of Father's money was lost. I still owe Mr Denton for some of my tailor's bills.'

'The unpaid tailors' bills in London would solve the national debt,' he quipped, steering her across the street and into the inn, a Tudor house with faded red bricks and oak beams that had a warm, welcoming atmosphere. 'It's a while since I was here, but they used to serve excellent beef.'

The inn was busy, its trade unaffected by the cider-wagon outside. Rosanna did not think they would find a seat, but when the host spied Justin, he came up to them at once.

'If you wouldn't mind sharing the parlour with another gentleman, Captain Sawle, I can find you a table more suited to your lady than the public rooms.'

'Thank you,' Justin replied with a smile. 'I am sure my wife would prefer it.' Dropping his voice, he winked at Rosanna and said, 'A mis-spent youth has its uses, it would seem.'

His look almost overset her, and she choked on a laugh as the innkeeper turned back to them. 'The Captain and I are old friends, ma'am. There's some folk as can always be sure of a welcome here.'

'You have known my husband a long time?' she asked as he led them into a cosy private parlour, where another rather ruddy-faced man was already tucking into a plate heaped with thick slices of roast beef.

'Why, bless you, ma'am, I've know him since he was knee-high! Liked my special lemonade and the treacle-toffee my Sarah made on purpose for him, did Master Justin. She always had a soft spot for him, my Sarah, young rascal though he was. Always into some mischief and as stubborn as a mule, but no real harm in him.'

'If you have finished ruining my reputation, Nathan, we'll have a jug of your best wine and some of that excellent beef.'

A broad grin spread across the host's face. 'Always one for a laugh, sir. Sarah has a lovely apple-pie in the oven. You'll want hot custard, and cream for the lady, I dare say?'

'Thank you,' Rosanna laughed. 'You obviously intend to spoil us, Nathan. I shall look forward to my meal.'

He had given them a seat by the window, and as he bustled away to fill their order and tell Sarah that her favourite customer was in the house, Rosanna turned to watch the busy scene outside. Absorbed, she was not at first aware of the curious glances directed towards them by the other diner, and was surprised when he addressed them.

'Quite a crush in the streets today, isn't it?'

'Yes. I had forgotten the fair,' Justin replied.

'You've forgotten *me*, sir. Henry Poughill. We met in Truro once. I have a mine myself, but not tin or copper. China clay, sir, that's the coming thing.'

'Ah, yes.' Justin stood up and went over to shake hands. 'You have a pit at St Austell, I believe?'

Poughill pumped his hand enthusiastically. 'That's it.' He sat down again as Justin returned to his seat. 'Thought you'd forgotten me. I hear you're having some trouble at Wheal Margaret. Sailing near the wind, what?'

'Indeed?' Justin's brows rose. 'Where did you hear that?'

'Can't just think at the moment. I get about quite a bit. Strange how these tales circulate, isn't it? Glad if it's wrong. Don't like to think of a fellow mine-owner in trouble.' He took a swallow of ale and dabbed his napkin to his lips. 'Thing is, I was thinking of offering myself as a partner if it would help. Still, I expect you're wishing me to the devil by now!'

'Since your intention was kind, sir, I shall bear you no hard feelings. If ever I do need a partner, I'll remember your offer.'

'Do that, Captain Sawle. I'm an honest man, though I say it myself. You won't hear that Henry Poughill ever did a man an ill turn, whoever you ask. I took a fancy to you when we met.' He pushed his empty plate away, and stood up. 'Well, now, I'll leave you and your good lady to enjoy your meal in peace. Remember me if you should ever need help. I'm not a man to see a friend go to the wall for the lack of a few guineas.'

As he walked from the room, Rosanna shot an amused look at her husband. 'What an odd man, Justin.'

His face was serious as he met her look. 'Stranger still, he seems to know more of my business than he should. Only Seth and I have access to the balances—and the bank. It appears that someone from the bank has been gossiping.'

Her smile faded. 'Are you in trouble?'

'We are just managing to hold our heads above water, but a serious accident could sink us.'

'I have perhaps fifty guineas left. If only I hadn't spent so much money on my trip to London!'

'Keep your money. We'll manage.'

'Mr Denton said that he thought he might be able to recover some of the money that was stolen from me. Perhaps, if I wrote to him...'

'No!' His voice rose sharply. 'You've done your share. If we need more money, I'll find it myself.'

There was a finality in his voice that silenced her. She realised that his pride had suffered because she had helped to finance the mine, and was surprised. He had married her for the fortune he believed she had inherited, so why was he embarrassed by her offer of help now?

CHAPTER EIGHT

'THERE'S no need to look at me with those wounded eyes, Rosanna,' Justin said harshly. 'I'm grateful for what you did, but any money you may get from Denton is yours. You must keep it for yourself and your children—when they come. I'll find the money I need somewhere. I could always invite Poughill in as a partner.'

'I suppose you could do worse.' Rosanna caught the look in his eyes, and giggled. 'He was rather sweet, really.'

'You are a minx!'

The slight atmosphere had passed, and by the time Sarah came bustling in with their dinner, they were the best of friends again. The landlord's wife was a plump, friendly woman with a curious nature. She would not be satisfied until she had heard all about their wedding, and Justin's trip to the war.

'Well, my loves,' she said at last, 'I must hurry back to my pots or the wretched kitchen girl will let the puddings boil dry. A terrible trial she is to me, and no mistake! Now don't you stay away so long in future, Captain Sawle.'

As she hurried off, the door was left ajar and Rosanna could see into the hall. A fair-haired woman in a rather fussy silk gown, and a gentleman several years her senior, were complaining loudly to the landlord.

'Why can't we have a table in your private parlour? I saw someone come out only a moment ago,' the woman said.

'What's to do, man?' Her companion struck the floor with his cane. 'I insist on being shown into the parlour at once.'

'But, my lord, I have customers in there already.'

'Then make room for us in a corner.'

'Very well, Lord Cornwallis.' Nathan shrugged his shoulders, giving Justin an apologetic look as he led the newcomers into the parlour. 'Since you insist, sir. I believe you are acquainted with Captain Sawle?'

'What?' Cornwallis halted abruptly, his glowering gaze flicking to the occupants of the table in the window. His thin, pale face turned ashen, and his eyes bulged with anger. 'Good God, why didn't you explain before, you dolt? Come, Anne, we shall go elsewhere. The air in here is stale.'

He grabbed hold of his wife's arm, almost unbalancing her as he pushed her from the room. 'Cornwallis,' she complained, 'you are hurting me!'

'Perhaps not as much as you deserve, you bitch. I ought to break your neck and shoot him!'

A deathly silence followed their departure. Nathan shook his head, clearly mortified. He opened his mouth as if to speak, then shook his head again. Obviously embarrassed by the unpleasant scene, he went out, closing the door behind him.

Rosanna sat stiffly in her chair, unable to look at Justin. Lord Cornwallis had been deliberately rude, and his reason for such outrageous behaviour was patently clear. He believed that his wife was still having an affair with a lover—and that the man concerned was Justin!

'I'm sorry,' Justin said at last. 'I would not have had you subjected to that for the world.'

'No, I do not suppose you would,' she replied quietly. 'It—It was unpleasant and embarrassing for everyone.'

'And unnecessary,' he said, a note of anger in his voice. 'Cornwallis behaved like a fool. He may have had a right to be angry once, I'll not deny that, but he has no cause for offence now. I have not spoken to Anne since Brussels...' He swore softly as Rosanna looked up. 'I danced with her at the Duchess of Richmond's ball. I did not wish to, but she made it impossible for me to refuse. I swear there has been nothing between us since before I married you, Rosanna.'

How much she wanted to believe him. It was true that he had had little opportunity of late to meet a mistress, but there were the months he had spent in London after the war. Why had he not come home as soon as he returned to England? Was it only that he had thought she would not welcome him to Rathmoor, or had he found other amusements to hold him in town? She could not be sure, but she did not wish the day to be spoiled by a quarrel. Besides, there was a look in his eyes that inclined her to accept his word.

'If that is so, I owe you an apology, Justin,' she murmured, a faint blush in her cheeks. 'When you left me alone just after our marriage, I believed it was to go to Anne Cornwallis. It was the reason I was often cold towards you.'

'Did you really think I would betray you, Rosanna?'

Her eyes opened wide and her heart fluttered. 'I—I don't know. I—I had trapped you into a marriage you could not want.'

'We were both at fault,' he said softly, 'and I believe it has cost us both dearly.'

'Justin...' She ran the tip of her tongue nervously over her lips. 'Justin, I wish...'

The door opened to admit Nathan. He was carrying a tray bearing an apple-pie with a browned sugar-crust straight from the oven, a jug of steaming yellow custard and a dish of thick cream. He beamed as he set it down on the table and cleared away the used dishes.

'There now, Captain Sawle, you and your good lady taste that, and tell me what you think.'

Rosanna cut the crust of the generous slice he had placed before her, giving a murmur of approval. The pastry was sweet and crumbled on her tongue, while the filling had a delicious sharpness slightly flavoured with cinnamon and cloves.

'Delicious,' she confirmed. 'Please tell Sarah that I have never tasted better.'

Her host's smile broadened as he picked up his tray of dirty dishes and departed, leaving them to finish their meal. When the door had closed behind him, Justin looked at Rosanna across the table.

'What was it you were saying?' he asked with an intent look.

She had been on the point of saying that she wished they could make a fresh start from the beginning, tempted to confess how much she cared for him. The moment had passed, however, leaving her uncertain again. She was sure he would not want a clinging, possessive wife. 'I was only going to say that I wished I had brought some money with me. I should like to buy some small gifts for Emily and Sally.'

He knew that she had changed her mind, but decided not to press her further for the moment. 'I believe I can oblige you, my love. Finish your pie, and we'll go to the fair. We'll buy something for everyone...'

It had been such a satisfying day, Rosanna thought, as she was preparing for bed. Justin had really thrown himself into the shopping expedition, bargaining with the stall-holders for the trinkets they had purchased. Lavender sachets for Sally and a length of muslin. A rag-doll for her daughter and a bag of sweetmeats. For Emily there was a pair of blue leather slippers and a lace collar; for the men, tobacco, fancy pipes and various treats from the confectionery stall. They had also bought gifts for Becky and her children.

'And what would you like?' Justin asked when they had found gifts for all their friends. 'You must have something, too.'

'No, there is nothing I need,' she protested.

'Something for the woman who has everything—what can we find?' His eyes glinted with humour as he glanced over the pedlar's tray. Spying a small crystal glass pot in the shape of a heart, he picked it up. 'This will do to keep your pins in, Rosanna.'

It was merely a fairing; a cheap trinket, but delicate and pretty. As she looked at it more carefully, she saw that it had an inscription inside: *'Love me for ever.'* She read the words silently, realising that he could not have seen them. 'It's lovely, Justin,' she said, smiling at him. 'I shall treasure it always.'

'A trinket from a fair?' His brows went up, but no more was said.

They had ridden home through Dunmere woods, past the banks of the River Camel, in a companionable mood, laughing and talking all the way. It was really the happiest day they had spent in each other's company, Rosanna thought, despite the unpleasant incident with Lord Cornwallis. They had behaved like a proper husband and wife, enjoying themselves without effort. Perhaps it was going to work this time? She ran a finger over the little glass fairing, which now had pride of place on her dressing-chest.

'Love me for ever,' she whispered. 'If only he...'

She caught the words back as Justin came in, turning back to the mirror and beginning to brush her long hair. He came and stood behind her, watching silently for a few seconds; then he held out his hand, and she gave him the brush. The touch of his hands smoothing her hair was soothing at first, but then the slow ritual of it became sensuous, arousing and stimulating desire in her. She put out her hand to stop him, standing up and turning to face him.

'Justin, I...' she began, but he placed a finger against her lips and she saw that there was no need for words.

His arms went round her slim waist, the heat of his body burning her through the thin silk of her night attire. She caught her breath, a shiver running through her as his hands began to stroke the slender arch of her back. His lips against her throat were like fire, making her groan as her blood quickened. She clung to him as he gathered her in his arms, carrying her towards the bed.

He lay down beside her, catching her to him as their lips met in an urgent, searing kiss. Rosanna moaned slightly, the desire moving in her hotly as his lips whispered down her throat in a trail of sheer delight. She arched and whimpered, feeling a sensuous pleasure in the way his lips nuzzled the delicate rose-pink nipples, then moved on down over her flat navel, caressing and teasing as it sent ripples of desire flooding through her. She was ready for his loving, her legs parting in moist invitation, but he did not immediately respond. Instead, he continued to stroke and caress her, holding back his own need until he had roused her to fever pitch and she gasped his name, begging him to come to her. She had never imagined that it was possible to feel such intense pleasure. Nothing had prepared her for the moment when something within her seemed to reach out and enfold him, taking him deeper into her. For one unbelievable moment the earth moved and they were flung into a whirling vortex of ecstasy that left them at last exhausted and drained.

Weeks later, Rosanna was to recall that moment; the moment that had perhaps seen the conception of their child. But by then it was a bittersweet memory.

'There's been a spate of accidents at the mine,' Justin said, striding into the long parlour. 'Seth says the men are threatening to strike. I shall have to sort it out myself, Rosanna. If I'm late, you go on to the Pardoes' card-party and I'll come when I can.'

'Oh, I'd rather not,' she said, pausing in the act of placing a pale pink rose in a silver vase. 'I could send our apologies.'

'No. It's the first time we've been invited out since we came home from London.' Justin frowned as he saw the stubborn look on her face. 'I want you to go, Rosanna. Benjamin will drive you over, and Sir Joshua will keep you company until I get there. No arguments, woman! You must go, or they will be offended.'

She gave in reluctantly. It was typical of Justin to insist that she go to a party while he was trying to avert a damaging strike at the mine. The men were growing restless after a long period of difficult working. So far no one had been hurt, but the pumps had been deliberately sabotaged and a tunnel had collapsed after seepage. Tools went missing; others were damaged, causing loss of working hours and reductions in productivity. The men wanted to be paid for the time lost, but Seth had refused to give into them, saying that they simply could not afford it.

'The line between profit and loss is fine enough,' Justin told his wife, 'but we'll have to give way or the men will strike. That could close us down.'

How could he expect her to enjoy herself, knowing that he was fighting for the survival of the mine? It was a sensitive subject, and one that she dared not mention unless he brought it up. Mr Denton had managed to salvage a further one thousand pounds from her father's estate, but when she offered it to Justin, he refused to accept more help from her.

'Ask your solicitor to invest it for you—or spend it on the house. There are ways of raising money, if I have to.'

She had not dared to ask how he intended to raise the funds he would certainly need in the coming months. They were on comfortable terms now, but there was still a barrier between them. Sometimes she thought that it was only Justin's pride that kept them from being completely happy. She knew he resented being in debt to her, and she was afraid that if the mine failed, the gap between them would be impossible to bridge.

Deciding to use her money to repair the worst areas of the house, Rosanna had recently called in a stonemason. It was specialised work that neither Rob nor Benjamin could do. After Justin had gone, she placed her last flower in water and went to inspect the work.

The mason had rebuilt part of a wall, and now the panels that Rob had re-carved so lovingly were being put in place. Rosanna found most of her servants gathered there to admire.

'This is how it must have looked when Rathmoor was first built,' Rob said to her.

'I think perhaps it looks even better,' she replied. 'Your carving is some of the finest I've ever seen.'

Sally moved closer to her husband, her face glowing with pride. Rob put his arm round her shoulders. 'As a lad, I always wanted to be whittling at a piece of wood, but my father called it nonsense and sent me down the mine to help feed the family. Being here—having a chance to restore this beautiful old house—has given new meaning to my life.'

Rosanna felt the sting of tears behind her eyes. 'I am so grateful for what you've done. I only wish I could pay you more—you certainly earn it.'

'I'd work for my keep rather than go down the mine again.'

She gave a choking laugh. 'Well, you won't have to do that. I'm not even sure that there will be a mine for much longer.'

Seth held the lantern higher as Justin inspected the damage. They could both see quite clearly that the pump had been deliberately sabotaged.

'When did this happen?' Justin asked. 'It was working well yesterday.'

'It must have been some time this morning. When the first shift came on, it was still going.'

'But how?' Justin frowned. 'No one saw anything un-usual. No one saw a suspicious stranger. I just don't understand.'

'It beats me how someone can come and go without being seen. I've recruited three sharp-eyed lads to patrol the access tunnels.'

'No one has reported seeing Nick Tregear lurking about?'

'No, why?' Seth looked surprised. 'You know how they feel about Nick.'

'Oh, it was just something I'd heard.' Justin frowned. 'We'll double the patrols, Seth. Somehow we've got to stop this.' He sighed deeply. 'Now, I suppose, we'd better go and reason with Zeb Tolly and his friends.'

'You look very lovely this evening, m'dear.' Sir Joshua kissed Rosanna's cheek. 'And where's that rascal? Surely he hasn't let you come alone?'

'He had to go to the mine.' Rosanna did not want to dwell on the subject. 'We haven't seen you at Rathmoor lately. You are not going to neglect us, I hope? You must come to dinner soon.'

'I've had a touch of gout,' Sir Joshua said, 'otherwise I'd have been over. I thought Justin would have told you. I ran into him in Truro the other week. Thought it was coming on then, and mentioned it.'

'Justin didn't tell me he'd seen you. I wasn't aware he had been into Truro.'

Rosanna frowned. It was not like Justin to go into town without telling her. At least, she had not thought so. She was about to ask more questions when her hostess bore down on them.

'Ah, my dear Rosanna, you mustn't hide yourself in a corner! I want you to meet one of my guests. In fact, I believe you may have met before...' Mrs Pardoe raised her brow. 'Harry Bellingham has recently become engaged to a friend of ours. Miss Bransen is such a delightful girl. They are staying at her aunt's house in Launceston.'

Rosanna allowed herself to be drawn across the room. She felt no embarrassment as she was introduced to Miss Alicia Bransen, smiling at her and then at Harry. 'I'm very happy for you both,' she said. 'Tell me, when is the wedding to be?'

'Oh, not for another six months,' Harry replied easily. 'There's no hurry, is there, Alicia?'

'No. No, I suppose not.'

Rosanna thought she looked a little doubtful; the reason was made plain to her in a few moments as Harry excused himself and went through to the card-room. Alicia's eyes followed him wistfully.

'Harry has never been able to forget you,' she said, looking at Rosanna resentfully. 'I know he is genuinely fond of me and he has promised to be kind and faithful, but he's still in love with you.'

'No, surely not! You are mistaken.' Rosanna looked at the thin-faced but pretty girl. 'I do not believe he was ever truly in love with me. If he had been . . .'

'Yes?' Alicia looked at her, her china-blue eyes misted with tears of self-pity. 'It was so cruel of you to jilt him. How could you break his heart like that? It's so unfair.'

'But I didn't,' Rosanna cried. 'Miss Bransen, I must tell you that I would never have jilted Harry if I had thought that he loved me. In fact, it was really he who jilted . . .' Hearing a slight noise behind her, she turned round, the colour leaving her face as she found herself staring into a pair of flinty grey eyes. 'Justin, I didn't see you come in.'

'That much is obvious.' He gave her a tight-lipped smile. 'I came as quickly as I could, thinking that you might miss me. Had I realised that Harry Bellingham was here, I would not have bothered.'

'Harry is engaged to Miss Bransen,' Rosanna said, her cheeks flaming.

'Miss Bransen, you have my sympathy.' Justin inclined his head. 'Excuse me, I think I shall retire to the card-room. Rosanna, do not wait for me. I may be late.'

Flinching as if he had struck her, Rosanna heard the girl at her side begin to cry. 'Oh, stop snivelling,' she snapped, her temper flaring. 'If Harry neglects you, it is your own fault. He is not in love with me. If you must know, he was more interested in my father's fortune than in me. As long as you are an heiress, you need not fear competition from me!'

'Oh, you hateful woman!' Alicia Bransen cried, and promptly burst into tears.

Rosanna stared after her, feeling penitent as she fled from the room. 'Miss Bransen, I'm sorry,' she called, regretting her flash of spite, but the girl did not look back.

Torn by guilt, Rosanna's annoyance turned to anger. It was all Justin's fault! He had stung her with his sarcasm, and she had retaliated by striking out at an innocent child. Sighing, she followed Alicia from the room. She had no choice but to go after the girl and apologise. Perhaps, if she explained everything all over again, but more kindly, Alicia would calm down. She had to try, otherwise the foolish girl might break off her engagement.

She was in time to see Alicia disappear into the garden. There was nothing Rosanna wanted less than a game of hide and seek with Harry's fiancée, but what else could she do? At least it was a warm summer evening and the sky was still light.

'Miss Bransen,' she called again, 'please stop. Please let me explain? I did not mean to be unkind.'

The girl had fled into the shrubbery, no doubt intending to sob out her grief in one of the little summerhouses. Quickening her step, Rosanna felt her gown catch on a thorny bush and gave a cry of annoyance, stopping to try to loosen the filmy silk without tearing it.

'Let me do that for you.' A man stepped towards her from the shadow of a clump of evergreens.

'Harry! I thought you were in the card-room,' Rosanna said, feeling surprised to find him alone in the gardens. 'Did you see Miss Bransen come this way?'

'No. I came out for some air—and to be alone for a while.' Harry disentangled the silk. 'There, I think no damage has been done. Why are you looking for Alicia?'

'I'm sorry, Harry, I think I've upset her.' Rosanna bit her lip. 'The silly girl imagines that you are still in love with me. I tried to tell her it was nonsense, but I was too harsh. I wanted to apologise.'

Harry looked at her strangely. 'If Alicia is upset, it's my fault, not yours. I know I've been neglecting her recently—but she clings so. She's right, Rosanna. I just cannot forget you.'

'Don't be so foolish! You know we agreed she would suit you very well.' Rosanna laid her hand gently on his arm. 'I am still fond of you, Harry. Please don't ruin your life because of me...'

She got no further. He reached out, pulling her into his arms and kissing her with an intensity that surprised her. He had never once kissed her like that while they were engaged.

'Harry!' she cried, struggling to push him away. 'What on earth do you think you are doing?'

He looked at her miserably. 'I adore you, Rosanna. I didn't realise how much you meant to me until it was too late. I don't think I can go on living without you. My life means nothing to me any...'

'Harry, stop!' Rosanna cried, shocked. 'This is wicked nonsense. You think you want me simply because you can't have me. But you can have Alicia. She's young and sweet—and so much in love with you.' She reached out to touch his hand. 'My dearest Harry, I love you very much...'

'Then come away with me. Leave your husband,' he interrupted eagerly. 'We could go abroad—to Rome, perhaps. Don't you ever think of that night in the gardens...'

'No, Harry, I do not. I love you as a friend.' She felt a twinge of pity as she saw the eagerness fade from his eyes. 'And, as your friend, I am telling you to go and find Alicia. Tell her I'm nothing to you any more. Remember how I used to dictate to you, Harry? You would have found me tiresome in time. You will be much happier with Alicia once you have forgotten me.'

'Shall I ever forget you?' Harry asked wistfully. 'But I know I forfeited my right to your love when I let you go. Goodbye, my darling Rosanna.'

She watched him walk away, feeling the sting of tears behind her eyes. Although she knew that their parting had been the best thing for both of them, she regretted his pain. He was the brother she had never had, and she would always be fond of him. 'Life is very cruel,' she whispered. 'Why could I not have loved you, my poor Harry? Why can Justin not love me?'

Turning, she walked slowly back to the house.

In the shadows of the veranda, a man was watching. He had witnessed the tender scene from a distance, and his eyes glittered with anger. So, she still loved Bellingham after all this time—after the nights of passion they had spent together!

The bitterness twisted inside him like a serpent, stinging him with its poison. He had followed her to apologise, thinking better of his angry words. He had never been quite sure if his jealousy was warranted. Now he knew! And the pain of it was killing him. In his rage, he wanted to strike out at someone. Rosanna! He should kill the cheating bitch or leave her. He could not let her go. He wanted her so badly at this moment that it almost choked him. She was like a recurring fever in his blood that would not let him rest. He had never believed that any woman could have this hold on him. Damn it, she was his wife! No matter that her every smile was a lie, he would never let her go to Harry Bellingham!

'It was good of you to see me home, Sir Joshua,' Rosanna said, kissing his wrinkled cheek. 'Goodnight. You will dine with us soon?'

'Next week, m'dear. I want a word with Justin, anyway.'

She waved as he climbed back into the carriage, yawning as she walked into the house. It was quite late, the shadows looming in the flickering flames of the light in the hall. She had stayed at the Pardoes' longer than she had intended, hoping that Justin would relent and accompany her home. He had not, but at least she had seen Harry and Alicia re-enter the house arm in arm. Feeling reassured on that point, she had asked her friend to take her home, leaving the carriage for Justin. If he had drunk a little too much, he might not be in any fit state to ride his horse. Stopping for a moment at Emily's sitting-room to tell her what was happening and to chat for a while, Rosanna went up to her room. She was feeling tired and she undressed quickly, slipping between the sheets and falling asleep almost at once.

The sound of something crashing to the floor awoke her with a jerk. She sat up and lit the candle, staring at the overturned chair and then at her husband. It was clear that he was drunk.

'You're home, then,' she said. 'Be careful, Justin, you'll wake everyone else.'

'Damn them,' he muttered thickly. 'Damn them all. All your faithful lapdogs! Well, I'm not one of them, do you hear me, waiting in line for a pat or a smile! I may live in your house and eat your bread, but I'm not a lackey...'

His eyes were glittering and he looked very strange. Wide awake now, Rosanna got out of bed, walking towards him with a coaxing smile. He was very drunk, she realised, feeling a little amused.

'No, of course you're not a lackey, Justin,' she said, 'you're my husband. It isn't my house; it's our house. Come to bed now, my love. It will all seem better in the morning.' She took his arm, trying to lead him towards the bed.

He struck her hand off, his face angry. 'Don't humour me, Rosanna. I may be drunk, but I know what I'm doing—and what I saw tonight. You cheating bitch! I should break that beautiful neck of yours, and I would if I didn't...' He broke off, flinging away from her as he began to strip off his clothes and drop them on the floor. 'Ought to teach the bitch a lesson...'

Rosanna stared after him, her eyes wide. She had never seen Justin in this mood before. He was letting his guard down in a way he never would when he was sober. He was jealous. He was out of his mind with jealousy! She ran after him, pulling on his arm so that he swung round to face her. 'Leave me alone, damn you!'

'Oh, Justin, don't be jealous,' she said, laughing, her eyes very bright. 'What you saw tonight meant nothing...'

She looked very beautiful with her long hair cascading down her back. Through the pale silk of her nightgown, he could see the outlines of her breasts and the shadows of rosy nipples. Her lips were moist and inviting, and her eyes mocked him.

'It may not have meant anything to you,' he muttered hoarsely, aware of the burning desire in his loins. 'You're probably playing him for a fool, too!'

Suddenly something snapped in his head as he saw the laughter in her eyes. She thought it was amusing to torment him, did she? Well, it was time she discovered what pain was all about! He seized her wrist, dragging her the last few paces towards the bed and thrusting her down as she stumbled. He knelt beside her on the silk coverlet, angry and bitter at the extent of his physical desire. He held her as she protested and tried to rise, still laughing, not yet realising what he was intending. She was so beautiful that she drove him mad, his jealousy eating into him. Had she looked at Harry like that earlier? The wanton! He was vaguely aware of her surprised cry as he threw himself on top of her, his mouth reaching greedily for hers.

When she finally understood what was in his mind, she struggled against him. He was drunk and upset; he did not know what he was doing. 'Stop, Justin,' she cried, pushing at him. 'Please don't hurt me.'

He said something she could not quite hear, his voice slurred. Then she felt his body drop heavily on hers and realised that he had fallen asleep. Smiling tenderly, she eased him to one side, making his head comfortable on the pillow. She knew that he had intended to force himself on her, but she felt no anger. He was far too drunk to know what he was doing.

Bending over him, Rosanna stroked the damp hair from his forehead. 'I forgive you, my darling. I don't know what devil drives you—but I love you. I shall always love you, no matter what you do...'

*   *   *

Justin woke as he felt something touch his face. The tantalising smell of hot coffee assailed his nostrils, and he opened his eyes to see his wife bending over him. She smiled, and indicated the tray she had set by the bed.

Sitting up gingerly, he regarded her with suspicion. 'To what do I owe this undeserved attention?'

'I thought it might help to ease your head,' she said, a hint of humour in her voice. 'Drink the tisane first, Justin, and then your coffee.'

He pulled a face, but took the cup she thrust into his hands, grimacing at the bitter taste of the herbs. 'Was I very drunk last night? I recall Benjamin putting me into the carriage, but the rest is a blur. Did I wake you?'

'Yes. I put you to bed. Don't you remember?'

'No. I hope I didn't cause you too much trouble?'

'No, not too much. You fell asleep very quickly.'

'If I'm going to be waited on like this, I may get drunk more often—or perhaps not! My head feels as though a hundred hammers are at work.'

'It serves you right,' Rosanna said cheerfully. 'I prefer you when you're sober. Now, if you've finished your coffee, I have something to say.'

He stared at her uneasily. His memory had holes in it, but he remembered the scene in the gardens clearly. He waited tensely for the blow to fall: she was going to tell him that she wanted an annulment.

'I'm listening.'

'You saw me with Harry last night. You were muttering about it when you came in.'

'Oh?' He looked at her warily. 'What did I say? I was drunk. You shouldn't believe a drunken man.'

'You seemed to believe I was having an affair with him. You called me names I would rather not repeat.'

'I saw you kissing him. I was angry.'

'No,' she corrected, 'you saw Harry kissing me. It was not with my consent, I promise you. I went into the gardens to apologise to Miss Bransen. I had upset her because you had made me angry. I did not expect to meet Harry.'

Justin looked at her intently. 'How can I believe you?'

'Harry wanted to marry me because I was heiress to a fortune. When he discovered that most of the money was lost, he said he couldn't afford to marry me, so I released him from his promise. He was concerned at what people would think if they knew the truth, and so...'

'You let everyone think that you had jilted him? You must have loved him very much to do that.'

'You will keep jumping to conclusions, and they are quite wrong. Please let me finish?' She smiled as he nodded. 'Harry thinks that he is still in love with me, but he isn't. We shouldn't have suited one another. I'm far too strong willed. I need a strong man to stand up to me. It isn't good for me to have all my own way.'

A reluctant smile twisted his mouth. 'That's true enough! But if Harry jilted you, you had no choice.'

'I could have made him keep his promise, if I'd wanted. He was always weak where I was concerned. The truth is that I'd realised I was not in love with him...'

'Are you sure?'

'Yes, quite sure.'

Justin looked at her steadily. 'Then I've been a damned fool! I thought you regretted the break with him. You even told me that you wished you had married him.'

'I was angry then. It was a cruel, foolish thing to say, and I'm sorry for it.'

'Why are you telling me all this now?'

'Because I care about our marriage, and...' she faltered, her courage failing. 'I care about you, Justin. I do not want that foolish incident in the garden last night to come between us.'

She had meant to tell him plainly that she loved him, but at the last moment the words stuck in her throat. Surely, if he truly loved her, he would speak now?

'Rosanna, I...' She waited, holding her breath. 'I am sorry for having doubted you.'

The disappointment was sharp in her, but she hid it behind a smile. Getting up, she turned her face aside as she said lightly, 'Are you gong to lie abed all day, lazybones? The stonemason has uncovered something interesting in the west wing. Will you not come down and take a look? I think there's a secret room, and there may be some passages that we didn't know existed. Who knows, we may find Lady Caroline's jewels at last.'

As Justin relaxed against the pillows, the thunder in his head made it almost impossible for him to think clearly. It would be ironic if the jewels were to turn up now. Rosanna would be a rich woman again. A soft curse escaped his lips. If only he could find the rich vein of copper he was certain the mine held. He had to repay the money she had invested—only then could he tell her of his love.

She cared for him. He had seen it in her eyes just now, and realised it had been there before. He was a blind fool to let his pride stand between them. The revelation of his bastardy had made him bitter. If it had not been for that, he could have given Rosanna all the things she had a right to expect, yet it was perverse to let his situation stand between them. He knew it, but it made no difference.

'You're a stubborn fool,' he told himself as he jumped out of bed. He was grinning as he began to shave. So she didn't give a damn for Bellingham—the minx!

There *was* a way to find the money he needed. It was risky, and he had hesitated to consider it. Smuggling was a common enough business in these parts, but he had always kept well clear of it. Some of the brandy in Charles Sawle's cellars had escaped the excisemen, and he had seen the men who delivered the goods under the cover of darkness often enough, but buying a few barrels was very different from what he was contemplating now.

He had been approached recently by the leader of a local group of smugglers. Jack Brendon wanted him to turn a blind eye to the contraband stored in a disused mine shaft. He had been aware of what was going on before the approach, and a few barrels of brandy had found their way back to Rathmoor. The smugglers constantly needed to find new hiding-places. The battle between the excisemen and the runners was finely pitched, each side gaining and losing the ascendancy in turn. It was almost a game of give and take. After the Revenue men had been allowed to find a few barrels, they left the smugglers alone. Perhaps the brandy reached only as far as their own cellars! Brendon wanted to bring his stuff further inland, to where there were no prying eyes. Justin knew he meant Rathmoor. Its isolated position at the edge of the moors was perfect. Only half an hour's ride from the cove, it would make an ideal hiding-place, and its cavernous cellars could hold a huge cargo. Brendon had approached him again only that week, for an important cargo was expected within a few days. If Justin accepted the bribe he had been offered, it would keep the mine running for at least six months—but did he want to become involved?

Pulling on his shirt and breeches, he put the troublesome thoughts from his mind. He would see Brendon tomorrow. Today, he would help Rosanna to look for the jewels. Hearing the sound of voices from the long gallery, he saw that half the household was gathered there. A large hole in the wall showed that there had once been a secret room behind the panelling.

'Oh, isn't it exciting, sir?' Sally cried as she saw him. 'Just think what you might find!'

Rosanna turned to her husband, her eyes shining. 'It is almost as exciting as Sally's own news. Guess what she has just told me!'

Sally blushed, looking shyly at her husband. 'Rob and me wondered if you'd mind another baby in the house...'

'Of course not,' Rosanna said at once. 'I think it's wonderful. Rathmoor needs young people; don't you agree, Justin?'

'Yes, of course.' He wondered at the odd note in her voice. 'It's marvellous news, Sally.'

'Shall we explore?' Rosanna asked. 'Give me that candlestick, Sally.'

'Let me have it,' Justin insisted. 'I'll go first. You stay behind me in case those steps are dangerous.'

He took the lighted candle, stepping into the opening. As he had expected, the steps leading down into the secret room were crumbling away at the edges, and he turned back to Rosanna, giving her his hand. 'There seems to be a passage leading downwards,' he said. 'I should imagine it leads to the cellars. It was probably used by a Roman Catholic priest at some time.'

Rosanna's eyes lit with excitement. 'I'm sure this passage was unknown to Jonathan,' she said. 'I really think we might find the jewels this time.'

Justin smiled at her enthusiasm. 'It may be yet another of those endless passages,' he warned. 'You mustn't be too disappointed if we don't find anything today, Rosanna.'

When she was nearing the bottom step, her foot slipped. Justin put out his arm to steady her, holding her against him for a moment. Her heart beat furiously as she looked into his eyes. There was a concern and tenderness that she had not seen before. 'Oh, I do not think I shall be too disappointed,' she murmured. 'Though it would be wonderful if we could find Lady Caroline's treasure at last . . .'

CHAPTER NINE

THE passage had led to the cellars, as Justin had predicted, but Rosanna was not too disappointed. The discovery of yet another passage had convinced her that there might be many more as yet undiscovered. She was quite sure in her own mind that the jewels were still where the unfortunate Lady Caroline had hidden them, just waiting to be found.

For herself, she was not over concerned about the treasure, but she knew it could mean an end to Justin's worries at the mine. Especially if he were to find them, for then he would feel that he was entitled to use the money for his business. The fact that they had spent the day exploring together, sharing a pleasant companionship, was enough for Rosanna. Her husband had kissed her lingeringly before he left for the mine that morning, and she was feeling particularly happy as she sat at her sewing in the little parlour. She looked up inquiringly as Sally came in.

'There's a lady to see you,' Sally said with a look of disapproval. 'She wouldn't give her name. I said I'd see if you were in.'

Rosanna was surprised. 'I wasn't expecting anyone. What is she like?'

'She speaks like a lady, but I doubt she was born one.'

'And you don't like her?' Rosanna laughed. Her servants were always trying to protect her. 'I think I had better see her. She did ask for me particularly?'

'Yes, Mrs Sawle.'

'Then you had better show her in.'

Rosanna put away her work-basket and stood up, feeling glad to be wearing a decent gown. She was even more glad when Anne Cornwallis was shown into the room, and she gave a little gasp of surprise.

'Lady Cornwallis, this is an unexpected pleasure. I—I'm afraid Justin isn't here at the moment.'

'I came to see you, Mrs Sawle. I did not give your maid my name in case you refused to see me.' Anne held a lace kerchief to the corner of her eye. 'Justin and I were...friends...once, and that is why I have come to warn you.'

'To warn me?' Rosanna stared at her. 'I fear I do not understand you, madam.'

'My husband is planning a terrible revenge. He—He thinks I have a lover, and he believes the man to be your husband. It isn't true—but there is someone else.'

'Then why should Lord Cornwallis believe Justin is your lover?'

'I have allowed him to think it. Oh, I know it was wrong, but I did not want him to guess the truth.'

'Why are you telling me all this?'

'Because I overheard my husband talking to someone.' Anne dabbed at her eyes again. 'I had no idea he could be so vindictive. He has been paying someone to cause trouble for Justin at the mine.'

'I had wondered if it might be your husband, ever since that incident at the inn,' Rosanna said, frowning. 'Do you know who he has employed in this?'

'No. I knew none of it until I heard him telling someone that he wanted to ruin Justin.'

'I'm sure my husband will be very grateful to know of this.'

'I should not have taken the risk of coming here if it were only the mine. They are planning something much worse.' She frowned. 'I could not hear everything, for they lowered their voices, but I do not think it was to do with the mine. Cornwallis seemed delighted at something he was told. He said it would be the end of Justin.'

'You have no idea of what they were planning?'

'No. One of the maids came into the hall, and I had to move away from the door at a crucial moment.'

'And when did all this take place?'

'Three days ago. I should have come sooner, but Cornwallis has been watching me like a hawk. I couldn't get away until he went into Truro this morning.'

'Justin has been to Truro several times recently.' Rosanna remembered that the last time had been four days earlier, the day after they had explored the secret passage. She had noticed that Justin had seemed very pleased with himself since then. 'Do you know what's going on?'

'No... Unless...' Anne screwed up her mouth. 'Someone told me that he had seen Justin with a smuggler, but I can't believe it.'

'Justin involved with smugglers—that's impossible!'

'Well, perhaps R—...he...said it only to tease me. He's a little jealous that I once cared for... Oh, I should not have said that!'

'It does not matter now. I'm grateful to you for coming.' Rosanna remembered her manners. 'Will you stay for tea?'

'No, I must not. I must get back before Cornwallis. You have no idea of the money I have to pay my coachman to keep my secrets! If Cornwallis knew I'd been here, he would kill me!'

'We must hope he does not find out.'

Looking at Anne's face, Rosanna realised that she was genuinely frightened of her husband. It could not be pleasant being married to such a man. Recalling the way Cornwallis had spoken to his wife that day at the inn, she pitied her. Perhaps it explained why she felt the need for a lover.

'I must go.' Anne got to her feet, and then hesitated. 'If I ever gave you cause to think...to doubt Justin, please forgive me. He never looked at me once he had met you.'

'There is nothing to forgive, madam. I love my husband...and he loves me.'

'How fortunate you are to be married to the man you love.' Anne sighed and dabbed at her eyes. 'Sometimes

I feel like running away...' She turned aside. 'I am being foolish. It would be no use. Cornwallis would fetch me back.'

'It was kind of you to come. At least, now, Justin will know who his enemy is.'

She walked to the door with her visitor, waiting until she was safely installed in her carriage. Then went to the west wing, summoning Benjamin.

'I want you to saddle my horse,' she said. 'I have to find Justin at once.'

Benjamin gave her an odd look. 'Shall I come with you?' he asked. 'You'll hardly ride there and back before dusk.'

'No...' Rosanna hesitated. 'If he should return before I do, tell him that he must do nothing foolish. He is in terrible danger...'

Rosanna's nerves were stretched tautly as she mounted her horse and set out across the moors. She was remembering that long, lingering kiss Justin had given her that morning. He had had an odd look on his face as he said goodbye, almost as though he wondered if he would ever hold her in his arms again. Oh, why had she not guessed that there was something wrong? It was Justin's foolish, foolish pride! He would never have become involved with the smugglers if he had not been in desperate need of money for the mine.

Urging her horse to a gallop, Rosanna whispered a prayer. Three days had passed since Anne Cornwallis had overheard her husband plotting against Justin, and she only hoped that the warning would come in time.

Emily looked at her husband angrily. She could scarcely believe what he had just told her.

'How could you let her go off on a wild-goose chase like that?' she demanded. 'And her in a delicate condition, if I'm not much mistaken!'

Benjamin stared at her sheepishly. 'I didn't know what to do, and that's a fact. She wouldn't let me go with her, and I promised the master I wouldn't tell her what was going on.'

Emily threw down her cooking-spoon in disgust. 'Men! You're all the same. I never took you for a fool, Benjamin, and that's a fact, but that's just what you are. It's not safe for the mistress to be out alone on the moors with all this trouble at the mine. I'd not like to be in your shoes if anything happens! You'd better go after her.'

'But what if she was right? What if the master is in danger?' Benjamin insisted. 'You know what's going on, don't you?'

'Ay, I know. I thought him a fool! Dabbling with the "gentlemen" always brings trouble.' Emily shook her head at him. 'The master can look after himself. You get after our Miss Rosanna—and don't you dare come back without her!'

It was a little misty over the sea. All the better for their purpose, Justin thought. They had signalled the French ship to come in as soon as dusk began to fall. She was riding at anchor just beyond a curve of dangerous rocks. Already the first boats had gone out to bring in the precious cargo of silks, laces, tobacco and brandy. It was no wonder Brendon wanted a new, safer hiding-place for his goods! This was no ordinary cargo. Most of the local cutters brought in a few barrels at a time, but this was a French merchantman loaded down with every luxury you could imagine. It must be worth a fortune! Watching the first boats begin to pull back toward the shore, he shivered, and blew on his hands. It was cold tonight. Autumn had set in early. He walked to the water's edge, joining the other men who were waiting to help to unload the contraband. There were rich pickings to be had tonight, and he knew every other man on the beach. Some were from his own mine, but they studiously ignored him. It was dangerous for one 'gentleman' to acknowledge another.

Justin felt guilt because the miners had been forced to risk their lives on this beach. He knew that some of them were hardly earning enough to feed their families because of all the setbacks below ground. Yet it was not only at Wheal Margaret that things were bad. Food prices were high and copper prices were low. It was a bad combination. Somehow he had to hold on until the tide turned for them all.

Surveying the scene, Justin noted that the Tregear brothers were missing. They were not popular with the other local men, and usually worked alone. Even the 'gentlemen' did not welcome murderers. Especially a man who had killed in cold blood. It was strange that Rosanna had seen Richard talking to Nick Tregear that day. Was it possible that the two of them were behind the accidents at the mine? Justin frowned. When this was all over, it might be a good idea to have a word with his cousin.

Rosanna reined in as she saw the men crowded in front of the mine house. She could hear voices raised in anger, and it was obvious that a demonstration of some kind was going on. Urging her horse slowly forward, she forced the men to part and let her through.

Seth was standing on the steps outside the house. Seeing her, he came to help her down, almost pushing her inside the house in his anxiety. 'What are you doing here?' he demanded. 'You shouldn't have come here alone. The men are in a dangerous mood. Surely Justin told you they were threatening to strike?'

'Where is he? I have to speak to him at once.'

'He isn't here,' Seth told her. 'He left three hours ago.'

'He isn't at home, and I didn't pass him on the way.' She grabbed his arm. 'Please tell me where he is, Seth? I have to warn him...'

'Warn him of what?' Seth stared at her hard. 'What has happened? I told him it wasn't worth the risk....'

'He's with the "gentlemen", isn't he?' Rosanna looked at him in horror. 'Oh, Seth, I'm so frightened! He has an enemy...Lord Cornwallis has been plotting against him. He was behind all the accidents at the mine—and now I think he means to kill him!'

'Then we'll have to warn him...' Seth began, breaking off as the door was thrown open. 'What...' He drew a sigh of relief as he saw who it was. 'Benjamin—you're just the man we need!'

'You must've ridden like the wind,' Benjamin said, looking at Rosanna. 'Emily made me come. She was worried about you.'

'I'm perfectly capable of looking after myself,' she replied sharply. 'You know where Justin is, don't you?'

Benjamin hesitated, looking at Seth. He nodded his agreement. 'You can't hide it from her—and one of us has to warn Justin that there may be trouble at the cove.'

'I'll go,' Benjamin said. 'If there's trouble, he may need me. You ride back with Mrs Sawle.'

'I can manage alone...' Rosanna began, but Seth shook his head.

'I don't anticipate more trouble with the men tonight. I'd just about managed to calm them down when you arrived, but Becky would never forgive me if I let you go home alone.'

'Oh, very well.' Rosanna turned to Benjamin. 'What are you waiting for? You have to warn Justin.'

Benjamin nodded grimly. 'I'll do my best, but I shall be too late to stop it. The drop was to take place at dusk. The ship will be unloading before I can get there.'

Justin glanced over his shoulder as the man came to stand beside him.

'It will soon be over,' Brendon said. 'Your five hundred guineas is as good as in your pocket. A bale of silk for your wife, too, if you want it.'

'You're in a generous mood tonight.'

'This has taken me over a year to set up. I had to have somewhere safe to store it. I plan to send it on when the price is...'

The roar of a cannon tore through the still night, halting him in mid-sentence. His face paled as he looked seaward. Through the mist, it was just possible to see a ship sailing fast towards the French vessel.

'My God, it's a Revenue-cutter!' Justin cried. 'How the hell did they get wind of this?'

'Someone has betrayed us,' Brendon said, his face marred with fury. 'Get away, sir! Get out of this while you can.'

'What of you and the others? The men in the boats…'

'There's nothing we can do for them; they're doomed, whatever they decide to do.'

The French ship was already hauling in the anchor in a frantic attempt to put to sea before the cutter could put a shot through her side. The men in the rowing-boats were pulling strongly for the shore, desperately trying to get away from the oncoming ship. Their only chance, it seemed, was to beach the boats and make a run for it. Now Justin could see a second Revenue-cutter further out in the bay, its obvious intention to cut off the Frenchman's escape. His attention caught by the furious activity at sea, he was unaware of what was happening behind him until he heard the shot. Spinning round, he saw soldiers pouring down the cliff-face and on to the beach. Brendon cursed and fled. Everywhere he looked, Justin witnessed panic as the smugglers tried to escape, deserting their comrades in the boats. It was every man for himself, now!

As Rosanna dismounted, she saw Emily waiting for her on the front steps. Fearing the worst, she hurried towards her. 'Is Justin here?' she cried. 'What has happened?'

'No, he's not here,' Emily said in a scolding tone. 'Thank God, you're back safely! I was that worried about you when Benjamin told me you'd ridden off alone—and you in your condition!'

Rosanna felt her cheeks growing pink as she followed Emily into the house. 'How did you guess?' she asked. 'I'm not really sure myself.'

Emily smiled, and shook her head. 'My eldest sister has five children, my younger sister three, so I know the signs by now. If you're not carrying a child, I'll be very surprised.'

'Well, I had begun to think I might be,' Rosanna said. 'I haven't said anything to Justin yet because...' She remembered the reason for her wild ride and broke off, her face anxious. 'I'm so worried, Emily. I know something is wrong.'

'You can't know that, lass. Why should anything go wrong?

Rosanna shook her head. 'I can feel it. I know Justin is in trouble.'

Emily looked at her anxious face. 'Well, there's no sense in telling you not to worry. Come on into the kitchen, and we'll have a cup of tea.'

Realising there was nothing he could do to help the men in the boats, Justin sprinted towards a spur of outlying rock. It was a dangerous climb this way, but the best chance of avoiding capture. Already there was desperate fighting on the beach. He could hear screaming, and he was afraid that people had been killed or wounded. The rock-face was steep and jagged. He cut his hands on the sharp surfaces as he sought for holds. What a fool he had been to get involved! It was a bad business, and he should have stayed well clear.

The climb was hard and dangerous. Twice his foot slipped, and he only just managed to hang on. He cursed beneath his breath, wondering what madness had driven him to risk everything for a few hundred pounds. He was a damned fool! He thought of Rosanna waiting for him at home, and the pain it would cause her if he were killed. She would never understand that he had done it for her. A bird, startled by his approach, flew out, making him jump. He leaned against the sheer rock-face to catch his breath, and then the sound of voices from somewhere just above reached his ears. Alerted to danger, he moved cautiously. Were there more soldiers at the top? Reaching the narrow plateau, he flung himself to the ground, crawling towards a hollow that would hide him while he took stock of his bearings. It was fortunate that he knew the cove so well.

Someone was coming towards him. Ducking his head, Justin hardly dared to breathe as they stood on a hummock just above him. There were two of them, so close that he could hear their voices plainly.

'So the information was right.'

Justin stiffened as he recognised the voice. Surely it couldn't be he! He lay tensely as the man went on, 'If it's all as Tregear promised, we'll have a good haul, eh, Cornwallis?'

'Nick Tregear is a frightened man. I promised I'd see him hang if he didn't do as I told him. You know what I expect from this—I want your cousin taken alive. He's to be tried and hanged for his part in this. You can have what you want of the rest. Money doesn't interest me. It's revenge I want.'

'You're lucky you don't have a miser of a father who refuses to pay your gambling debts! I'm sick of his lectures. The sooner he's in his grave, the happier I shall be.'

'Why don't you give him a helping hand?' Cornwallis laughed, then peered at something moving in the grass a short distance away. 'What's that—over there?

Justin got to his feet as he heard the shout of alarm. He had no choice now but to make a run for it. If he could reach his horse, which he had taken the precaution of hiding in a small disused barn, he might have a chance. In any case, he would rather take a ball in the back than be caught like a rat in a trap.

'My God! I think it's him. Don't let him get away, Richard! He must have heard everything.'

Justin heard the shouting behind him, and then a pistol-shot. The ball whistled past him harmlessly, for he was almost out of range. He was going to make it ... The second ball caught him on the run, lodging high in his shoulder. The impact sent him stumbling to his knees;

for a moment, the pain took his breath away. He gritted his teeth, rose to his feet and staggered on for a few steps, knowing that he was done for. He could never get to his horse now. The faintness was washing over him. He could scarcely see. As he tottered unsteadily on, refusing to give in, a shadow came swiftly from the darkness.

'It's me, sir,' a voice he dimly recognised called to him softly. 'I've got you Captain, don't worry.'

The blackness was closing in as he felt a strong arm catch him, and then he knew no more. Mercifully, he felt no pain as he was hoisted over Benjamin's broad shoulder and carried swiftly away from danger.

Her worst fears had been confirmed. As Rosanna heard the voices in the hall, she knew that Justin had been hurt. Hurrying into the front parlour, she was in time to see her faithful servant carry in the unconscious body of her husband.

'Is he badly hurt?' she asked, her heart hammering. 'We had better take him up to my room.'

'He has taken a ball in the shoulder, but he's still alive,' Benjamin reassured her. 'Don't you think it would be safer to hide him in the secret room? They may come looking for him here. If the trap was set to catch him, they won't give up so easily.'

Rosanna hesitated, hating the thought of Justin lying wounded in the small, dark room they had discovered in the west wing. Yet it might be the safest way. As Benjamin told her of the terrible scenes on the beach, she realised that she must do anything to save her husband from arrest and possible imprisonment.

'You are right,' she said. 'Lay him on the sofa while we make up a bed in the concealed room.'

'I'll see to that,' Emily said. 'You stay with him, though I doubt he'll come to himself just yet. We'll have to stanch the wound for the time being. If there's to be a search of the house, it will be soon. As soon as they realise he isn't among the dead or wounded.'

The whole household had been roused, and everyone was eager to help. A mattress was fetched from one of the spare bedrooms and a bed hastily prepared in the secret room. Only chance had revealed its presence to the men repairing the west wing, and it was unlikely that any excisemen would discover it.

While they were binding his wound, Justin regained consciousness for a few seconds. He became restless, trying to rise from the sofa, and muttering words that no one could understand.

'There's nothing to worry about, my love.' Rosanna soothed his brow. 'We're going to hide you for a while, and then, when it's safe, we'll see to your shoulder.'

It was doubtful if he heard her. He lost consciousness again as Benjamin carried him to the hiding-place they had hurriedly prepared.

'You must go to bed now,' Emily said, once he was settled and all traces of stained cloths had been removed from the parlour. 'No arguments, Rosanna. If you are up and dressed, it will seem suspicious.'

'I can't leave him. He might wake or cry out...'

'I'll stay with him,' Rob offered. 'They'll expect to see you and the others, but I'm a cripple as far as anyone outside this house is concerned. They'll not bother to ask where I am.'

Rosanna had no wish to leave her husband, but a cry from Sally gave the alarm. She had been watching from an upstairs window, and now came rushing down the stairs.

'There's three riders come into the courtyard!'

It was past ten by the longcase clock in the hall, Rosanna noticed as she fled upstairs to her room. Emily would delay opening the front door for as long as possible, but already someone was banging loudly, demanding admittance. She had never undressed so quickly. Kicking her discarded gown under the bed, she slipped between the sheets without a nightgown. Her heart was thudding as she lay down, feigning sleep. Emily had coached the others in what to say. There was nothing to worry about, so why was she trembling?

The knocking had ceased now. Emily must have let them in. How long before they came upstairs? She imagined the scene, picturing her housekeeper's angry protests at being so rudely woken. Would the soldiers believe her? 'We keep country hours at Rathmoor,' she would be saying. 'The whole household is abed and asleep.'

Rosanna's skin crawled with tension as the seconds ticked by. What was happening? What was going on? Then she heard voices and the sound of heavy, booted feet in the hall. Everything was working out as Emily had predicted. She heard her friend protesting shrilly, 'I told you you can't go in there! Mrs Sawle is asleep, and the master's been gone to town these two days past.'

The door of the bedroom was suddenly flung open, and a young man wearing the scarlet-coated uniform of a captain in the Dragoons entered, closely followed by a loudly protesting Emily. Rosanna counted to five, then screamed and sat up, clutching the covers to her naked breast.

'Oh, don't be frightened, ma'am,' Emily cried, pushing past the startled soldier. 'I told him you were in bed...'

'But...I don't understand...' Rosanna let the cover slip briefly, to reveal a tantalising glimpse of one breast. 'Why are you in my room, sir? How dare you invade my privacy like this?'

A deep brick-red flush had swept up the young officer's neck and into his cheeks. He licked his lips nervously, trying not to look at her naked shoulders or imagine the delicate curves he had briefly glimpsed.

'I—I beg your pardon, ma'am,' he said, backing towards the door. 'I—I thought your husband might be with you. He—He escaped when we rounded up a gang of smugglers this evening.'

'Impossible!' Rosanna looked at him haughtily. 'My husband is on his way to London. If you will wait downstairs, I shall dress and come down to you. There has obviously been a terrible mistake.'

'Yes. Yes, of course.' He retreated hastily, looking flustered.

As the door closed, Rosanna allowed herself a little smile. So far, everything was going according to plan. Emily had been right. Finding her in bed had put the officer at a disadvantage, and letting the sheet slip had been a master stroke.

She dressed carefully, taking her time and making certain that every hair was in place before going down. It would do that impulsive young man no harm to be kept waiting. She had never looked more regal than when she swept into the hall, to find the officer and his subordinates restlessly pacing the floor. Her eyes moved over them scornfully.

'Now, sir, first you will tell me your name—and then you will kindly explain this ridiculous story of my husband being involved with smugglers.'

'Captain Harley of the royal Dragoons, on assignment to the Revenue.' He quailed before her flashing eyes. 'I have been given information which leads me to believe that Captain Sawle was the leader of a desperate gang of smugglers. It is a very serious charge, ma'am. Several of my officers were wounded, and two local men were killed.'

'That is indeed a serious business,' Rosanna said. 'But why should you imagine that my husband was involved? Captain Sawle fought for his country under the Duke of Wellington. He was wounded, and commended for his bravery by the Duke. He is also a respectable mineowner. Why should he become embroiled in smuggling?'

Captain Harley ran a finger round the collar of his jacket, which suddenly felt tight. 'We were given information...'

'By whom? I demand that you tell me!'

'It—It was one of the smugglers.'

'Indeed! And you believed the word of a man like that? You would take the word of a criminal rather than mine—and my servants? You may question any member of my household.'

'I already have.' He was distinctly uncomfortable now. The information had come from a dubious source, and he believed there was malice behind it. 'Your servants all confirm that their master set out for town two days ago. Perhaps I owe you an apology.'

'You most certainly do! However, you are only doing your duty. You have come to search the house, and I shall not hinder you.'

'Th—That will not be necessary, Mrs Sawle.'

'Indeed it *is* necessary. I insist that you search the house now. Your men will begin in the cellars, so that they can see for themselves that we are hiding no contraband. You will accompany me on a tour of the house.' She held up her hand as he would have spoken. 'Benjamin, please show these gentlemen the cellars and the outhouses—and the barns. Don't forget the barns.'

As Benjamin led the two soldiers away, she turned to their officer. 'If you will follow me, sir. Please carry that candelabrum. We shall need plenty of light. They are repairing the walls, and you must watch where you step.'

'This isn't necessary, ma'am. I'm prepared to accept your word.'

'That is not sufficient.' Rosanna's eyes flashed in the candlelight. 'My husband has been slandered. When you leave here, you will be able to report that a thorough search was made and nothing found to incriminate him.'

'As you wish.' He inclined his head, looking uncomfortable.

The tour of the west wing was made in silence. Rosanna led the way, opening every cupboard door and every coffer where a man might possibly be hiding. She insisted that he look under the beds and up the chimneys. Her heart beat very fast when they passed the panelling that concealed the room where Justin was lying. She held her breath in case he should cry out, but there was not a sound. Because of all the building, there was a lot of dust and dirt, and by the time they returned to the main hall, Captain Harley's uniform, hair and face were all streaked with dirt.

Rosanna did not spare him. A search was conducted throughout the house and the attics. It was more than an hour before she finally allowed him to leave. He went with abject apologies, promising to make a full report and assuring her that she would not be disturbed again.

'And that's the last we shall see of that young man,' Emily said, as she bolted the door behind him. 'I almost feel sorry for the lad!'

Rosanna smiled slightly. 'Captain Harley certainly won't return in a hurry, but the men who informed against Justin won't give up so easily. We must be prepared for a surprise visit at any time. Seth will have to be warned.' Her face took on an anxious look. 'That ball has to come out of Justin's shoulder, but we daren't risk sending for a doctor.'

'You leave that to me,' Benjamin said, coming into the room. 'Emily, I want the kitchen table scrubbed and gallons of boiling water.'

Rosanna was surprised to see the normally gentle giant taking charge. 'Are you sure you can do it? He has lost so much blood.'

'Not so much as you might think.' He gave her a reassuring smile. 'The Captain is awake now, and he knows what must be done. I cared for your grandfather for many years. Isolated as we are, we've learned to cope with broken limbs and cut fingers—and gunshot wounds. It won't be the first time I've taken a ball out of a man's shoulder. You can help Emily to get things ready.'

She accepted his suggestion, knowing it would ease her tension. Yet even as they scrubbed the wooden table, boiled pans of water and tore one of the best linen sheets into strips, she was worrying about her husband. Supposing he were to die? He had lost so much blood, and there was always the possibility of a fever... Her throat caught with emotion as they carried Justin into the kitchen. He was conscious and clearly in pain, but he smiled at her as she went to him.

'Go away now,' he murmured. 'Leave it to Benjamin and Emily. I don't want you here for the moment.'

'Oh, Justin,' she protested, but acquiesced as she saw his look. The operation would have to be carried out without the benefit of laudanum, and she knew he did not want her to see him in agony. 'As you wish, my dearest,' she whispered, her throat closing.

Sally followed her into the long parlour, while Rob stayed with the others. Rosanna knew that it might be necessary to hold Justin down when the knife cut into his flesh. She could hardly bear the thought of what he must suffer. It was in her eyes as the two women sat down, their faces white and strained.

'They'll see to it,' Sally said. 'The master's a strong man. He'll pull through.'

Rosanna twisted her hands nervously in her lap, trying not to think about the agony Justin must even now be enduring. 'I couldn't bear it if he died,' she whispered, bowing her head as the sobs began to shake her body. 'I love him so much...'

Sally knelt beside her, putting an arm round her shoulders. 'I know how you feel. I thought I'd die of grief the night they brought Rob back from the mine with his legs crushed. They said he might die of the shock—and they were sure he would never walk again. The master was good to us; then you brought us here, and Rob had a reason to get on his feet again. He'll never be the man he was; he can't work for more than an hour or so at a time, and there's nights he could weep from the pain. But he survived, and so will your man. They're both as proud and stubborn as they come.'

'Oh, Sally...' Rosanna smiled through her tears.

They clung together, crying and comforting each other. It was a long time before Emily came in. A long, terrible night that left everyone pale and exhausted, but at last it was over.

'It's done,' Emily said, smiling despite her own weariness. 'The master's in his own bed. You can go up.'

'Is he conscious?' Rosanna asked, getting to her feet.

'Ay—though I doubt you'll get much sense out of him. Benjamin made him drink that much brandy. He was singing and cursing loud enough to waken the dead by the end of it. If the soldiers had come now, they'd have heard him right enough!'

Rosanna nodded, her throat tight. 'We must count our blessings.' She caught back a sob. 'Thank you. Thank you all for everything you've done tonight. I don't know how I would have managed without you. I love you all...' She ran from the room before the tears could fall.

Hurrying upstairs, she struggled to bring her emotions under control. Justin must not see how upset she was. He was lying with his eyes closed when she entered the room. She walked softly towards the bed, not wanting to disturb him if he was sleeping, but he opened his eyes as she bent over him.

'Damned fool,' he muttered thickly. 'Wanted to... Wanted to tell you...'

She leaned over him, smoothing the damp hair back from his forehead. His skin looked waxen in the candle-light, and she felt a frisson of fear along her spine. He was not out of danger yet. He had lost a great deal of blood, no matter what Benjamin said, and there was always the risk of infection.

She felt his hand moving feebly towards hers and took it in her own. 'What is it, my darling? There's nothing to worry about. You're safe now. Everything will be better soon.'

'Don't pamper me, Rosanna!' The words came out clearly with a flash of his old fire. 'Too much damned brandy... Can't think... Danger... Have to warn him...'

'It's all over now. There's no more danger.'

Justin's head moved negatively on the pillow. 'Richard...' he muttered. 'Planning to kill...'

His voice slurred the last words into each other and she could not understand him. 'Yes, my darling,' she whispered, stroking his hair. 'We'll warn him. Go to sleep now.'

He gave a deep sigh as the fight became too much, and his eyes closed. Rosanna sat by his side, watching until she was sure that his sleep was natural. Then she retired to the sofa at the foot of the bed, curling up with a cushion under her head. She would be near at hand if he should wake and cry out for her in the night. All she could do for now was to pray that he would wake refreshed and free of fever.

As her eyes began to grow heavy, she wondered what his muddled words had meant. Why was he worried about Richard? Did he imagine that his cousin was mixed up in the plot against him? She wished she had been able to tell him that his enemy had been Lord Cornwallis! Sighing, she gave up the struggle, drifting into sleep.

Anne Cornwallis had been cutting flowers in her garden when she saw the man coming down the path. Her heart quickened its beat, and she glanced round guiltily before going to meet him. 'Richard,' she said, the excitement bringing a glow to her eyes. 'You shouldn't have come. Oh, I'm glad to see you, of course, but Cornwallis is at home.'

'Why are you so scared of him?' Richard Mountjoy's mouth curled in a sneer. 'I could break his skinny neck if I'd a mind to it.'

'You must not say such things!' She looked at him, faintly alarmed. Although he had been her lover for over a year, she was still unsure of him. He had such strange moods. If he had not been a skilled lover, she would have found him less than amusing. She had taken him up because he was Justin's cousin, but had soon discovered that he was nothing like the younger man. Sometimes he was almost as boring as Cornwallis!

Richard laughed, reaching out to pull her against him so that she dropped her basket. His kiss was savage, bruising her lips. She gave a cry of protest and thrust him away, her eyes reproachful as she looked up at him.

'Why did you do that? You know I do not appreciate brutality.'

'I really do not care what you like any more, Anne. You have served your purpose. I came here to say goodbye. I am going away.'

'What do you mean?' Her eyes narrowed in anger. 'How dare you treat me like this?'

'Like a whore?' Richard's scorn had the sting of a whiplash. 'Isn't that exactly what you are? A very generous, willing whore, my dear Anne?'

Her cheeks flamed. 'You are insulting, sir! If my husband knew of our affair...'

'But he doesn't!' He laughed triumphantly. 'You let him believe Justin was your lover. The old fool has spent a fortune trying to ruin my beloved cousin. He was wasting his time. I told him so, but he wouldn't listen. He had to do it his way. He even bungled the affair last night by blabbing to the Revenue men. We should have let Brendon's men land the cargo and take it to Rathmoor, so that we could have caught them red-handed. But your husband brought in the Revenue, and Justin got away. They searched his house but couldn't find him, and now he's in the clear.'

The colour drained from her face as she looked at him; she felt sick as she realised that he had never cared for her at all. He had used her and her husband as a means of hurting his cousin. He had probably taken her as his mistress only because he thought Justin still wanted her.

'So Justin was cleverer than you both,' she said, beginning to laugh. 'My poor Richard, after all your scheming and plotting! I'm so pleased. He's worth two of you any day—in bed and out of it. You thought you could take his place, but you could never match him.'

'You bitch! I ought to break your neck.'

Anne was suddenly afraid as she saw the murderous look in his eyes. He was a cold, evil man. Her hands went to her throat and she gave a cry of fear. 'Don't you dare to touch me! Lay one finger on me, Richard, and I shall tell Cornwallis that you have been my lover for a year.'

'Do you imagine that I care what you tell that old fool?' Richard laughed nastily. 'This is goodbye, Anne—but perhaps I shall have you one more time.'

As he reached out, she screamed loudly, backing away. In that same moment something caught the corner of her eye, and then she saw a man move from behind a large bush. She gasped with fright as she saw the fury in her husband's face, but then she realised that it was directed at Richard.

'You insolent dog!' Cornwallis yelled, charging at the younger man, his cane held aloft. 'So I'm an old fool, am I? Well, I can still teach you a lesson, sir!' He struck at Richard as he spoke, catching him on his face and the side of his head.

Richard gave a snarl of rage, grabbing the stick and trying to wrest it from its owner. 'Stop it, you buffoon,' he muttered. 'Don't you know she'll put a permanent pair of horns on you? She's not worth the trouble.'

'You are a swine, sir!' Cornwallis shouted, beside himself with anger, his cheeks mottled with a strange purple colour. 'No man insults my lady and lives to gloat over it! I'll kill you!'

The cane snapped in Richard's hand, cutting him across the palm. He cursed, and threw the useless tip away. Seeing his moment, Cornwallis raised his arm again, intending to bring it down on Richard's face, but the blow never fell. He began to cough and splutter, his eyes bulging in sudden fear as he fought for breath. A strangled cry left his lips and a crimson froth began to fill his mouth, choking him. The broken stick slipped from his fingers as he fell, face down.

'Cornwallis!' Anne screamed, falling on her knees beside him. Tears were streaming down her face. She had never loved him, but his last words had shown her clearly that he had loved her in spite of everything. 'Cornwallis, speak to me!' She rolled him over on to his back, staring in horror as the colour drained out of his cheeks and his eyes glazed. 'Oh no! He's dead! *He's dead!*.' The last words came out in a hysterical scream

as she looked up. 'You killed him. *Murderer!*
MURDERER!'

'I never laid a finger on him.' Richard's face was
ashen. 'You saw what happened. He came at me. He
struck me. I didn't touch him.'

'Murderer!' She screamed again and again. 'Help!
Someone help me! Murder! *Murder!*'

Richard backed away from her, fear flickering in his
eyes. 'I didn't touch him, Anne. You know it!'

Her eyes narrowed, glittering with hatred. 'I may know
it, but no one else does. You'll hang for murder,
Richard.' She saw some of her husband's servants
running towards them, and began to scream again.
'Murder! He killed Cornwallis! He killed my husband…'

Richard stared at her in horror, backing as she began
to laugh and scream hysterically. 'You won't get away
with this,' he hissed. Then he began to walk swiftly away,
his pace increasing as he heard the alarmed cries of her
servants. All at once, he started to run.

CHAPTER TEN

THERE was only one small candle burning on the table beside the bed. Justin had been resting peacefully for a while, and Rosanna had her eyes closed. She opened them as someone came in.

'How is he?' Emily whispered. 'He seems a little quieter now.'

'Yes. I think perhaps he is,' Rosanna replied. 'Thank God for it.'

'I'm sorry to disturb you,' Emily said. 'But we've just heard some news...'

Rosanna realised that it must be important, so she followed her from the room. 'What is it, Emily?'

'I'm not sure whether... But Benjamin thought you should know.'

'You'd better tell me. Has someone discovered that Justin is ill?'

'No...' Emily took a deep breath. 'It's about his cousin Richard—and Lord Cornwallis.'

'Are they causing trouble at the mine?'

'Lord Cornwallis is dead. They say it was Richard Mountjoy who killed him.'

'Oh no!' Rosanna cried. 'Has Richard been arrested?'

'No. He seems to have disappeared. The talk is that he's gone abroad.'

'I do hope so,' Rosanna said. 'Justin's uncle will be so distressed.'

'Yes, well, we thought you should know,' Emily said. 'And Seth Miller was over an hour or so ago. He asked me to let you know that things seem to have quietened down at the mine for the time being.'

'Thank you.' Rosanna sighed. 'We have enough problems without a strike just at the moment. I'm going back to Justin now.'

'Why don't you rest for a while? Let me sit with him.'

'Thank you, but no—not until I know the fever has gone.' Rosanna smiled at her. 'I've managed to rest for a few hours. I believe the tide is turning.'

She turned away and went back into the room. Justin had lain in a fever since they brought him to his own room over a week ago. For the first few days she had been terrified he would die, but his fits had begun to lessen and he had been resting for the best part of the afternoon. As she approached the bed, he opened his eyes, staring at her blankly for a moment, then he smiled.

'Rosanna?' he whispered. 'My throat is dry.'

'I'll bring you a glass of water.' She went to the wash-stand in the corner, pouring from the china jug. 'Here you are, my dearest.'

Justin gulped several mouthfuls, then fell back against the pillow. 'How long have I been here?'

'Eight days. You've been in a fever.'

'A fever?' He blinked at her as he struggled to remember. 'Ah, yes, Benjamin brought me home . . . I was wounded . . .'

'Don't worry about it yet. It will all come back when you're feeling better.'

He frowned, trying to recall something. 'Did you hide me in the secret room while the soldiers searched?'

'Yes. They made a search of the house and went away. We thought they might come back, but they haven't returned yet.'

'I shouldn't have brought all this trouble on you. Benjamin should have left me to die!'

'How dare you say that?' Anger flared in her. 'How dare you wallow in self-pity, you stubborn, foolish man! Don't you know by now that you mean the world to me?'

Justin smiled, reaching for her hand on the coverlet.
'Forgive me. I know I'm an awkward patient.'

'Oh, Justin.' She reached down to brush her lips over
his. 'I'm so glad you are better. Don't worry about anything for the moment. Go back to sleep, my love.
Nothing matters except that you should get well.'

'I don't deserve that you should care,' he murmured,
but his eyelids were growing heavy, and Rosanna smiled
as he drifted into sleep. It was a natural, peaceful sleep
and she whispered a prayer of gratitude. He would soon
recover his strength now that the fever had waned.

It was three days later that Rosanna saw a definite im-
provement in her husband's health. As she opened the
door, he was sitting up in bed, waiting for her.

'How are you feeling?' she asked as she set the tray
down beside the bed. She leaned across to plump up a
pillow and found herself caught and held. Justin pulled
her down across his body, imprisoning her as he took
possession of her lips. She did not resist, her hands
moving up into his thick, dark hair as she gave herself
up to the sweet sensation flooding through her. 'Obviously you are very much better!'

'I've been better for days, woman, but how much
longer do you intend to keep me prisoner? If I stay in
this room another day, I shall go mad!'

She shook her head, pretending to scold. 'You are the
most ungrateful man I've ever met! We've all been
waiting on you hand and foot. Benjamin saved your
life—and I told thumping lies so that your reputation
would be as spotless as ever, and all you do is complain!
You have to stay out of sight for as long as it would take
you to ride to London and back. If anyone outside this
house guesses you were involved with the smuggling, it
will ruin everything.'

'I know. Do you think I don't realise what a damned
fool I was? I risked everything for the sake of a few
hundred guineas.'

'Yes, and without a word to me! Can you imagine how I felt when I discovered what was going on? Sometimes I could shake you!'

A glint of humour showed in his eyes. 'I adore you when you're angry! You look so—so queenly. But you're right. I've realised I was wrong to involve all of you in this. You took so many risks for me.'

'Of course we did. We all care about you.'

'Please forgive me,' he said with unusual meekness. 'I know it was madness, and I feel so stupid for having caused so much trouble.'

'Oh, Justin,' Rosanna sat on the edge of the bed, smiling down at him, 'I don't care how impatient you are. I was teasing just now. I do love you. All that matters to me is that you are alive. Don't you understand that, my darling?'

'I'm beginning to,' he replied with a rueful smile. 'But that makes it even more important . . . I thought the smuggling would be an easy way of getting money for the mine.' He played with her hand as it lay beside his on the silk covers. 'We're so near a break-through, Rosanna. I suppose I'll have to take a partner in, but I'm reluctant. When it comes, that money is for you. Why should I give away half of what we've struggled for for so long? I want to buy you all the things you should have had. I want to hang diamonds round your throat and buy you pretty clothes. I'd like to snatch the moon from the sky and lay it at your feet.'

Tears stung her throat. 'All I've ever wanted was your love. I thought at the start that I was marrying you to save Rathmoor, but it was never truly that. I was attracted to you the first moment we met. Even though I was too proud and stubborn to admit it.'

'You've had my love from the beginning,' he murmured. 'I thought you must have guessed it long ago. That first night we danced in London, I wanted to catch you up in my arms and run off with you, but you were engaged to another. Afterwards, when you were free, I found myself in an awkward position. I needed money for the mine, and so I told myself that I had to marry an heiress. I was afraid to admit, even to myself, that I loved you, and then it all started to go wrong. I've wanted to tell you how much you mean to me, but I couldn't. I knew that I would have to tell you the whole story—and I was too proud...'

'I don't understand, Justin.'

There was an odd, vulnerable expression in his eyes. 'I wanted the mine to succeed so that I could give you something. Something that was truly my own.'

'I've told you, all I want or need is your love.'

'You have a right to expect your husband's name, if nothing more.'

'What are you trying to say?' She saw the pain in his eyes and caught his hand. 'Please tell me. I have known that something was between us—something that has hurt you badly.'

'I am a bastard, Rosanna.' His hand gripped hers so tightly that she almost cried out. 'I did not know it until the night after I met you. I expected to inherit the estate. Within a few seconds, I lost everything: my name, my right to a fortune—and the memories I cherished of my mother. I had always adored her. She was lively, intelligent, beautiful. When I realised that she had foisted another man's child on her husband, it nearly destroyed me. She—the most perfect of women—was little better than a whore!' His voice faded to a groan.

No wonder he had despised women so much!

'You mustn't think that,' Rosanna said, feeling his pain. 'She was your mother, and you loved her. If she married a man who was not your father, it may not have been her fault. If her lover deserted her, she would have been desperately afraid. She had to marry or bring shame on her family. Please, Justin, don't keep this bitterness inside you. Love her or pity her, but don't hate her. She was probably thinking of you when she married a man she did not love. She wanted to make her child safe.'

'Yes, perhaps you are right. Recently, I have begun to wonder about the man she loved but did not marry. Who is my father?' He frowned as he gazed into his wife's eyes. 'Yet the fact cannot be altered: I am still a bastard. I have no right to the name I have borne all my life.'

'For myself, I do not mind that,' Rosanna said, 'but for your sake, I wish there was some way we could discover your father's identity.'

'There is only one person who might...' Justin sat up with a jerk as something stirred in his memory. 'I had forgotten! Richard was there the night I was injured. I heard his voice, and I believe it may have been he who shot me. He was talking to Cornwallis, saying that he wished his father were dead. I recall Cornwallis suggesting he should... My uncle's life may be in danger!'

She pressed him back as he would have risen. 'No, Justin, your uncle is not in danger—not from his son. Richard has fled the country.'

'What are you saying? What do you know of Richard?'

'They say he murdered Lord Cornwallis.' She bit her lip as she saw Justin frown. 'I would have told you sooner, but you were so ill. It happened the day after that business at the cove. Everyone is talking about it. It seems that Richard tried to attack Anne. She screamed, and her husband came to her assistance. Richard tried to strangle him, and he choked to death.'

'Cornwallis is dead?' Justin's frown deepened. 'Is there a warrant out for my cousin's arrest?'

'I suppose there must be. I only know what Sir Joshua told us when he came over to see how you were.'

'Ah yes, our faithful herald.' Justin laughed as she shook her head in mock reproof. 'I like the fellow, Rosanna; he's been a good friend—but you must admit that he loves to gossip!'

'Well...' She smiled and agreed. 'He has nothing else to do, Justin. Besides, we should never know what was going on if he did not tell us. We are so isolated at Rathmoor.'

'That's just as well—or they would put you in prison for harbouring a desperate felon.' His eyes glinted with mischief. 'And I shall be desperate if you do not let me out of this bed today, Rosanna. I'm warning you, you will pay for your stubbornness!'

'And how shall I pay, sir?' She tilted her head to one side provocatively. 'Will you beat me or...' She gave a little scream of laughter as he grabbed her, pulling her on top of him. 'Justin, you are a sick man!'

'Be damned to that,' he muttered, and rolled her on to her back, trapping her with his body. 'If I prove to you that I am well, will you at least let me leave the bedroom?'

'Perhaps.' She pouted at him. 'Perhaps I shall keep you here forever as my slave.'

'Then you will stay with me,' he murmured. 'Oh, Rosanna my darling, I never knew it was possible to love and need someone so much.'

'Justin,' she whispered, her lips parting invitingly for his kiss. 'I've waited so long to hear you say those words. Say them again, please. Say that you will always love me.'

'I shall love you for ever.' He touched his lips to her forehead, then to her eyelids and finally her lips. 'You are the woman I have longed for all my life.'

She arched towards him, her arms going round his neck as he began to kiss her throat, his hands pushing aside the soft frill of lace that covered her breasts. Already the sweet, slow throb of desire was building within her. She gave a sigh of content as she surrendered willingly to his urgent demands. She had it all now. Everything she had longed for: his love and his child growing in her womb. After they had made love, she would tell him.

*   *   *

Justin entered the secret room, carrying a chamber-stick, spare candles and a silver matchbox. He had at last persuaded Rosanna that he was well enough to leave his bed, though he had promised he would not leave the house. Indeed, he had not much inclination for it; his shoulder was still stiff, though the wound was healing well. Restless and bored with the enforced inactivity of the past weeks, he had decided to explore the possibilities of the tiny room in which he had lain hidden while the soldiers searched the house. It had occurred to him that it was in fact the most likely hiding-place for Lady Caroline's jewels. He was sure Jonathan Whitby had not known of its existence, and there was no mention of it in any of the records of the house. It must have been long forgotten.

He knew that Rosanna had always been fascinated by the legend. For a while he had let his own bitterness blind him to the truth. It was no longer so important that he should provide the money himself, though it would of course give him great pleasure to do so if the mine started to pay. Now he was more concerned to give his wife happiness in any way he could. What did it matter if it was her inheritance or his that provided the things he wanted her to have? If he could find the jewels, it would be enough to see the delight in Rosanna's face— her beautiful, beloved face. He was smiling as he began to tap the walls, moving slowly so that he covered them inch by inch.

'Well, Lady Caroline,' he murmured, 'where did you put those damned jewels? Or was it always just a legend?'

When one of the stones he was knocking suddenly slid back to reveal an iron handle embedded in the wall, he felt a tingle of excitement. Pulling it hard, he heard a grating noise behind him and swinging round, he saw that a large section of the wall had slid sideways, revealing what was obviously a passage. For a moment he wondered if he should fetch Rosanna and let her explore it with him, but then he decided to go on alone. It looked as if he might be on the verge of discovering the truth about the jewels at last!

Rosanna walked slowly, enjoying the autumn sunshine. It was very warm for the time of year, and she had come out into the garden to make the most of it. She had gathered the last of the roses. There was no point in leaving them for the frost, when the dried petals would make fragrant sachets for the linen-chests—chests that would soon hold the tiny garments she was making for her child. It would be a spring baby...

Hearing a rustling sound somewhere behind her, she straightened up and turned round, an odd prickling sensation at the nape of her neck. 'Is someone there?' she called. 'Is that you, Benjamin?' There was no answer. She shivered, feeling cold suddenly, despite the warm sunshine. Someone was watching her. Someone hiding in the shrubbery. She must not panic, she told herself. Whoever was watching knew that she had heard something. Perhaps he would go away if she acted as if nothing had happened. She bent to pick up her basket, and then she saw the man move from behind a large bush. She gave a cry of alarm.

'Don't be afraid, Mrs Sawle,' he said. 'Please don't scream. I mean you no harm. I'm a friend of your husband.'

She stood very still, clutching her basket in front of her. 'Who are you? What are you doing here?'

'I have a message for Captain Sawle.'

'Who are you?' she demanded again. 'If you're from the Revenue, my husband is still in town.'

He chuckled deep in his throat. 'I'm Jack Brendon, Mrs Sawle. You need not fear me. Will you give my message to your husband, please?'

'I might. What is it?'

'Tell him that the traitor was Nick Tregear. He's hiding up at the old tin-mine. It was he and his brother who caused all the trouble for Justin.'

'How do you know all this?'

'I know it, believe me. Nick betrayed us all, and he'll pay for it. It's our way.'

'Why are you telling me this? What do you want of Justin?'

'Nothing. I thought he should know, that's all.' Brendon went on, 'Someone else is hiding out at the old mine. Someone who has sworn to see your husband dead.'

'And who would that be, Jack?'

'Where did you come from?' Brendon swung round in surprise as Justin came up behind him. 'Damn it, man, you startled me!'

'You've a guilty conscience,' Justin replied, grinning. 'I'm glad to see you got away. Are you sure Richard is at the mine?' He laughed harshly as he saw the surprise in Brendon's face. 'It has to be my cousin. Cornwallis is dead.'

'I'm as sure as I can be. We've been watching Tregear, and there's someone with him. Tregear will be dealt with tonight—your cousin, too, if you wish.'

'No! I'll deal with Richard myself.' Justin's eyes narrowed dangerously. 'If you're after Tregear tonight, I'll have to go this afternoon.'

'No, Justin!' Rosanna cried, 'you can't. You're not well enough. Please don't get involved in this.'

He came and stood before her, looking into her eyes. 'I can't stand by and see Richard murdered, Rosanna. I have to try and persuade him to give himself up to the authorities. I don't believe he killed Cornwallis—not in cold blood. Richard is many things, but not a murderer.'

'How can you be so sure? He plotted with Nick Tregear and Cornwallis against you.'

'Exactly. How much easier it would have been for him to put a ball in my back as I rode home from the mine one night. It might have been days before anyone found me out there on the moors. No, Rosanna, he simply hasn't the stomach for it. Richard is a coward, and because he knows that I know him for what he is, he hates me.'

'Oh, Justin,' she whispered, seeing that stubborn look in his eyes and knowing that this time he would not listen to her. 'I wish you wouldn't go.'

'I'll go, then,' Brendon said, making them look at him. 'You have until tonight. My men will leave no witnesses. You'd best be gone yourself before dark. I'll warn them to leave you alone, but you'd best be gone, sir.'

'Your business is your own,' Justin said. 'Don't come here again, Brendon. I made one mistake; I'll not make another.'

'Understood.' Brendon nodded. 'I'm sorry if I frightened you, Mrs Sawle. Revenue officer—that's a good one!'

They watched as he strode away, chuckling to himself. Then Rosanna looked up at her husband, her eyes dark with emotion. 'If you must go, let me come with you?'

'You know the answer to that, my love.'

'Please don't go, Justin.'

'He is my cousin. I owe it to his father to try and save him.'

'You said he wanted to kill his father.'

'No, when I thought about it, I realised it was Cornwallis who said that. Richard might pray for his father's death, but wouldn't actually do anything. I told you, he hasn't the guts for it.'

'You're saying that only so that I won't worry.'

'Would I do that?' he asked with a teasing smile.

'Yes, you would,' she replied crossly. 'You're always trying to protect me, as if I were made of delicate china. I'll have you know I can shoot better than most men.'

He laughed deep in his throat. 'I'm sure you can defend yourself, my sweet, but you are too precious to me. You and my son will stay here and wait until I come back. Do you hear?'

'Yes.' She pulled a face at him and then gurgled with laughter. 'How do you know it's a boy?'

'He wouldn't dare to be anything else!' Justin slipped his arm about her waist. 'I've been looking for Lady Caroline's jewels, my love. That's how I managed to sneak up on you. I've found another passage that leads out behind the barns. The house is perfect for hiding contraband. I wouldn't be surprised if some of your ancestors were smugglers or pirates.'

'Neither would I—you should look at some of the portraits! They were surely a disreputable lot.' She said sternly, 'If you're thinking of...'

'I'm not.' He kissed her on the lips. 'Stop nagging me, woman! You heard me tell Brendon that I don't make the same mistake twice. From now on I intend to be very respectable. I want my daughter to be proud of me.'

'You said it would be a boy,' she protested.

'A son first and then a daughter.' He caught her against him, smiling down into her eyes. 'I don't care, my darling. You are all I want of life, but I know you want children.'

'I want *your* children, Justin,' she said, 'but I want you too. You most of all. Promise you won't do anything foolish out at the mine. Please?'

'Seth and some of the men will be with me.' He touched his lips to her brow. 'I promise I'll come back to you—and if you say another word, I shall put you across my knee!'

Her eyes sparkled as she gazed up at him. 'You are becoming a tyrant, sir!'

'You said you needed a strong hand on the reins,' he replied with a twist of his mouth. 'You may wish you had married Harry Bellingham after all.'

'No, I won't,' she said passionately, pressing herself against him. 'You are the man I want, Justin. Now, always and for ever...'

'And you are my woman,' he said, kissing her. 'Please understand, my darling. I have to do this. Richard is my cousin. We were friends once—and I owe it to his father.'

She nodded, releasing him and standing back. 'Yes, I know you have to go, but please come back safely.'

He smiled, his eyes sparkling with some of his old mockery. 'Yes, my love. Of course I will.'

She watched as he strode away, fighting her tears.

'Are you sure he said the old tin-mine?' Seth asked. 'No one has been down there for years. It ran out in your grandfather's day. The tunnels will have caved in by now.'

'I know it must be in a dangerous condition, but apparently Tregear has been hiding there for some time. If he's the one who's been causing all the accidents, there must be a tunnel that connects the new workings with the old. If he had come across land, someone must have seen him long ago, but if he has found a passage leading from the old mine...'

Seth nodded, beginning to see what Justin was getting at. 'Yes, I see what you mean. I thought it had to be one of our own men who was causing all the trouble. I've had my suspicions about Zeb Tolly. He's been stirring the other men up over all this.'

'Tolly is a troublemaker, but he's honest,' Justin said. 'I doubt he'd have a hand in this.'

'You say your cousin is there, too?'

'I've been warned to get him out before tonight.'

'What about Tregear—will you warn him?'

'It would do no good. The fool should have gone to France as soon as the raid was over. He must have known that those who managed to escape would take vengeance for their friends.'

'He was never popular. Too sullen by half. It's a wonder someone hasn't done for him before this. Especially after he killed that Revenue officer. It caused a lot of trouble for the ''gentlemen''. A few barrels of brandy slipped ashore is one thing; murder is quite another.'

'Cornwallis must have had some hold over him.'

'Or someone else did.'

'You mean Richard?' Justin frowned. 'He may have passed on his knowledge to Cornwallis. We shall probably never know for sure.'

They had left the mine house and were walking towards the deserted workings beyond Sawltry village. All that remained to show that there had once been a mine were mounds of earth, long grown over with grass and furze-bushes, and some dilapidated huts, their roofs blown off and windows broken. The two men made a brief search of the ruins, but did not expect to find anything. At the entrance to the main shaft, though, they found signs that it had been used recently: footmarks, flattened earth and an empty wine-bottle.

'I thought it was just a rumour,' Seth said, frowning. 'But it looks as if your information is right.'

'We shall have to go down,' Justin said. 'I'll lead the way.'

They were both wearing hard hats with hempen candles fixed at the front. It took a moment to kindle the flames, then the light flared to reveal the steep, sloping tunnel that had first been hacked out of the earth well over a century before. Set in the hillside, it slid away gradually for some distance and was high and wide enough for them to walk comfortably side by side; then it began to narrow sharply and they were forced to go slowly, in single file. The air became less fresh and the walls were slimy with a green mould.

Seth coughed, and held his breath. 'I wouldn't fancy hiding out in here myself.'

'No. Richard must be desperate.'

Seth touched his shoulder, lowering his voice to a whisper. 'I thought I heard a sound.'

Justin stopped and listened. He could hear nothing, but he was sure that Seth was right: there was definitely someone in the mine. He cupped his mouth with his hands, shouting his cousin's name. The sound echoed eerily, but there was no answering shout. He tried again, speaking slowly.

'Richard, can you hear me? It's Justin... Listen to me, Richard. Your life is in danger!' He paused, listening intently. This time, he heard it himself. Loose stones shifting beneath someone's feet. It seemed to come from somewhere deeper, on the lower level. 'Richard, I've come to help you. I don't believe you killed Cornwallis. Come with me now, and I'll help you.'

'He won't come up,' Seth said. 'He's frightened. We'll have to go down after him.'

The air was fresher now. Looking up, Justin realised they were below a shaft. It went deep into the mine, with a wooden bridge across the gap. As he hesitated, a figure appeared at the other side. In the darkness he was not certain it was Richard, until he called out.

'Don't come across, Justin. I have a pistol. I'll use it if I have to.'

'Don't be a fool! I want to help you.'

'You want to see me hang!'

'Why should I? I know we've not been friends these past years, but I don't hate you. For your father's sake, if not your own, give yourself up. I'll help you. I give you my word.'

There was silence. Justin peered into the gloom, straining to see the face of the man on the other side. What was Richard thinking? What was he doing? Surely he must know that he could not go on hiding in this awful place! If Richard would not come out, he would have to go and get him.

'I'm coming over!' He put one foot on the wooden planking, but a shout from Richard made him draw back.

'Stay there, or I'll fire. I'm warning you, Justin. I mean it!'

'For God's sake be sensible, man! You can't stay here for ever. There's danger if you don't get away tonight. The "gentlemen" know you're here. You'll be caught like a rat in a trap.'

'I don't believe you.' Richard sounded strange. 'You're trying to trick me.'

'No, Richard. It's the men Nick Tregear betrayed. They want the traitor, and they'll kill you too if you're here. Come with me now, and I'll help you.'

There was silence again, the seconds ticking by tensely as the sound of trickling water somewhere reached Justin's ears. He dug his nails into the palms of his hands, muttering a prayer. Somehow he had to get his cousin clear!

'Why should I believe you?'

Justin drew a deep breath. He was drawing him. He was slowly winning! 'You know me, Richard. You know I wouldn't lie to you. I might knock you down in a fight; I might thrash you if I had cause, but I would never trick you. I'm telling you the truth. Come on, man, we're cousins. Blood stands for something—you know I care about your father. I'm doing it for his sake.'

'Yes, I believe that.' There was a harsh laugh from Richard. 'You were always closer to him than I—he liked you more than me.'

'You're his son, Richard. He cares what happens to you. We'll both stand by you, I give my word. We'll get you out of this.'

'I didn't kill Cornwallis. The old fool came at me with a stick. We struggled, and he had some kind of a choking fit. Anne screamed "murder", but she lied. It was her revenge because I'd insulted her.'

Justin could hear the fear in Richard's voice, but he was weakening. He was beginning to realise that he must face what had happened. 'I thought it might be something like that. Don't worry, Richard, her testimony won't stand up in court. I'll talk to her. I'll make her tell the truth.'

'Why should you?'

'I told you, I care for your father. I'll help you, for his sake as well as your own.'

There was silence again, and Justin held his breath. If Richard would not come now, he would have to go after him.

'Stay there, Justin. I'm coming over.' Richard moved on to the bridge. 'Wait for me—this damn thing isn't safe.' He began to walk cautiously across the narrow bridge. There was an ominous cracking sound and he paused, clinging to the rail. 'It's giving way. I'll have to go carefully.'

The bridge seemed to be swaying as Richard inched his way across. To the two men on the other side, his progress looked painfully slow, but there was nothing they could to to help him. It would only make things worse if they interfered. All they could do was to watch and shout encouragement.

'Take it easy, Richard! Keep to the side and hold on to the rail.'

'He's going to make it,' Seth said. 'It's holding...'

Almost as he said that, a man rushed out of the darkness of the opposite tunnel. He yelled Richard's name, falling on his unprotected back and striking him with some kind of weapon.

'You damned fool!' Nick Tregear shrieked. 'You'll hang us all.'

The struggle between them was violent and desperate. The bridge began to sway wildly. Justin gave a cry of alarm and took a step forward, but Seth grabbed his arm, pulling him back.

'No!' he yelled, 'don't be a fool. There's nothing you can do.'

Even as he spoke, there was a terrible cracking and the planking in the middle gave way. Dust and splinters flew everywhere as a large hole appeared beneath Nick Tregear's feet. He made a grab for the rails, but missed and pitched forward into the gaping blackness. At the same moment, Richard lurched forward, falling face downward on the trembling wooden struts.

'Richard! Get up, man!' Justin cried.

Richard scrambled to his feet. The bridge was breaking up completely, pieces falling into the void. He began to run across the single remaining plank. Justin yelled encouragement, leaning forward from the edge, trying to reach him, while Seth held on to him from behind, bracing him. The earth was crumbling beneath their feet, showers of loose stones slipping away. It was all happening so quickly; no one had time to think. The last plank gave way, falling into the deep pit below, and Richard jumped in desperation, his fingers clawing at the rocky ledge. Justin caught his hand, their fingers gripping. He tried to pull back, but the weight of Richard's body was dragging him forward. Seth dug his feet in, hauling them both back with all his strength.

Richard was hanging on, his legs dangling over the shaft. He called out to his cousin. 'Help me! For God's sake, don't let me fall!'

'Hold on, Richard.'

The pain in Justin's injured shoulder was intense. He groaned with the effort, gritting his teeth. Sweat was trickling down his face, into his eyes. He could feel a pounding at his temples, the strain making the veins bulge in his neck. He felt that he was gradually winning. One more effort...

'Get a foothold, Richard,' he said hoarsely. 'Don't let go.'

'I can't... I'm going...' Richard screamed, as his fingers slipped from Justin's and he felt himself falling back. He scrabbled for the edge, but could not hold on. 'Justin...' His scream faded to a whisper as he slid away from them, slithering down and down, deep into the mine. Then a last, terrible cry echoed in the darkness.

'Damn it! Damn it! Damn it!' Justin cried, striking the wall of the tunnel in frustration. 'I had him! I had him, but I couldn't hold him.'

'He almost took you with him,' Seth said. 'Don't blame yourself, Justin. No one could have held on.'

'I should have. He trusted me, and I lost him.'

'It wasn't your fault. If it hadn't been for Tregear, he would've made it. The bridge was rotten. The struggle between them caused it to give way.' Seth pulled him away from the edge, back to safety. 'There's no more you can do here now. We'll need more men, ropes and ladders. We'll recover the body if it's possible. Come away now, Justin. He's gone.'

'God rest his soul.' Justin turned away, his face strained. 'How shall I tell his father?'

Seth shook his head, understanding his sense of shock and frustration. 'You did your best,' he said. 'No one could have done more.'

'It's getting late,' Rosanna said, her face white as she looked at Sally. 'Something has...' The words died away as she heard footsteps in the hall. Getting to her feet, she started towards the door. As it opened, she gave a cry of relief. 'Justin! Thank God!'

He held out his arms, and she ran to them. She felt a deep surge of emotion as he clasped her, and their lips met in a passionate kiss. Tears glittered in her eyes as she gazed up at him.

'What happened?'

'Richard is dead,' he said in a strangled voice. 'I tried to save him, Rosanna. If he had just held on for a little longer...'

Rosanna made a little sign to Sally. As her servant slipped away, she drew Justin to a sofa, making him sit down. He seemed almost in a daze, unable to realise what had happened. She poured a glass of brandy, pushing it into his hand. He drank it without tasting it, then looked at her.

'What am I going to tell my uncle? Richard was all he had.'

'You will tell him the truth,' she replied. 'There's nothing else you can do.'

'Yes.' Justin nodded, the doubts clearing from his face. 'Yes, you're right. I have to tell the truth—the whole truth.'

CHAPTER ELEVEN

'BE CAREFUL, my love,' Justin said as he helped Rosanna down from the carriage. 'Well, what do you think of Greenslade?'

Rosanna looked at the graceful lines of the Georgian house. It was much bigger than Rathmoor and built of buff-coloured bricks, with white pillars on either side of the front door, and mullioned glass panels.

'It's a beautiful house, Justin,' she said, 'but it's not Rathmoor.'

He laughed and touched her cheek, thinking how beautiful she looked. She was carrying her child easily, and her skin had a healthy bloom. 'You and your house! Anyone would think Rathmoor was the only house in the world.'

'It's special to me,' she said, pulling a face at him. 'There's just something... I can't explain it.'

'You don't have to. I know how much it means to you.'

'As much as this visit means to you?' she asked gently.

It was Justin's first visit to his uncle's house since Richard's death. He had of course written to Lord Mountjoy, telling him what he was doing, but had received only a terse reply. Rosanna knew that he was feeling apprehensive about his reception. He had not ceased to blame himself for his cousin's death, though he had done everything in his power to put matters right—even at the risk of great danger to himself.

A little nerve flicked at his temple. 'I can only hope that he will find it in his heart to forgive me.'

'He cannot do otherwise when he learns what you have done, Justin.'

He smiled, but said nothing, and she took his arm as they went into the entrance hall, looking round with interest. There was a beautiful wrought-iron stairway leading to the gallery, and a floor of pale shining marble. Large gilt-framed mirrors hung between narrow windows, with gilded pier-tables beneath them. They walked through the hall to a long room behind it. Here the floor was of polished wood, covered with rich Persian carpets; a big circular table had pride of place in the centre, its polished surface inset with different-coloured woods spraying out like the rays of the sun. The walls were hung with magnificent paintings and mirrors in ornate frames. In front of the elegant Adam fireplace were two large sofas with winged backs. Sitting on one of them was Lord Mountjoy, his leg propped up on a footstool. His face wore a sombre expression, and he seemed to hesitate a moment before he got to his feet to greet them.

Rosanna felt Justin stiffen, and she knew that this was a moment of great strain for him. She squeezed his arm gently, encouraging him. He smiled down at her, then looked Lord Mountjoy straight in the eyes.

'It is good of you to receive us, Uncle,' he said.

The sombre expression lifted as he held out his hand in welcome. 'I am pleased that you have brought your wife to see me at last.' He took both her hands in his, studying her face. 'Yes, I can see why Justin married you. You have beauty, but there is more besides. Welcome to Greenslade, my dear.' He kissed her cheek, then turned to Justin. 'I had your letter. Richard's death was a great shock, as you may imagine. I do not fully understand all the details, and it would help if you could explain.'

'There was no hiding the truth at the inquest into Richard's death, sir.' Justin looked at his wife, and smiled. 'Rosanna did her best to shield me from the consequences of my folly, but I decided to make a clean breast of it.'

'As Richard should have done.' Lord Mountjoy shook his head. 'It was a bad business—that Richard should try to ruin you! I know you two were never the best of friends, but this shames me.'

'There is no need for that, Uncle. Although there seemed to be good reasons for the antipathy between us, I never hated him. I went to the mine to try and save him. I never believed that he had killed Cornwallis.'

'At least you managed to clear his name of the charge of murder.' Lord Mountjoy sighed. 'I shall be forever in your debt for that, Justin.'

'It was easy enough, once Anne Cornwallis told the truth.'

'But you risked imprisonment for smuggling.'

'I took no real part in what happened at the cove that day. When it all came out about Cornwallis's attempts to ruin me at the mine, I received considerable sympathy, but my main concern was to clear my cousin's name. I owed you that, sir.'

'Nonsense!' The frown left Lord Mountjoy's brow. 'I know the incident at the mine was not your fault. I do not blame you, my boy. Indeed, I thank you for all you have done.' He rang a bell, summoning refreshment. 'Now, both of you, come and sit down and tell me what I can do for you. Your last letter made me curious, Justin.'

They moved to the sofas before the fire, and sat down. Justin's eyes dwelt affectionately on his wife's face for a moment before he replied, 'Rosanna is with child, sir. Before my son is brought into the world, I should like to know the name of my father. I know you and my mother were very close. If she told anyone, it would have been you.'

'I wondered how long it would be before Charles Sawle told you that you were not his son!' Lord Mountjoy steepled the fingers of both hands, nodding as he looked at his nephew's face. 'Margaret did not deceive him, you know. She was honest from the start. He knew when he married her that she was carrying you. He took her for her dowry.'

Justin's gaze did not falter. 'I know there was some sort of compact, but I was too angry to listen when we quarrelled. I'm glad she told him. We did not always agree, but he was decent enough when I was a child. Did he know who my father was?'

'Margaret would not tell him. He tried to force it out of her many times, but she never spoke. I don't know why. It could not have hurt Kilamorin.' Lord Mountjoy paused briefly, then explained, 'Your father was Lord Kilamorin. It's an Irish title, Justin. I brought Michael home with me from Oxford, and Margaret fell in love with him at first sight. He was a very charming man. Unfortunately, he was married, so the situation was impossible. Even if he had been single, my father would never have accepted the match. He was as poor as a church mouse. Their love was doomed from the start. She didn't even tell him she was carrying his child. He went back to Ireland, and we heard later that his ship sank in a terrible storm. He was dead before you were born, Justin.'

'That explains so much. Thank you for telling me.' Justin held his wife's hand tightly. 'Poor mother. How she must have suffered!'

'She had you, Justin. She was a remarkable woman. She survived, and she made the most of her marriage. Charles Sawle had no reason to complain. I believe he was in love with her at the start, but he brooded over his inability to have a child of his own. It turned him bitter. I'm surprised he didn't tell you the truth long ago.'

'Perhaps he meant to keep his side of the bargain. We quarrelled, and he couldn't hold it back any longer.'

'So he disinherited you. I promised Margaret that you would not suffer if that happened. Why didn't you come to me?' He shook his head. 'No need to answer. You're as proud as she was. Well, you'll be my heir now, whether you like it or not: I've no other blood kin. The title will be yours as well as all the rest.'

'Not for a good many years yet, sir.'

'Maybe not, but I'd like you to take my name now, Justin. I shall adopt you as my heir and give you the allowance due to you.'

'I shall be proud to bear your name, Uncle. As for the rest...'

'No nonsense now! You're entitled to it, and it will give me pleasure. All I ask is that you invite me to your son's christening.'

'We'll bring him—or her—here to be christened,' Rosanna said, smiling. 'My foolish husband is too proud to accept your gift, sir, so I shall say thank you for him. When he has thought about it, he will realise there is no shame in accepting your generous offer.'

'You're a sensible woman. I can see you mean to keep the rascal in order.'

She laughed, and looked at her husband. 'I do my best, sir, but he is rather a tyrant. His pride is his undoing, but I shall teach him to behave decently in the end.'

Justin smiled ruefully. 'What can I say? Of course I accept most gratefully. It would be churlish to refuse.'

'And foolish.' Lord Mountjoy chuckled. 'I never thought to see you under petticoat rule, my boy—but so charmingly done! Now you are going to stay with me for at least a month, I hope? I like company, and I want to get to know this beautiful wife of yours.'

'I'm not sure we can stay that long,' Justin replied with a smile, but Rosanna shook her head at him.

'I see no reason why not. I think you can be spared from the mine—and I'm looking forward to some long talks with Lord Mountjoy. I want to hear all the secrets he can tell me about you as a child...'

*   *   *

'Home at last!' Justin flung down his gloves and hat in the hall. 'Greenslade is all very well, but there's nowhere quite like home.'

'I believe Rathmoor has cast its spell over you,' Rosanna said, laughing up at him. 'I'm glad to be back, too. Lord Mountjoy was very kind, and I enjoyed meeting all his friends, but it was so exhausting! It will be good to be alone for a while.'

'Alone—that sounds wonderful!' Justin looked at her teasingly. 'If I were a jealous man, I should have challenged half the men in the county this past month.'

'You had no cause to be jealous, and you know it!' They had progressed into the small sitting-room. She let her eyes move over the familiar surroundings, feeling the warm glow that always came to her when she returned to Rathmoor. 'Oh, it's so good to be back! I shall not stir from this house again until after our child is born.'

'Come here, woman, I want to kiss you.' Justin reached out, drawing her against him. 'At last I can kiss you whenever I want without someone watching.'

A little cough behind them contradicted his words. He turned round with a resigned look. 'Yes, Emily, what is it?'

'Mr Miller is waiting to see you, sir. He came over two days ago, and I told him you were expected back today.'

'Then I suppose I had better see him. Show him in, Emily.' Rosanna giggled, and he turned back to her with mock severity. 'This is merely a temporary respite, madam.'

She shook her head at him, but was saved from replying by Seth's arrival. It was obvious at once that he was very excited, and he began to speak immediately.

'We've found it, Justin! A vein of red copper that looks like lasting from now to kingdom come!'

'Red copper? That's worth three to four pounds a ton more on the open market than the lower grades.'

Seth nodded in vigorous agreement. 'I told you it was there, Justin. I knew it. I could feel it in my bones. I found it myself after we explored the passages Nick Tregear had been using, and I took some of the men in to investigate. We were nearly through to it, but now we've taken a new route and it's saved us weeks of tunnelling. It's coming out so fast that we can't keep up with it. It will put the mine into profit before the month is up!'

Justin clapped him on the shoulder, laughing triumphantly. 'We've done it together, Seth. By God, we've done it! I'll make you my partner. You deserve it.'

'No, Justin, I want only the percentage you promised at the start.'

'Be damned to what you want, man! Think of Becky and the children. You'll be my partner, or I'll throw you out.' Justin punched the air with delight. 'Wine! We must have wine to celebrate. It's not every day a fortune drops in your lap.'

'I think we have some champagne, Justin,' Rosanna said, shaking her head at the pair of them. 'I'll tell Benjamin to fetch it from the cellars. Everyone must share this with us.' She hurried away, laughing as she heard Justin demanding to hear all the details of the find all over again.

'All we need now is to find Lady Caroline's jewels,' Rosanna said, after Seth had gone and the rest of the household had discreetly melted away. 'Two months ago you were so desperate that you risked everything for a few hundred guineas—now you're a wealthy man.'

'I shall be soon,' Justin said, putting down his wineglass to take her hands in his. 'What do you want first, Rosanna? A diamond necklace, emeralds, rubies?'

'First, I want the roof in the west wing repaired. Then I want to furnish the nursery and schoolroom. After that . . .'

'I might have known you would want something for your beloved house!' His eyes glinted with humour. 'Shall we go exploring, Rosanna? I found several passages the other week, but I didn't have time to look in them all. I feel lucky tonight. We might find Lady Caroline's jewels—and if we don't, at least I'll have you to myself for a while. No one will follow us in there!'

She gurgled with laughter. 'Yes, let's explore together, Justin. We don't need the jewels any more, so we'll probably find them.'

They collected the things they would need, feeling like a pair of children setting out on an adventure. The discovery of a rich copper lode at the mine had changed everything. It gave Justin the independence he had always wanted, and though he could not refuse his uncle's gift of an allowance, that could be put aside for his children. Rosanna saw a new pride in his eyes. She joined in the game he had suggested, not because it mattered whether they found anything, but because it pleased him. It was exciting and silly, and they stopped to embrace every few seconds. She had everything she had wanted and more, much more.

So she was not unduly disappointed when they ended up in Lady Caroline's bedroom an hour or so later, dusty from exploring dark passages that led nowhere in particular. All she had to show for the expedition was a broken heel on her shoe.

'Oh, look,' she said, laughing, as she sat on Lady Caroline's bed. 'I've broken the heel. That ancestor of mine has a lot to answer for. I give up. I refuse to look for the jewels ever again. I don't believe she hid them at all!'

She lay down on the bed, throwing the shoe hard at the silken canopy above her head in exasperation. There was a sharp ripping sound, and the whole thing suddenly dropped in the middle, seeming to split apart.

'Rosanna!' Justin yelled as he realised what was happening. He made a desperate dive across the bed, rolling her to the side and covering her with his own body. 'Lie still!'

There was a heavy thud on the bed beside them; then it seemed as if all hell had broken loose as an avalanche of objects rained down from all sides. The sound of metal striking metal reverberated in the room, making Rosanna flinch, and then it was suddenly quiet. Justin slid his legs over the bed and pulled her to her feet, holding her tightly against him. She felt the deep shudders run through him and looked up in concern, gasping as she saw the stricken look in his eyes.

'What is it? Are you hurt?'

'No,' he said in a strangled voice. 'You could have been killed. God forgive me! I almost lost you.'

She saw how shocked he was, and reached up to touch his cheek. 'You saved me, Justin. I'm not hurt. There's nothing to worry about, my darling.'

'Thank God! I would rather die than lose you, Rosanna.' His arms tightened their hold about her. 'None of it—the mine, anything—none of it means anything without you, my darling.'

'Oh, Justin,' she whispered, tears in her eyes. 'I'm here, my love. I'm with you.'

'Never leave me,' he said. 'Love me for ever, Rosanna. Never stop loving me. I need you so much.'

'How could I?' she asked, her eyes bright with emotion. 'You are my life. I shall never want anyone but you. Surely you know that?'

'Yes. Yes, I know it,' he said, the fear leaving him as suddenly as it had come, and taking with it all the bitterness that had soured his life for so long. She was here in his arms, and the world was his. 'Yes, I know it, my darling.'

Releasing her, he turned to look at the array of silver trays, tankards, candelabra and a heavy wooden casket that lay where Rosanna's head had lain seconds before. The treasure of Rathmoor had remained hidden in the thickly padded silken canopy, which stretched between four wooden struts and covered the whole of the bed, for over a hundred and fifty years. The silk had gradually rotted through, stretched by its heavy load almost to bursting-point. When Rosanna's shoe hit it, it had finally given way, almost resulting in tragedy. But she was safe, and the mystery was solved.

'Well, my love,' he said, a hint of mischief in his voice. 'I believe we have discovered the secret of Lady Caroline's jewels at last. She hid them all above her bed. All those passages to choose from, and she hid them in the canopy!'

'So it would seem...'

Rosanna looked up into his eyes, and suddenly they were laughing.

'Everyone has been searching the house for years, tapping the walls,' Justin said, 'and all the time the jewels were close enough to touch!'

'Perhaps she didn't know about the passages?'

'No, my love. It was the first place she thought of.' Justin's eyes glinted with devilry. 'It's quite typical of a woman's logic...' He retreated before the fierce glow in his wife's eyes. 'I apologise! I apologise...'

It was too late for apologies. He was under attack, retreating until his back was against the wall and he could go no further. Then, at last, he surrendered...

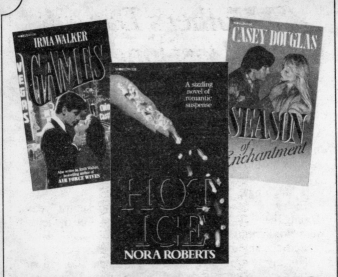

IS PASSION A CRIME?

HOT ICE *by Nora Roberts* £2.95

A reckless, beautiful, wealthy woman and a professional thief. Red hot passion meets cold hard cash and it all adds up to a sizzling novel of romantic suspense.

GAMES *by Irma Walker* £2.50
(Best selling author of Airforce Wives under the name of Ruth Walker)

Tori Cockran is forced to save her son by the same means that destroyed her marriage and her father – gambling. But first she must prove to the casino boss she loves that she's not a liar and a cheat.

SEASONS OF ENCHANTMENT *by Casey Douglas* £2.75

Ten years after their broken marriage and the loss of their baby, can Beth and Marsh risk a second chance at love? Or will their differences in background still be a barrier?

All available from February 1989.

W♦RLDWIDE

From: Boots, Martins, John Menzies, W H Smith, Woolworths and other paperback stockists.

A Mother's Day gift that will last longer than Flowers

We need your help!

Help us out and we'll send you:

☆ A FREE MILLS & BOON ☆ MASQUERADE NOVEL

At Mills & Boon we always do our best to try and ensure that our books are just what you want to read. To do this we need your help! Please spare a few minutes to answer the questions below and overleaf, and as a special thankyou we will send you a FREE Mills & Boon Masquerade novel .

Don't forget to fill in your name and address so we know where to send your FREE BOOK.

PLEASE TICK THE APPROPRIATE BOXES TO INDICATE YOUR ANSWERS

1 **Where do you get your Masquerade books from?**

   ❏ Shops   ❏ Reader Service

2 **How long have you been reading Masquerade historical romances?**

   _____

3 **How often do you read a Masquerade historical romance?**

   _____

4 **Do you read other historical romances apart from Masquerade?**

   ❏ Yes   ❏ No

   If yes, which authors do you read?

   _____

   _____

   Please turn over page to complete ⫸

CONTINUED FROM OVERLEAF

5   When you read an historical romance, how important
    are the following?

	Very Important	Important	Not Important
a) A strong romantic relationship			
b) A good fast plot			
c) Lots of historical details e.g. clothes, way of life etc.			
d) Use of real historical characters.			
e) Use of real historical events.			

6   Which of the elements in Q.5 would you say is the
    MOST IMPORTANT to you and why? _____

    _____

    _____

7   Which period in history do you most enjoy reading about and why?

    _____

    _____

    _____

8   Do you read any of the following series? Please tick

    a) Mills & Boon Romances   ☐   e) Silhouette Desire   ☐
    b) Mills & Boon Best Sellers ☐   f) Silhouette Sensation   ☐
    c) Mills & Boon Doctor/Nurse ☐   g) Silhouette Special Edition   ☐
    d) Mills & Boon Temptation   ☐   h) Mills & Boon Collection   ☐

9   Which age group are you in? Please tick

    Under 25 ☐   25 - 34 ☐   35 - 44 ☐   45 - 54 ☐   over 55 ☐

10 Please tick which applies to you?...

    Married ☐   Widowed ☐   Work full time ☐   Unemployed ☐
    Single ☐   Have children ☐   Work part time ☐   Retired ☐
    Divorced ☐   No children ☐   Housewife ☐

                                                                    RAR
Name _____

Address _____

    _____

    _____ Postcode _____

Thank you very much for your help. We hope that you enjoy your free book. Please
send your completed questionnaire to... **Masquerade Survey,**
FREEPOST, P.O. BOX 236, CROYDON, SURREY. CR9 9EL.
Your address details may be retained by us for mailing you with other offers.

NO STAMP
NEEDED